No Looking Back

No Looking Back

Alex Kane

hera

First published in Great Britain in 2019 by Hera

Hera Books
28b Cricketfield Road
London, E5 8NS
United Kingdom

A CIP catalogue record for this book is available from the British Library.

Print ISBN 978 1 78863 610 0
Ebook ISBN 978 1 912973 05 7

Printed and bound in Great Britain by Clays Ltd, Elcograf S.p.A.

For Alexander Clapperton, and William Kane,
two men I am incredibly honoured to be related to.

This book is for anyone who has ever been faced with the
ordeal of an abusive relationship and has had the courage to
walk away. For anyone who has yet to find peace,
I hope you can.

Prologue

Thinking back to our wedding day, my memories are mostly happy ones. I remember the music I chose to walk down the aisle to, our favourite song, 'Here Comes the Sun', by The Beatles. I never actually liked them before I met my husband, but when someone plays a particular band on repeat, you kind of get used to the tunes, the guitar riffs, and their individual sound. Jimmy used to say I was his little ray of sunshine. I often wonder how such a benign thought was possible. So evil.

I recall the aftershave Jimmy wore that day, one I had picked out for him. Every time I smell it now, I think of that song, the dress, the look on his face when I made my journey down that aisle towards the rest of my life. Tonight, and every night as far back as I can bring myself to think of, my memories are tarnished with panic, with anxieties which are at the surface of my being and I cannot stop the tears which are brimming in my eyes.

–

The gravel scraped my back as I was dragged by my long hair along the path towards the wagon at the end of the site. It was the one thing he often used as grip, he knew I liked my hair and he used it as a weapon against me.

He said nothing as I used my left hand to try to prise his fingers open to release my hair. He was much stronger than me and laughed sadistically at my attempts to escape. I kicked my feet in protest but he continued to pull me towards the wagon. Those once caring and soft hands now held such a threat. My face still throbbed from the impact of his fist. I knew exactly where I was headed, but I was determined to fight. I knew what was in there, waiting for me, and I was not prepared to go through it again, even though in my heart I knew there was nothing I could do about it.

It was my punishment for... for what? For loving someone with my everything? Because I had done nothing wrong, but no matter what I did, I couldn't stop the punishments which were becoming a daily occurrence. Although this particular chastisement was kept as an *extra* punishment, if I had done something truly awful. Choosing my own outfit to wear was a stupid decision. I should have known not to do that; he always picked out my clothes, unless he couldn't be bothered. In that case I would be left to choose, and then I would get a slap for choosing wrong.

Cold rain cascaded down from the darkened sky, mixing with my tears. I wanted my dad. I wondered what he would think if he was looking down on me being dragged across the ground.

If the residents of the site were awake, surely they would be able to hear the commotion? But turning a blind eye to this sort of thing was not unusual in my community, and especially so in my case, since most people wanted nothing to do with my family, anyway.

I tried to block out the pain in my back as the gravel peeled away tiny particles of skin, exposing the under-layer. It's strange, the things you think about in times of trauma; the miracle of life and how some people just don't seem to appreciate it. It would break my parents' hearts if they knew I was being treated like this. I had been conceived and grown up with love, cherished by them.

Another wedding day memory flashes in front of me and I feel my throat swell. We'd written our own vows at Jimmy's suggestion. I'd expected his to be short and to the point. However, his words ran deeper than I'd ever imagined they could, promising to take care of me now that my parents were gone. He'd held my hands, giving them a little squeeze from time to time, as he promised to love me unconditionally and protect me from the world; saying that I'd never be on my own and he would always have my back.

Now when I think of it, I am translating his words into what I believe he actually meant. He would protect me from the world, meaning that he'd never let me out of his sight. He'd always have my back, meaning if I ever betrayed him in any way, he'd make sure I only did it once.

I didn't dare speak, but I wanted to cry out in protest from the pain. The waistband of my leggings had become damp from the blood and rain water which now soaked my back. I twisted my body so my left hip took some of the gravel. Quite quickly, the leggings began to tear and fresh skin was exposed to the elements.

A gap in the rain clouds appeared, and I noticed the brightest star I had ever seen. It lined the edges of the surrounding clouds with a beautiful white shimmer. It was so bright I wondered if it was another sun, far away in our galaxy. I imagined it was Dad. He would never allow this to happen if he was still here. Come to think of it, why was *I* allowing this to happen?

I kept my eye on the star above as the anger began to build in my stomach. Suddenly, we stopped moving and my hair was released; relief overwhelmed me as my scalp stopped burning. I listened to his heavy breath, knowing just what he was going to do next but hoping I had enough strength to stop him.

'Get up!' the voice from behind me snarled.

I did as I was told, not allowing him to see my face in case he could read me.

'What do you have to say for yourself?'

How the hell did I know? I was never fully aware of my actions which led to punishment, anything could set Jimmy off at any given moment. I knew what I *wanted* to say; question was, did I have the guts to say it out loud?

'Well?'

'Fuck you!' I said, aiming for firm and loud but managing only a frightened rasp. He frowned, shocked at my audacity.

'What did you just say?'

I took a deep breath, ready to collapse in fear. I attempted to say it again but something stopped me. The glint in his eye, perhaps? Or the fact that I did know better than to give him backchat.

He grabbed my face, digging his filthy nails into my cheeks. I wrapped my hands around his wrist, willing myself to push him away.

'Please, don't do this,' I whimpered, but he only tightened his grip. I glanced back up at the sky but no longer could I see that single star; the clouds were no longer lined with a white shimmer. I was alone, as always, fighting the demons I could never defeat. The light went out inside me with the absence of that star and I began to feel numb as memories of the day I promised to love Jimmy forever flooded my vision.

I heard the familiar sound of the Allen key opening the entrance to hell: the belly box, stuffed full with boxes of God knows what kind of crap; darkened corners littered with old newspapers, buckets and paint tins stretching across the floor. It was cold at this time of year. I was thrown to the ground because he needed two hands to open the box. It was my chance to escape but I had nowhere to run to. Fear rooted me to the ground. I wanted it to open up and swallow me. Hell itself would be better than what was ahead of me. Another set of hands held on to my shoulders and my heart sank. Two against one was just not fair.

'Why are you doing this to me?' I asked meekly.

There was no reply. The second pair of hands hauled me up from the ground.

'In you go,' a voice said. But was not my husband; it was Rab, his sidekick and the man who would do absolutely anything Jimmy told him to.

I got to my feet, heart thudding against the wall of my chest. I stared at them both, Jimmy who had said, 'I do,' and Rab, who had signed our register. How could the lives of three people and the relationship they shared have become so distorted, twisted, and evil?

'Are you deaf?' Rab said, a grin spreading across his face so widely I imagined the corners of his mouth might crack.

'Nah, she's not deaf. Just defiant,' Jimmy said, his tone flat and cold, matching the temperature of this freezing night.

'Please,' I pleaded again, feeling pathetic.

Rab took a step forward and I felt myself cower back. Jimmy held a hand up, stopping Rab from coming any closer.

'Kat, if you don't do as you're told, we'll have to do it the hard way.' His sing-song voice chilled me to the depths of my soul and I shivered, not because of the wind and rain.

I stared down into the box and something inside me shifted. On one hand, I wasn't scared that I might die in there, in fact I wondered if falling asleep in the cold and darkened cavern would be the easiest way out. On the other, I was determined I *wouldn't* die in there.

'No,' I said, wriggling my toes to feel my grip on the ground.

'Have it your way,' Jimmy said, dropping his hand from Rab's chest, as if releasing a wolf on hunt.

I was thrown into the box before I could react. Thrown onto my back, I looked out at them, unable to sit up due to the depth of the box, waiting for them to take mercy on me.

Two pairs of eyes glowered at me but I stared up at Jimmy. I pleaded silently with him not to allow this to happen.

'Kat, just remember that if it wasn't for me, you wouldn't be alive today. The least you can do is respect me as your husband,' Jimmy said, his soft voice the opposite to his expression. I glance at Rab, unable to believe that they were using my existence as an excuse to treat me this way.

'Night night,' Rab said before the plank of wood holding the entry open was snatched away. The noise of it falling shut was deafening. I was plunged into darkness. I strained my ears as the sounds of their footsteps faded.

I lay still and in silence, the only sounds were those of my breath and beating heart. There was no way I could escape from the belly box unless someone let me out.

They could have left me here to die, on my own in the cramped space below the abandoned wagon. It was at that point I decided that death would be better than what lay ahead of me; it was likely that more of this lined my future.

Did I want that? Was I prepared to go through this until one of us died? It was possible I could be in my eighties before I was released from this hell.

I wrapped my arms around my body and tried to make myself as comfortable as possible. I closed my eyes, hoping for release, whatever that meant.

Chapter One

Jimmy looked across the crowd at me with a glint in his eye as I took the admission for the waltzer machine from the man and his son. How dare I breathe in the same direction as another man? Of course, it didn't help that this same man had returned three days in a row and had been very friendly towards me. I had tried to be distant, even if he was extremely handsome and had a pleasant manner. I supposed any manner was pleasant compared to my husband's.

'That's a fiver,' I said, keeping my head down, trying to let Jimmy see I wasn't meaning to do anything to upset him. 'Make sure the wee one is secure, please.'

'Are you kidding?' the man said, smiling as I raised my head. 'He'll be keeping an eye on me. I don't know how he manages to talk me into stuff like this.'

In the background, I was aware of Jimmy still staring at us. I looked past the man and his child towards my husband. Jimmy smiled, turned away, and started talking to Rab. My mind played havoc with my stomach. Was he angry with me or was I imagining things? These days I couldn't do right for doing wrong. I was always checking myself, making sure I was behaving appropriately towards him and others. It was best to remain neutral towards other people, but sometimes even that caused problems.

Although I knew that was the way he liked it. It kept him in control.

The machine started up and the music began to blare. My ears buzzed as teenagers and children screamed to go faster. I hadn't meant to, but I accidently and continuously made eye contact with the man who had returned three days in a row. He smiled every time our eyes connected.

'Who's your mate?' Jimmy suddenly whispered in my ear. His breath warm against the side of my face and I detected a hint of vodka on his breath, masked by a minty scent. Otherwise, he smelled good, which cast a black cloud over me, making me think of better times and how bad things had become between us. The scent reminded me of when we first got together and our wedding day. He knew I liked Davidoff Cool Water so would wear it all the time. I felt his arm slide around my waist.

'Don't know, he's a punter here with his boy,' I replied, as gently as possible but loud enough that he would hear me over the banging music and screaming punters.

'He's been here three days in a row. Either his kid has him wrapped around his finger or he fancies you.'

I felt as if he was asking me a question. 'Oh God, who would fancy me?' I attempted a laugh.

'You think he's good looking, don't you?'

I couldn't pinpoint his tone. It was either sarcastic or accusatory. Either way, I didn't have a death wish. No matter what I said, Jimmy would make up his own mind. And if it didn't go in my favour, I was going to get a battering, no matter what the truth was. I turned to face my husband and put on the most loving smile I could.

'You know that's not true, Jimmy.'

'Oh do I now?' He pinched my waist. My stomach flipped. 'And do you still fancy me?'

'Of course I do. I don't have eyes for anyone else. You know that.' My heart began pounding in my chest.

His attitude annoyed me when it came to our marriage. He would never admit it and I had no proof, but I knew he had cheated on me with other women. Punters, most likely. They were easy to come by, and he did have a certain charm about him, which I suppose is why I fell for him in the first place.

So Jimmy was allowed to go out and shag whoever he wanted behind my back, but God forbid another man even look in my direction. I'd often see him flirting with girls younger than me but I would never challenge him on it, or I'd get a slap.

He walked off, back to the hook-a-duck stand. I watched him, rooted to the spot. My stomach flipped again, my skin tingled and my head swirled. The palpitations began and my chest froze, my lungs aching with every deep breath. I tried taking shorter breaths, but this made my skin tingle even more. I hated not knowing what he was thinking. Jimmy was a passionate man. By 'passionate', I mean often aggressive and violent. He liked things done a certain way. But nothing I did was ever the right way. I had become tired. I had tried to leave him, twice.

Around a year after we had got married, and after careful thought and consideration, I'd sat him down and told him how I felt. It turned out not to be my best move, I'll admit.

'No,' he'd said. 'You're not leaving.'

I felt my brow furrowing. Had I asked his permission? Everything about his response had suggested I had even though I knew that wasn't the case.

'I'm not asking. I'm telling you,' I replied, my tone firmer.

Jimmy was midway through lunch, fork hovering between the plate and his mouth. His eyes bored into mine and something in the air around us changed. Placing the fork down on the plate, he then wiped his mouth with a tissue and stood up to face me.

'You're *telling* me?' he'd said, head cocked to the side as if talking to a puppy, his eyes narrowing.

'Yes, Jimmy. This just isn't working.' A blunt force caught me on the jaw so suddenly I fell to the floor.

I hadn't thought there was pain like it, or that someone could be so cruel to another human being. He punched me, kicked me, and slapped me across the back of the head. To be honest, none of that was as bad as when he ended the beating. He could have done anything to me and it wouldn't have been half as bad as that. He stood over me and spat. Several times. He looked at me as if I were a piece of shit on his shoe.

'If you want out, you're going to have to get past me. You'll never leave me, do you understand?' he said, words hissing through gritted teeth.

I would have looked him straight in the eye had my own eyes not been swollen shut. Bastard. And to think I'd loved him once. I suppose you can't help who you fall in love with, and if I could have helped it, I would have told myself to leave well before then.

'I said, do you understand?' He was calm; the calm scaring me more than the prospect of another beating. I knew what his relaxed manner at this point meant for me. More beatings or worse.

My mind was screaming at him. I wanted to tell him I hated him and that he deserved nothing other than death. I hated him, more than anyone could ever hate anyone or anything else in the world. But I had also loved him more than anything. I was torn.

I couldn't say the words. I knew if I said anything other than yes, he would start on me again.

'Yes,' I replied. I could feel the blood trickling down my chin as I released the word.

'Good, now get to the bathroom and clean yourself up.'

I hadn't made my second attempt until much later in our marriage. The second had a far worse outcome.

I remembered it like it was yesterday. No matter how much I tried not to think of it, it always crept its way back into my mind. Like a slow leak, I could keep it hidden for only so long before the memory began to trickle in, turning into a flood in my brain. To think I had actually sat down and tried to reason with him. But I had to do something to get away from the godforsaken site.

Talking to him the last time hadn't worked. So this time, I'd decided to leave unannounced. I'd work out the logistics of my life later, I'd thought. All I needed was to get away from him. So I waited until it was dark, until the site was silent and he'd fallen asleep, drunk. My prayers were not answered that night.

I'd heard him snoring, having passed out on the sofa an hour or so earlier. I'd packed a small bag of clothes and tiptoed towards the front door of our trailer. I'd held my breath as I gripped the handle and pulled it down. Locked. Shit!

I'd begun turning the key which clicked loudly in the mechanism. My heart lurched at the sound, as did Jimmy.

Silence held me there for a few seconds and only when I thought he was still asleep had I pulled the handle down again. The door had opened just a crack when the sound of his voice stabbed at my chest like a red-hot blade.

'You're leaving?'

My throat dried up as I opened my mouth to speak. *Lie, say anything.*

'You don't love me anymore?' Jimmy said, his voice soft. I hadn't expected that question. It pulled at my heart. I had loved him once, of course. Otherwise, I would never have ended up marrying him.

'Of course I love you. But...' I pause. 'You know things aren't good between us.'

'What things?' Jimmy shifted into a sitting position.

I hadn't known what to say. I was digging a hole and I wasn't able to stop myself.

'You don't fancy me anymore? Is that it?' he asked, looking into my eyes suddenly.

I gripped the handle of my bag. 'It's not that. It's—'

'Because you still do it for me. You always have.' He was by my side now, his hand on my shoulder, leading me towards the couch. His grip tightened as my heart raced.

'Jimmy,' I said. He hushed me. I froze, my breath cold on my lips.

'Baby,' he said, sliding his hands around my waist. He held me tight. 'You can't leave. You belong here. Where would you go? What would I do without you?'

I tensed in his embrace. This was the first time I realised that he made my skin crawl. 'I... I don't know.' It came out as a whisper. But he was right, where would I go? I hadn't planned that far in advance.

'See? You don't want to leave, not really. You belong here with me. You don't have anyone else, do you?' He pulled me closer. 'You're a Denton. You were destined to be a Denton; we are supposed to be together. So, let's stop this nonsense, eh? You're not going anywhere.' Tucking my hair behind my ear, he pushed his tongue into my mouth. Bile rose in my throat but I held it back.

It wasn't what I had expected. I had believed he would go crazy at me. When I think back to it now, I would have preferred a beating. I would have preferred death.

He forced me down onto the couch. I hadn't realised what was happening at first. When reality kicked in, I began to fight him. 'No, Jimmy.'

He hushed me again, pulling at the waistband of my jeans. 'Let me give you a reason to stay.'

'Stop it. I want to stop.' My words were muffled as he forced my face into the cushions.

'Come on, Kat.' His breath was fast and heavy as he held his full weight on top of me. I was pinned down. I couldn't stop him. His weight pressed down on my rib cage, forcing the air from my lungs. I was sure he would crush me to death, the pain in my body causing alarm, my senses going into overdrive as I came to realise what was happening. My mind stirred, dark thoughts crept in as he continued his attack. Could a husband rape his wife? I couldn't be sure. But the more I thought about it, the more I understood that when I said no and he went ahead and did it anyway, it was most definitely rape. Even after everything he had done in the past, the way he treated me and the way he spoke to me, I was still shocked at his

14

behaviour. How he thought it was perfectly fine to abuse me in all sorts of ways. My head was a mess then, even more so than it had been before. The man I had fallen for was not the man I was married to. The term *mind-fuck* was an understatement when Jimmy was involved. He only did it the once and it was four years ago. Had it been that long? Since that night, I've barely slept in fear that he would do it again and I have been trying to behave in a way that is acceptable in his eyes, just to protect myself.

I had been planning to get out of the travelling community ever since I could remember, even before Jimmy. My parents were travellers, too. They died when I was fourteen years old. I hadn't expected to still be here at thirty years old.

Jimmy's family were a big part of our community, respected but not at all liked by most of the families. Most of the kids on our site growing up were warned to stay away. Of course, I didn't listen to that warning. When my parents died, his mum felt sorry for me so the Dentons took me in. I had no one else to turn to. My mam's parents died when I was little, so little I don't remember them at all. I never knew my dad's family.

There were five members of the Denton family, including his parents. He was two years older than me and the eldest out of his two siblings. I was a mess and I never really felt like I belonged anywhere, since we were travellers.

Of course, we had our trailer, but I never felt settled. Jimmy had a certain sort of charm when I were fourteen and because I was vulnerable, I fell for it. He was so nice to me in the beginning. I never saw how controlling he could be until it was too late. Soon, I wasn't allowed to choose my own clothes or food. I've never really known what it's like to have a mind of my own. I slept with him for the first time after about six months of living with him and his family. It was after that first time that I realised I was in love with him, and he knew it. He would show me off to the other teenage travellers; he called me his property. Being a teenager, I never really thought it was a bad thing. In fact, I found that word 'property' quite reassuring in a way, as if it gave me a sense of belonging. I was wrong.

The Denton family were a mess. His dad would batter his mum on a daily basis, still did by all accounts. So it was clear where Jimmy got his aggression from. Jimmy's youngest sister, Mandy, was quiet – if you didn't bother her, she wouldn't bother you. She would often fly off the handle if someone got on her bad side and even though people knew this, they still seemed to do just enough to anger her, even if it was never their intention. I saw another kid on the site get lippy with her once and she broke her ankle by stamping on it. His other sister and second in age to him, Ellie, was one of those girls you just wouldn't mess with. She was into drugs, boys, alcohol; you name it, she'd done it. She was as hard as nails and I avoided her as much as I could. She never really liked me. Come to think of it, she never really liked Jimmy either, but I never knew why. I often wondered if she didn't like the male species at all because of how her dad behaved.

My mind back on the present day, I kept my eyes on Jimmy as I tried to move my feet. Even though I knew what was coming, it was always in the back of my mind; would tonight be a double whammy? Would he batter me senseless then rape me, just for good measure? I worried about that every time, but he had never repeated that abuse, thankfully. I think he preferred my fear of the threat rather than the act itself.

The day dragged on, and I was not looking forward to returning to my shitty trailer and my shitty life. Maybe I could just slip among the crowd and be gone? Again, I was kidding myself. He would catch up with me in a minute. I looked down at my watch and found that it was time for us to shut down the machines and clear out the punters. Shit. My punishment was creeping closer, snaking towards me and taunting me as the hands on my watch moved closer and closer to the end of the day.

Jimmy appeared in front of me, that evil glint still in his eyes. He didn't have to say anything; I knew that I was not going to escape this. I wished I could just disappear. We approached the trailer, and he opened the door and, not daring to let me out of his sight, he made me go inside first. I was entering the gates of hell, the only thing missing was the fiery blaze.

I closed my eyes, fully expecting the worst so that he couldn't shock me. I had become my husband's punch bag, and I was nothing other than property. He did not love me, he only loved to control me.

The slap across the back of my head came quickly. But it was lighter than expected. Jimmy was goading me.

'So, does your new boyfriend have a name?' Jimmy said.

I knew better than to backchat; I knew better than to reply with denial.

'No,' was all I said.

'He came to see you three days in a row and he didn't tell you his name?' Jimmy said, his breath in my ear.

I shook my head. I was too terrified to speak. Not that it would make a difference; nothing I could say would stop him from what he was about to do to me. I just hoped it was quick.

'Cat got your tongue, Kat?' he laughed.

My stomach rolled. I wanted to close my eyes; I didn't have the desire to watch his fist approach my face. But I didn't close them, I couldn't. They remained fixed on him, intent on not backing away and reverting into the pathetic foetal position he often forced me into. I stood strong.

'What the fuck are you looking at?' he bellowed at me, making me jump.

Jesus Christ, I couldn't even look at him now?

'On your knees,' he said, quieter this time.

I did as I was told. I wanted this to be over as quickly as possible. Before I had a chance to look up at him, his left boot caught the side of my face. I heard a crunch as my teeth crashed together. I fell to the side and stayed still, eye throbbing. I had trained myself not to make a sound; his satisfaction at my suffering often prolonged the abuse.

'Don't cross me, Kat. And if I see that prick anywhere near you again, he'll get the same as you.'

I knew Jimmy meant it but I wasn't sure that he would actually go through with it. Women were his pick, not men. No: men fought back, not women. I'd love to see someone stand up to him. The only one I had ever witnessed putting Jimmy in his place was his dad.

Jimmy left the trailer, slamming the door at his back. I got up and went into the tiny bathroom to wash my face. I managed to open one eye and reluctantly looked in the tiny mirror on the wall.

'Shit!' I said as I examined my eye.

My face burned with pain. From previous beatings, I knew nothing was broken, although I couldn't understand how; he had caught my jaw with some force. I heard the trailer door fly open and my heart sank. Jimmy was back for round two. I braved going out into the tiny hallway and found Ellie standing in the kitchen with a cigarette in one hand and a bottle of vodka in the other. She looked up at me through drunken eyes and frowned.

'What the fuck happened to you?' she slurred, as the smoke filtered through her nostrils.

'Nothing.'

'Aye, right, heard that before,' she laughed. 'That arsehole Jimmy laying into you again?'

'That *arsehole* is your brother.'

'Some fucking brother.' Ellie laughed so hard she started to cough. 'So, what was his excuse this time?'

I shook my head. I didn't want to go into detail about why her brother had almost broken my jaw, even if I had done nothing to deserve it. Hate him or not, she was still his sister. Blood's thicker than water, isn't it?

'Come on, what happened?' She took another swig from the bottle. How the hell she could drink that stuff straight was beyond me.

'If you must know, a punter's been giving me the eye. I said nothing was going on and the guy was just making small talk.'

I waited for her to go nuts, to accuse me of being unfaithful. But she didn't, she just nodded as if she knew it was coming. 'And I assume from your face that Jimmy disagreed?'

'Pretty much sums it up,' I said, as I spat blood into the sink.

Ellie offered me one of her cigarettes. I allowed her to light it as the pain intensified as I pulled my lips together to hold the tip.

'Why are you still here after everything he's done to you?' Ellie asked, as she took yet another gulp from the vodka bottle.

'Is this a trick? Has he sent you in here to ask me questions so he can lay into me again?'

Ellie shook her head then drew her eyes away. 'You know I can't fucking stand him, Kat.'

'And why is that?' I asked wearily.

Ellie avoided eye contact. 'It doesn't matter. The point is, he's a prick who needs to be put in his place, taught a lesson.'

'And what lesson would that be? How to break more bones with fewer punches?'

Ellie sniggered. 'Aye, right.' I saw venom in her eyes. 'No, the lesson he needs is for him to wake up one day and for you to be gone.'

Now it was my turn to laugh. 'Like that's ever going to happen.'

'Why not?'

Could she not *see* my face? And anyway, how could I tell her what had happened the last time I had tried to make a late-night getaway? Ellie didn't like me or her brother, but I still couldn't trust that she wouldn't kick off towards me if I told her what he had done to me. I couldn't quite understand where this conversation was heading.

'It's not important.'

'Isn't it?'

It was now or never. I had never spoken of my rape to anyone. Could I trust Ellie? I wasn't sure.

'Well?'

'Why are you so concerned with me leaving Jimmy? He's your brother. And, let's face it, you've never been my biggest fan.'

Ellie stubbed her cigarette out in the ashtray next to the sink. I looked over her shoulder and out of the large sitting area window to the site. I could see Jimmy standing next to his dad's wagon, talking to his mam as if nothing had happened.

'I'm not a fan of *anyone* who gets involved with Jimmy. That is no choice to make; life would be a downward spiral with him involved. Look at you. It hasn't exactly been a happy marriage, has it?'

'I wouldn't exactly say being a traveller is a life I would've chosen for myself.'

Ellie took a deep breath. 'Me neither.'

My knees began to tremble as I thought about telling Ellie everything about that night four years ago. I didn't know how she would react, but I had never conversed with her this way before. I decided that taking one more chance wouldn't be so bad. I was used to taking chances that backfired on me, used to getting a slap or worse. One more wouldn't make a difference.

'Jimmy raped me.' The words were out before I could stop them.

Ellie stared right through me. 'I thought you were going to say that. Kat, why do you put up with it?'

Not the response I was expecting.

'Because I have absolutely nowhere to go. I don't have any family or friends out of this fucking site and I wouldn't even know where to start.'

Ellie reached over and took my hand, leading me to the couch. She sat me down and looked over at Jimmy, who was now going inside his mam and dad's wagon.

'If I tell you something, do you promise to keep it to yourself?' she asked, words slurring again.

I nodded. I had never seen this side to Ellie before. I didn't know what to expect.

'When I was wee, I used to hear my dad battering Mam most nights. Sometimes he'd do it in front of us. I used to try to keep Mandy from seeing it, but me and Jimmy weren't so lucky. It wasn't until Jimmy reached twelve years old that he changed. He started acting out what Dad was doing to Mam.'

'What do you mean, acting out?'

'He used to hit me, which I could handle. I'm not a complete wuss. He'd threaten Mandy, so I used to take it for her. But then, one night he climbed into my bed.' She took a deep breath. Her eyes did not fill with tears the way mine did every time I thought about how he had abused me. They filled with hatred.

'I tried to stop him.' She took a large glug from the vodka bottle. 'He was so strong for a twelve-year-old. I threatened him and said if he ever did it again I'd take his dick off with Dad's pocket knife. He never touched me again after that.'

We were quiet for a while. I couldn't believe what she had just told me. Of all people, I would never have thought she would have kept something like that quiet for so long. Ellie was ballsy, and people knew not to mess with her, along with the rest of the Dentons. But then, I suppose that attitude came afterwards. Me, on the other hand, I became a blubbering wreck who was scared of my own shadow. Everyone deals with things differently, I suppose.

'Are you ok?' Ellie asked, and I suddenly felt stupid.

'Ellie, this family is a fucking joke!'

Ellie nodded. 'Aye, it is. But you can get away.'

Something outside caught my eye: Jimmy. He was heading back towards our trailer. The terror I felt was unbearable.

'What do we do?' I asked, fear clearly present in my voice. I didn't want another kicking.

'We act normal,' Ellie replied. There was no fear in *her* voice. I envied her for that.

What the fuck is normal? I thought it would be evident that we had been discussing what Jimmy had done to me, but when he came inside, he didn't even look in our direction. He went to the fridge, opened the door, took out a can of beer, and slammed the fridge door shut before going into our bedroom. I opened my mouth to speak but Ellie placed her finger over her mouth to quieten me, shaking her head.

Before we knew it, we could hear Jimmy's snores coming from the cramped bedroom.

'I've never hated you, Kat. I just didn't want to get involved in your relationship with Jimmy. To be honest, I wasn't sure I had the energy to deal with his bullshit.' Ellie's words slurred more as she spoke. Her behaviour towards me was the polar opposite of what I had been used to over the years; she was actually more like me than I thought, only stronger.

23

'You're a good actress, then, because I thought you wanted my head on a plate.'

'If you want out, you're going to have to get out soon.'

I knew she was right, but where would I go? What would I do to earn money? And would she even remember this conversation in the morning?

My vision for my life was never anything like this, even if this was all I had ever known. My parents' history as travellers was never quite clear to me. I was never told about other family members or where I really came from. My first memory was of my mam hanging out the washing beside our trailer as I crawled around on the long grass beside her. I had a good upbringing aside from all the travelling around, the different schools every year, and never really having any friends. I was educated as well as I could be, but I held no real qualifications. My parents were the only constant in my life back then. And then they were gone, and I fearfully faced life alone. Was being alone a better prospect than a life with Jimmy?

'I can't leave, I don't know how to live out of this site.'

'Then we'll just have to learn, won't we?' Ellie said.

'We? You mean you're planning on leaving too?'

Ellie nodded. 'I've wanted more from life than this shitty campsite and if this is my chance, I'm not going to let anything stand in my way. We didn't get the choice about how we lived when growing up, did we? Apart from the trailers and wagons, we never really had a home. I want a home. Don't you?'

Ellie had surprised me today, but I still wasn't sure if this was a trick or if she was genuine. Jimmy was here, and I couldn't help but wonder if he had put her up this just to land me in the shit again. Ellie took another swig from

24

her vodka bottle and, just as she was about to speak, her eyes became fixed on the door which Jimmy was behind.

'Yes, I'd love to leave and start a new life for myself. But I know nothing else other than this place,' I said. 'Jimmy told me that we're not moving again. That we can travel with the machines, but this would be our base. I've never felt at home or that this life was meant for me, no matter where we were. I've never felt like I belonged, even when my mam and dad were alive.'

Ellie nodded. 'Aye, and that bastard lying in his pit has only gone and made that feeling worse, right?'

So, what was I supposed to do now? Just up sticks and leave? I knew there was a women's refuge place in the city, but I didn't want Jimmy to find me.

'I'm not sure I can go through with it,' I said.

'Kat, we'll do it together. We'll change our names so no one can trace us and start a new life together, away from this shit-hole.'

I couldn't be sure that when she woke up the next morning, hung-over to her back teeth, she would remember all of this. Another thought crossed my mind, one which had been there since the beginning of our conversation.

'Ellie, why all of a sudden do you want to take me away from all this? You've never liked me, not really. We've never been friends, never been close. What has changed?'

'Look, I told you that I don't like anyone who gets involved with Jimmy. But you weren't to know what he was like before you married him, not really. I've watched my dad abuse my mam for years, watched Jimmy abuse you. I should have left years ago. But I didn't, we're both still here and now is the time to change things. Jimmy shouldn't be in charge of your life; that's your job.'

Ellie eyed me, and I wondered if she could see through my bravery and into my soul, that I was terrified and didn't trust her, not fully.

'Look, I know I've had a drink, but I think we should stick together on this, Kat. We Denton women should change the tradition of being the ones who are not in control; become the ones who are *so* in control that there is nothing the men can do to us.'

I stare into her eyes and I know now that she is serious. I don't know what it is in me that has changed so quickly from not trusting to trusting Ellie, but my heart tells me she is right.

'And the way to do that is to leave with no trace?'

'Let's just go.'

My eyes widened. 'What, *now?*'

Ellie smiled. 'Not now, but soon. When he least expects it. Let's face it, he's going to expect you to try it tonight after the beating he's just given you. So if he wakes up tomorrow morning to find you here, he'll relax a bit, think his message has sunk in and he'll lay off you for a while.'

'God, it's like you and Jimmy share the same brain or something.'

'Shame we share the same blood, but that's as far as it goes. Anyway, one of the nights he's out at work, we can just leave. We'll leave all our stuff 'cos that'll throw him off. Then by the time he realises you're gone, it'll be too late to find you.'

Ellie was becoming manic with her idea, and loud. 'Sssh!' I hissed. 'Talk any louder and he'll fucking hear you.'

Jimmy and the rest of the male travellers made their living by travelling around the country with the machines and fronting the carnivals and festivals throughout the spring and summer seasons. I, along with the other women, got dragged around in our trailers and made to work the ticket stands on the machines. But I always knew that I wanted more from life. I wanted a real job and a normal life, to be part of how the world works.

'So, are you with me?' She was quieter this time.

I paused, considering my only two options. Stay here and risk beating after beating and constant abuse. Or, run and build a life for myself? It would be hard, and I would be looking over my shoulder for the rest of my life, but at least it would be a life and not just an existence. Although, I was aware that I was contemplating making a life-changing decision with a drunk woman.

'Well?' Ellie prompted.

A sudden crash came from the bedroom, followed by muffled swearing. I looked over at Ellie, who had a look of repulsion on her face at the sound of her brother waking up. The bedroom door swung open and Jimmy fell out of the room. It was obvious that the effects of a full day's worth of drinking had eventually knocked him senseless, which was good in a way as it meant he wouldn't be able to hit me again, even if he concentrated hard enough. Jimmy would often work the machines with a drink in him. It was the first thing he did when he woke up in the morning and I was used to that. It was a wonder he hadn't killed himself yet.

'What the fuck are you two looking at?' Saliva dripped down his chin as he slurred his words.

'Fuck off, you drunken arsehole,' Ellie replied.

Jimmy sniggered, clearly amused by his sister's bravery.

'Aye, I will. Bunch of tarts,' he replied as he went into the bathroom, slamming the door closed behind him and causing the trailer to shake once more.

'You're not seriously considering staying here with that disgusting pig, are you?' Ellie whispered.

'Not a chance. I'm in.' I tried to move my mouth as little as possible as I spoke, so my jaw ached less.

This was it. I had finally decided that after all these years, I was going to leave Jimmy and get out into the real world. I didn't care what my new life threw at me. Surely I couldn't end up worse off than I already was?

Chapter Two

I woke to the sound of Jimmy clattering around in the kitchenette. The smell of fried eggs and bacon made me salivate before I'd even opened my eyes. The sun shone through the small bedroom window creating a warmth I didn't normally feel when I was there. Perhaps because Jimmy was in another room, I didn't feel so threatened. The night before, I had crawled into bed as quietly as I could. But the bastard was waiting for me, with 'I'm sorry,' and 'I love you,' so he could worm his way back in. That used to work on me, in the beginning. When we first got married, his abuse caught me so off-guard that I genuinely believed that the odd punch here and there was just stress-related on his part. He'd seem so full of guilt and would shower me in compliments, apologies, and assurances that it would never happen again. I'd believed him, every single time. Not now. Someone can't make the same mistake that many times and still expect people to believe it wasn't intentional.

All those years of pretending he was sorry, and I just had to accept it so the situation wouldn't escalate, so he didn't get angry at my reaction and resort to violence once again. Now I had to put on a front, pretend that it would all be ok, and we would get through things as a couple, so that he wouldn't suspect I was trying to leave again.

I heard him open the door but pretended to be asleep.

'Breakfast is up. Get your arse out here and fill your boots, girl,' he bellowed into the room.

I sat up and out of nowhere the smell of grease made me feel sick. I fought the urge to vomit and got out of bed, ensuring I wrapped myself up properly in my dressing gown. I walked out to the kitchenette and watched as Jimmy set the small table.

'Sit your arse there and I'll serve. It's the full shebang today.' Jimmy was chirpy. Even in this mood, though, he made me jumpy. Something in my stomach gave way when I saw the plate in front of me.

'Tuck in, hen, we fair worked up an appetite last night.' He laughed, stuffing his mouth with greasy food in between the words.

Looking down at the plate, my stomach heaved. In the blink of an eye, I was staring into the bottom of the toilet.

'My cooking isn't that bad, is it?' Jimmy laughed from the kitchenette.

I shook my head as I flushed the toilet. Jimmy Denton really was all heart. My own heart ached as I thought of what had happened to the Jimmy I had fallen in love with. Yes, he was rough round the edges back in the day. But now, he was just cold. I imagined evil ran in his veins. I thought of how he used to react if I was ever ill. He'd rub my back, hold my hair out of the way. He'd wrap me in the duvet and bring me tea. It was obvious to me now what he had been doing; luring me into a false sense of security, making me think that even though I'd lost my parents at such a young age, he'd be there to look after me. But in reality, he was setting his trap so that I would have no one to turn to other than him.

Getting to my feet, I caught sight of my reflection staring back at me from the mirror. I was white as a sheet. I opened the cabinet to get some mouthwash and my tampons were staring me square in the face.

'Jimmy, what day is it?' I shouted before I could stop myself.

'Why?' he replied, through a mouthful of food.

Think, Kat. Why would you want to know what day it was?

'I'm supposed to be going up to the shop to see when they next get their stock of that whisky you like, and I can't remember what day they said I should go in.' *Quick on my toes with that one. Nice one, Kat.*

'It's Wednesday, you idiot.'

'Thanks,' I called back.

Shit! I was late, by almost a week. I was never late, not ever.

I heard the dishes being slung into the sink and Jimmy shouted, 'You don't fancy doing those dishes before I'm back, eh?'

'Ok, see you later.'

This couldn't be happening, it couldn't be. Not now. I'd been so careful over the years, hiding the fact I was on the pill. Jimmy'd wanted us to have a child almost as soon as we got married. In the beginning, I was definitely on the same page as him. But after the first beating I took from him, I had decided that bringing a baby into a violent marriage was not the right thing to do. That and raising a child as a traveller was something I didn't want. I remember as a child how hard things were at school, especially since we'd moved around a lot. I was teased because I was different. The way I spoke was different too. I didn't want that for my child. I'd been lucky enough to find a hiding place for my pill in the cleaning cupboard. Jimmy never went in there. Fourteen years of being on the pill and there had never been one ounce of suspicion from him. We'd been careful during the first two years and luckily it had worked.

Now my period was an entire week late, for the first time I could remember. My heart sank.

Hearing him leave, I ran into the bedroom and got dressed. I got the fright of my life when I heard Ellie behind me. 'You haven't changed your mind, have you?'

'Jesus Christ, Ellie, you nearly gave me a fucking heart attack.'

Ellie smiled as she leaned against the small door.

'No, I haven't changed my mind but there's a spanner in the works.'

'What do you mean?' Ellie frowned, massaging her temples.

I sighed. This was not what I needed. 'My period, it's late.'

Ellie stood up straight although swaying a little from the lasting effects of the alcohol from last night. 'You'd better be kidding.'

'I wish I was.'

'Then get your arse up that shop and get a test.'

What was it with that family, referring to my arse when they wanted me to do something? 'What did you think I was going to do, just hope for the best?'

'Well, come on then. I'll go with you.' She was pulling at my arm. We were speed-walking towards the local shop.

'You're going to have to buy it,' I said.

'What?'

'If anyone sees me buying a pregnancy test, they'll tell him and the whole bloody site probably. You know what this place is like. We can't risk it.'

Ellie sighed, and I wasn't sure if she was about to have a change of heart.

'Ok, I'll buy it. And if anyone asks, I don't know who the dad is. That way, Jimmy can't do any damage. But we're ahead of ourselves here. There might not be anything to worry about yet. You could just be late due to stress. You don't exactly have the easiest lifestyle, do you?'

I nodded as she dragged me into the shop. I wanted to believe her. Deep in my heart, though, I knew what the outcome was going to be. Ellie picked up the cheapest test and before I knew it, we were back outside.

'Where are we doing it?' Ellie asked.

'I don't remember a pregnancy test consisting of two people having to piss on a stick,' I said.

Ellie laughed, but then quickly stopped. 'Oh, don't make me laugh or my head will explode.'

'If you hadn't tanned that bottle of vodka last night, you'd be fresh as a daisy,' I replied. '*I'll* do the test where no one will see. You just keep watch.'

This was not what I'd had in mind when I imagined myself taking a pregnancy test for the first time. I climbed the small wooden fence at the back of the shop and checked to make sure nobody was around. I couldn't go back to the trailer to do it. What if Jimmy came back and found me? I'd never be able to get away from him if he thought I was carrying his baby. There was no way in hell I would willingly have a baby with someone like him. If he was capable of battering the shit out of me, eventually he would do it to our child. No chance I'd allow that.

I went behind the large hedge at the back of the fence and hid. The hedge was over seven feet tall, so there wouldn't be a chance of anyone seeing me. I took the test out of the box and did what I had to do. The leaflet told me to wait for five minutes to check the result.

'Done it yet?' Ellie appeared in front of me.

'Ellie!' I gasped, pulling my jeans up.

'What?'

She lit up a cigarette and offered me one.

'I'd better wait, see if I can smoke or not.'

'You mean you'll keep it if you are?' she said through rings of blue smoke.

I shook my head. 'To be honest, I have no idea what I'll do.'

I thought about the last twenty-four hours; in fact, I thought about the last sixteen years. I had put up with a lot. And now I was about to find out if I was pregnant by a monster. It would not be the child's fault I was in this mess. If Jimmy could hurt his sister and wife, he could do the same to his son or daughter. It was different making stupid decisions when I only had myself to think of. I didn't want to make the wrong choices when a baby was involved.

'Five minutes is up,' Ellie said, taking my hand.

I had never seen this side of Ellie before. Was this the real Ellie, who had been hiding behind a hardened exterior because of what Jimmy did to her?

'Shit.' I realised the next few seconds could change my life forever.

'It'll be fine, whatever the outcome. If we have to leave as a three, we will. But we'll have to be extra careful because you know he'll come looking for us. If he finds out you're pregnant, he'll be on the rampage. So, if you are, you have to act completely normal. Only we will know about it, ok?'

I nodded, the lump in my throat growing at a rapid pace. I turned the stick over. My eyes filled with tears.

'Well?' Ellie prompted.

I looked into Ellie's eyes. I couldn't speak. She took the stick of fate from my quivering hands and stared down at it. She was quiet for a few moments before she looked up at me.

'We'll be fine.'

Could this really be happening? A baby, growing inside me?

'Kat?' Ellie was shaking me. 'Kat, we need to make a plan now. We have to leave tonight.'

'Tonight?'

'Yes, we have to go with nothing. We have to do it now more than ever. If you stay, there's a chance he'll kill you both.'

Ellie was right. It was one thing to allow him to push me towards death, but I wasn't about to let him do it to my baby. *My* baby, not his.

'Ellie, why now?' I ask, suddenly realising I had no idea why she wanted to help me.

'Why now, what?'

'Why after all these years do you want to leave now?'

'I see what he does to you. I see what Dad does to Mum. I might be a bitch, Kat, but I'm not evil like the men in my family. You don't deserve this. No one does. I want out of here as much as you do. Why not now?'

We stare at each other in silence and she hands me back my pregnancy test. My lifeline. My whole reason to get the hell away from hell and the devil himself.

'Ok, we go tonight. And we fucking *run*, as far as we can.'

And if I wasn't successful in my attempt at escape this time around, then I was sure I would die at the hands of Jimmy, along with my baby.

Chapter Three

My mam and dad were the best parents I could have wished for. From what I could remember, they were happily married and even though we lived on a traveller site I wanted for nothing. I was heartbroken when they died.

I remember my dad fondly. He was a gentle man who adored me and my mam. I never knew why they chose their way of life. I remember them talking about when my dad used to live in a house in the outskirts of Glasgow, but I never found out why they ended up as members of the travelling community.

I always imagined that my mam and dad could have done something big with their lives. They were clever people. My dad was always reading; I remember there being stacks and stacks of books in our trailer, despite the lack of space. He would read just about anything; my mam, too.

In the weeks leading up to their deaths, I'd started seeing Jimmy. He had managed to charm me. I have to admit he had a way with words, even though he was only sixteen at the time. He had the brightest smile and, much as I hate to admit this now, he made me weak at the knees. Dad had warned me to stay away from Jimmy, said that he was bad news. I tried to do what my dad said but I just couldn't help myself. Jimmy had me exactly where he wanted me, I see that now. Sixteen years down the line and now here I was, pregnant and planning to run away from him with his sister.

'Don't take any of your belongings tonight. Just make sure that you're ready to go when I say.'

I nodded as Ellie spoke. 'Have you told Mandy?'

Ellie shook her head sadly. 'No, she thinks the sun shines out of Jimmy's backside and she's oblivious to my dad's behaviour. If I told her what we were doing, she would tell them. We can't risk it.'

Ellie looked worn out. She was holding everything together for me and I would be eternally grateful to her for that.

'Thank you.'

Ellie looked at me. 'For what?'

'For giving me the strength to do this. If it weren't for you, I would probably be stuck here forever.'

Before I could say anything else, Ellie wrapped me in a tight hug.

'No need to thank me, we're in this together.'

'If you don't stop squashing me, you'll be going it alone.' I laughed gently.

I looked around the trailer that had been my home for the past twelve years. Jimmy and I had moved into our own after living in the cramped wagon with his family. It might have been my home, but it had never felt like it. Not after Jimmy had turned my life upside down. And come to think of it, the whole traveller way of life had me feeling unsettled for as far back as I could remember.

'I'll come and get you when I know everything is clear.' Ellie left the trailer. I watched as she walked across the site to the wagon she shared with the rest of the Dentons.

I couldn't believe my life had come to this. I had allowed someone to take control of me and waste my time. My dad had always said the same thing to me over the years, *'Never waste your time on someone who doesn't love you for who you are.'*

I had allowed Jimmy to wear me down and mould me into the person he wanted me to be, someone who would bow down to his every word just for an easy life. What had happened to me?

Jimmy Denton was going to learn what it was like to feel lost and hurt for a change.

The door opened then, and I kept facing the window to the Dentons' wagon. I knew it was Jimmy coming in because every time he did, the atmosphere in the room would turn heavy. I didn't dare look at him in case he could see in my eyes that something was wrong.

'You just going to ignore me, aye?'

I took a deep breath. 'Not at all, I was just daydreaming. How are you?'

His presence was close. I felt his breath on my ear. 'Aye, I'm fine. Cannae say the same for that sister of mine, right enough. She's got a face like a well-skelped arse. She's not said anything to you, has she?'

I played it cool. 'Which sister?'

There was silence for what seemed like hours. I held my breath. I still couldn't bring myself to look at him.

'What's the matter with you?'

I turned around. 'Nothing. Why do you always think there's something wrong with me?'

Jimmy shrugged. 'Must just be a woman thing, then. Your lot always have a face like you're hard done by.'

He sat down and turned the TV on, putting his feet up on the table. I tried to remain brave and act normal. His words were like acid.

'Are you and the rest of the guys working tonight?' I asked.

'Aye, some of us are doing the doors. Trying to get the ticket sales up for the carnival coming up. Why?'

'Just wondered if you wanted dinner before you go?' I asked sweetly.

'Nah, I'll grab something when I get back. We're not planning on it being a late one anyway.'

I suddenly felt sick. Without wishing to draw attention to myself, I started to walk to the bathroom, taking deep breaths as I did. Once I was in there, I locked the door behind me and switched on the shower, praying that the sound of the water hitting the base of the cubicle would drown out the retches coming from my throat. I suppose I had all this to look forward to while I was on the run. I still couldn't imagine my life without Jimmy, but not because I would miss him. I loathed the man, even though my heart had told me differently in the past.

I knew he wasn't good for me and that anyone who truly loved someone could never hurt them the way he had hurt me. He didn't love me; he possessed me. I was his and no one would ever be able to change that. Even if I did manage to get away from him, I would always belong to him, until death, I really was beginning to believe that myself even though I know I shouldn't.

There were times when I was alone with Jimmy and he would be sitting quietly watching the television, or reading the paper, and I would look at him and wonder what had happened to the man I had fallen for. I often wondered what it would be like to turn the tables on him, to see him express fear for a change. I remembered when we were younger, not long after my parents died, him teaching me how to use his father's gun. We were out in the fields and he asked me if I had ever wanted to shoot something to see what it felt like. I had said no, I couldn't imagine killing or injuring a life like that.

But the chemistry between us that day had been so intense. We couldn't keep our hands off each other, and having sex with him in that open space, while he had a gun in his hand, had filled me with the most intense adrenaline rush I had ever felt. Afterwards, he shot a crow as it flew over the field. I was horrified, but I didn't show it. When we got back to the trailer that day, he put the gun in what he called 'the safe place'. Not so safe if the television ever got stolen as the gun was taped to the back of it.

Years later, when we moved into our own trailer, Jimmy had his own gun and brought it with us. He put it in a safe place, taped to the back of the old television set, just like Stan's, swearing me to secrecy about where it was. I often imagined what it would be like to bring it out and shoot him with it. But if I was completely honest with myself, I knew that if I couldn't handle watching a crow fall at the mercy of a bullet, I would never be able to put one in my husband.

I wiped my mouth and climbed into the shower. It was likely to be the last shower I would have for a while, depending on how long it would take before Ellie and I found some sort of shelter. I imagined what it would be like to be on the run from Jimmy; what kind of life would

I lead away from the site? Would I be able to integrate into society properly? Would I be able to look after my baby? I was pinning all my hopes on *yes*.

'I'll see you when I get back. You will be in, won't you?' I heard Jimmy call through the paper-thin bathroom door.

'I've nowhere else to go. I'll see you soon.' I tried to sound sincere, but the more I relived everything he had done to me over the years, the harder it became to pretend everything was fine.

I heard the door close and turned off the shower. As I climbed out and wrapped a towel around me, I heard Ellie. 'I saw them leave in the wagon. We need to be out of here in the next thirty minutes if we have any chance of getting away.'

I opened the door to her and was surprised to see that she looked terrified.

'Are you ok?'

'No, not really. I'm leaving the only life I've ever known; I'm allowed to be a little scared, am I not?' Ellie replied.

'You can't be any more scared than I am right now. Do we have an actual plan?'

Ellie nodded as I passed her to go into the bedroom. I dried myself and got dressed, throwing my wet hair up in a ponytail. I didn't care how I looked. All I cared about was getting as far away from Jimmy and this site as fast as possible.

'The plan is to run like hell and not look back. I know a few Women's Aid centres in Glasgow, and there are some in Aberdeen and Edinburgh.'

'And how the hell are we supposed to get to Aberdeen or Edinburgh?' I asked.

Ellie sighed. 'I'm not saying we're going there today, but they are there if we need to go further. Glasgow might seem like a big place but Jimmy will find us eventually, Kat.'

Ellie was right. I was going to spend the rest of my life looking over my shoulder, expecting to find Jimmy's eyes burning into me. He would kill me if he ever found me. I had to be so careful. I would have to change my name and basically be in hiding for the rest of my living days. But when I thought about it, all I found myself caring about was the fact that I had a little life growing inside me and so long as I could protect it, I didn't care what I had to do to stay safe.

'Are you ready for this?' Ellie asked.

'No, I'll never feel ready. But we have to go and we're going now.'

Ellie took hold of my hand and looked dead into my eyes. 'Let's go.'

We decided a relaxed attitude was the best form to adopt as we left the trailer, so as not to raise any suspicion. The sun was low as it set over the Old Kilpatrick Hills. The sky was a lovely pink colour and the air still warm. I looked over the site for the last time and remembered my parents. They would have been proud of me for doing this. I missed them so much, especially in times like this. They were taken from me far too soon and I had never truly recovered from their deaths. As we walked towards the site exit, Ellie and Jimmy's younger sister, Mandy, was walking towards us, holding hands with a spotty teenaged boy.

'And who's this?' Ellie asked, letting go of my hand and holding her own out, gesturing towards the boy.

'None of your bloody business,' Mandy replied, a smirk spreading over her face.

'Maybe not, but you know Dad and Jimmy will make it their business.'

The smirk on Mandy's face disappeared instantly. 'This is Davie, he plays in the darts tournament at the pub down the road.'

'The Tavern?' Ellie replied.

'Ellie?' I heard myself saying. 'She's a grown woman.'

Mandy was a nineteen-year-old Denton daughter; this Davie character wouldn't last five minutes once Jimmy and Stan heard about him. Poor guy.

'Thank you, Kat, at least someone understands me.'

I didn't understand or care. I was just very aware of time. I couldn't give two shits if she brought someone back to the site with her. Once the guy was introduced to Jimmy and Stan, he'd be off like a shot before he got his head caved in anyway.

'Just take it as a warning. Look after yourself, Mandy, you hear?' Ellie said softly.

'Eh?'

'You heard me, look after yourself.'

Mandy's brow furrowed. 'You say it like you'll never see me again.'

Ellie was quick off the mark. 'Well, if Dad sees you with this one,' she pointed at Davie, 'then there's a chance I *won't* see you again.'

Mandy shook her head. 'Shut up, Ellie. I'll see you later.' She skulked off, dragging her newest friend with her. The poor guy didn't know what he was letting himself in for. I looked at Ellie and noted how strong she was being. She was leaving her little sister behind to help me get away from Jimmy.

'Are you ok?' I asked, as we began to walk away.

'I'll come back for her one day. I can't leave her here.'

'Jimmy wouldn't do anything to her now that she's older, would he?'

'Who the hell knows? He's capable of anything.'

We walked casually out of the site and I could tell that it was killing Ellie to leave Mandy behind. I felt guilty that I was the main reason. 'I'm sorry for dragging you into this. You don't have to leave her behind because of me, you know.'

'I'm not doing it just for you. I'm doing this for me too. I can't stand the thought of staying here any longer and living this fucked-up life where everyone thinks we're the strongest family there ever was when, in fact, we're the most fucked-up family there ever was.' Ellie stops and for a moment I think she is going to cry, but she doesn't. 'Kat, look at you. You're a shell of who you once were, who you should have become. I am too, I've recently realised. For years I've watched Dad grind Mam down until she no longer fought against him, until she decided it was best she just nod her head, and do what she's told. I should have left years ago when Jimmy first started showing signs of turning into dad.'

'Ellie,' I say, and then I falter. I don't know how to respond. A multitude of lives, destroyed by the same men.

'If the best thing to come out of the Denton family is your little one, then we have to get as far away from here as possible. This is why we have to leave today, no time like the present. If we stay, we'll never be free. Your daughter, my niece would face a lifetime of misery. We can't let that happen, Kat. We can't. My mam couldn't protect us from it, but we can protect her. Or him,' she said, gesturing towards my stomach.

We kept our eyes on everything around us as we walked, and my heart skipped a beat every time I heard a car or footsteps close by. I had a clear vision in my head of what would happen to me if Jimmy caught me making my break from him.

Ellie and I climbed the back wall which enclosed the camp site. We had travelled with the camp for years, as far back as I could remember, but we had been at this site for close to a year now. The view was outstanding, with the Old Kilpatrick Hills in front of us and the Clyde leading west to Dumbarton and Greenock. The only thing I would miss would be looking at that view as the sun went down. This was the last time I would see it.

I drank it in as I straddled the back wall and we began our getaway. We climbed the hill leading up to the back end of the Dalnottar Cemetery and found a hole in the wire fence which surrounded the grounds. We stayed close to the top end so that we could take cover behind the trees should Jimmy or anyone else happen to pass through. It was highly unlikely, but we couldn't be too careful.

As I looked down onto the A82, I could see the whisky distillery and beyond, over towards Paisley. The sun was strong as it set behind us and the view in front of me looked like it had been sprinkled in golden glitter.

Glancing over the graves as we hurried along the top of Dalnottar, I read some of the memorials and began to think about my parents. I missed them so much it still hurt like it had the day they died. I felt my eyes fill with tears and my heart swell as I thought about them and the fact that they wouldn't meet my own son or daughter.

'We're almost there,' Ellie's voice interrupted my thoughts.

'Where?'

'The exit of the cemetery. But I don't want us to walk along the main road. If Jimmy and the rest of them pass us, we'll be caught. We have to use the back road and go through the streets of Duntocher.'

I considered the chance of us being caught and dragged back to the site. I didn't want to risk it, so I agreed.

'Do you know the way?' I asked.

Ellie nodded. 'As soon as we get out of the gate, there's a farm road which leads up to Beeches Stables. If we follow that and then turn right at the horse field, we'll be beside the primary school and can get into Duntocher from there.'

I was surprised at how well Ellie knew the route we had to take. She had barely left the site the whole time we lived there.

'How do you know all this?'

'I snuck out of the camp last night and did a trial run. I had to be sure there were alternative routes to the main road.'

'You were absolutely hammered. How the hell do you even remember this?'

'I forget nothing, Kat. Living with Jimmy and my dad, you have to remember every detail to protect yourself.'

It was ridiculous that we were grown women, and yet we were never allowed to leave that bloody site unless we had a Denton man by our sides. Life had become a sorry

47

state of affairs. Ellie seemed focused; I was so glad she was with me.

'You really don't know what this means to me, Ellie.'

'Just keep walking, we've a lot of ground to cover before it gets dark. You can get sentimental later,' she half smiled.

We exited the cemetery and made our way up the farm road to the stables. This was it, the start of my new life. I was terrified.

Chapter Four

We made it out of the farmland and into Duntocher, where the streets looked almost identical, lined with cosy-looking houses, lights shining in nicely dressed windows. It was then I realised that this was what I wanted for my baby – a proper life with a proper home, where we wouldn't be moved around constantly. A home we would be settled in, near a school where my child would make friends.

We began climbing the steep hill in front of us. There were houses running up the left side, with gardens and driveways contained in small spaces. On the right-hand side was a large patch of grassland and further up were more homes. This road seemed to go on forever, but I enjoyed looking in the windows and seeing families sitting around the television or the dinner table. I wanted that for my little one.

'This place is lovely, don't you think?' I asked.

'Pity we can't stay here. But there will be plenty more places like this,' Ellie replied.

We reached the top of the hill, and there was a street to my left which led downhill to another street with rows of flats down one side. Ellie grabbed my hand and pulled me into an opening which led to some old, crumbling garages.

'Why did you take us this way?' I asked.

'Any roads which lead us away from the possibility of Jimmy seeing us are better than main roads.'

She was right. I hadn't thought of that. We came out of the garages and crossed through a small car park, passing a shop which was still open.

'We should get some supplies for the journey. I know it's only Glasgow but I don't know what will happen when we get there.'

'What do you mean?' I asked.

'Well, the refuge centre might not have space; we might have to wait for them to find something else for us. So we should get some food in case.'

Great. Now I had visions of us not only hiding from Jimmy and the scum he no doubt had out looking for us, but also sleeping on the streets. In Glasgow.

'And you didn't think to tell me this before we left?' I snapped.

Ellie laughed. 'What, because you would've stayed with your caring husband if I had and lived happily ever after?'

I fell silent.

'Nah, I didn't think so. Come on, we can get plenty of the things we need.'

'Ellie, we don't have any money other than bus fare to get into Glasgow.'

Ellie winked at me. 'That's what you think. I took the stash that Jimmy keeps at Dad's wagon. And the best thing is, he doesn't know anyone knows about it. So he'll have no idea it was me who took it. Unless he finds it's missing after he realises we're gone.'

'What stash?' I asked, trying not to think about how he would react when he realised what we had done.

'You didn't know he kept money at Dad's wagon?'

I shook my head. 'No, he tells me nothing but expects me to know everything. He uses my lack of knowledge as an excuse to mess me up.'

Ellie shook her head and lit a cigarette. 'He has over five grand stashed there. Fuck knows where it all comes from but I couldn't care less. And if he owes someone money then even better, there's a bit of karma for you.'

'What a risk to take, Ellie, well done.' I didn't feel sorry for Jimmy. I felt sorry for me; another reason for him to batter seven bells out of me, if he caught me.

Ellie laughed and smoked the rest of her cigarette before going inside the shop. I followed her and threw anything I could find that didn't have to be cooked into a basket. We paid quickly and as we stepped outside there was a bus sitting at the stop.

'Let's see if it's going to Glasgow.' The words hadn't left her mouth before she was on the bus. I followed quickly behind.

'Do you go to Glasgow?' Ellie asked the driver.

'Aye hen, do you want a return?'

'We're not coming back, a single is fine,' I replied. It felt good to say it, but just as I did I looked out of the front window of the bus and down the hill, to see Jimmy and his scummy friends from the site doing their door-to-door sales.

'Nice one, Ellie, you've put us in the middle of the lion's den,' I hissed in her ear.

'Just pay the fare and keep your head down.'

We sat at the back of the bus and slouched down as far as we could. The bus began to pull out and I could feel it moving downhill. The little window above me was open, and I knew we were passing the group as I could hear them talking. When the bus stopped, I thought my heart had too. Jimmy was right outside my window. I felt like I could throw up from the fear I felt rushing through me.

'Any sales yet?' I heard Jimmy ask.

'Aye, a few folk have bought family tickets, but that's about it. Got about twenty quid so far,' Scum Number One replied.

'Well, get a fucking grip and get round more doors, we're going to need more than that to get by.'

So, I wasn't the only one he spoke to like a piece of shit. I kept myself so low I was almost on the floor. It felt like a lifetime had passed since the bus stopped moving, but it slowly began to pull away again. I could feel blood rush back to my face and after about five minutes I sat back up.

'I've just realised that was the last time I'll ever hear his voice.' I looked at Ellie and smiled. 'I was right there and he had no clue. By the time he's back at the site, we'll be long gone.'

Ellie nodded. 'Don't get too excited. It's Jimmy. He'll stop at nothing to find us, especially you.'

It was true. Even though I intended that to be the last time I would hear his voice or be anywhere near him, I knew that as soon as he realised I was gone, he'd be after me. And Jimmy Denton would stop at nothing to get what he wanted.

The bus was empty, except for us. It was almost a clear run all the way into Glasgow, with only a few people getting on and off before we hit the city centre. I took in the sights of the city as my imagination trailed off to somewhere far away. We had done it; we had managed to get away. It seemed too easy and too good to be true. I just hoped it wouldn't be short-lived. Glasgow wasn't that far from the site, but it's far away enough that I know he won't find us right away. Jimmy is a lot of things, but clever isn't one of them.

–

We stepped off the bus in Argyle Street and gazed around for a few moments, not really knowing where to go or what to do next. I had left it to Ellie to figure out the details. Central Bridge was just ahead of us and I felt vulnerable as I realised just how much open space we were standing in the middle of. Of course, there were people everywhere, but I felt like Ellie and I stood out like a sore thumb.

'Now what?' I asked.

Ellie grabbed my hand and pulled me towards her. 'We find the refuge and stay there for the night.'

'Can we do that? What if there's no room?'

'We'll deal with that if it happens. Now, get a move on.'

We walked along Argyle Street for a short time before Ellie pulled us up to the left and onto Hope Street. There were bars and restaurants filled with people. Everyone looked happy and carefree. I didn't know how that felt; come to think of it, I hadn't felt like that since before my parents died. The combination of car fumes, fast food, and beer invaded my senses, and I began to feel sick. My legs became wobbly and I stopped on the pavement. Ellie turned as she felt my hand tug on her jacket.

'What's wrong?'

'I feel sick,' I said, through deep breaths.

'We're almost there, Kat. You have to keep going. You can rest when we get to the refuge.'

I moved my legs, this time putting all my effort into making them cooperate. I tried not to make eye contact with anyone, fearing that when I did look up, I'd be face to face with Jimmy. Funny how I felt more terrified now that I was away from him than I ever had been when I was there. I suppose in a sense I knew what to expect back at the site. I was fully aware that my next reign of abuse was just around the corner.

The air brakes on the double-decker bus beside us gave me such a fright I almost shot up into the air. I must have let out some sort of noise because two girls standing outside a pub smoking a cigarette began giggling. I shot them a look of disgust. Not intentionally, but through embarrassment. They dropped their eyes from my gaze and continued their conversation.

This was what my life would be like from now on; every little noise, every footstep behind me, I would be on edge for the rest of my days. I would be expecting him everywhere I went.

'Yes, I knew we'd find it,' Ellie said. I looked up and was faced with a large building. It was nothing special, just bricks and glass. But it would be our haven for the night.

We went inside and found a woman sitting behind a desk. The place was quiet, and I instantly felt safe.

'Hi, I'm Ellie, we spoke on the phone this morning.'

Before I knew it, we were in what looked like a flat. I had concentrated on my breathing on our way up the several flights of stairs.

'Make yourselves comfortable. If you need anything, this phone connects to the site office downstairs. Just lift the receiver and press nine,' the woman said, pointing to a black phone on a small table in the corner of the room.

'No one will know we're here, will they?' I found myself asking.

'Not unless you want anyone to know,' the woman replied. 'I'm Louise, by the way. I'm on duty until six tomorrow morning, so if you need anything, you'll get me on the phone.'

I nodded and Ellie thanked her.

Louise left the room, and I sat down on a small couch. I didn't pay any particular attention to the details of the room we were in. All I wanted to do was lie down and go to sleep.

'Do you think he'll have figured it out yet?' Ellie asked as she sat down next to me.

I shook my head. 'I hope not. That'll give us more time.'

'Well, you should rest. I'm going to go downstairs and find out what we can do next. I'll put the food in the kitchen if you're hungry.'

'You're leaving me up here on my own?' I said, trying to keep calm. My hands were sweating with panic, and I knew that she could hear the tremble in my voice. 'What if he knows we're here and comes after us?'

Ellie put her hand on my shoulder. I was shaking violently as if I were convulsing. 'Kat, no one knows we're here. How could they? We haven't left a trail, we've not even packed a bloody bag. We literally fled with nothing. We're safe here until we can move on.'

My eyes stung with the tears that filled them. 'And when are we moving on?'

'That's what I'm going downstairs to find out. I promise I'll be back inside the hour. The phone is there if you want to phone down to check I'm still here.'

Inside twenty-four hours, Ellie had become my rock. Inside twenty-four hours, my life had changed so drastically that it made me feel sick.

Ellie, I thought. How was it possible that we had avoided each other over the course of sixteen years, yet I was facing the prospect of spending the rest of my life with her? I couldn't begin to imagine what our lives were going to be like away from the site. Neither of us had known anything else. Neither of us knew how to exist outside the gates of that place.

I'd never have imagined that I would literally have placed my life in Ellie's hands. Or the life of my unborn child.

Starting over in a strange city, out of my depth with a baby on the way. On the run from the most violent man I could imagine. My life was better just for getting away from him for a few hours, and worse for not knowing if he would find me or not, all at the same time.

'Don't be long,' I said.

As Ellie left the room, I locked the door behind her. I stayed away from the windows and curled up on the couch. As I sat alone in the unfamiliar room, a churning feeling of uncertainty set in. I wanted to be in my own bed, wrapped in my own duvet.

I shook my head. Why was I feeling home sick? Or was it just insecurity about what lay ahead of me? I'd never lived on my own, had never been responsible for anything in my life. All I knew was that life, the familiar faces of the people who I had travelled with, how I grew up

I pulled my knees up and thought about the last sixteen years. Jimmy Denton had robbed me of my life. He had beaten me into submission over the years, and I had become a shell of what I had once been. I had wanted to do something with my life, something worthwhile. Jimmy had made damn sure that I would live for him and only him, that I would do as he said and if I stepped out of line, I would pay the price. I had blocked it out for years, but now that I was in a refuge centre, away from his abuse and carrying a new life, I should have felt relief.

So why did I want to scream? Why did I feel sheer terror? Why did I feel more terrified than I had ever been before?

Chapter Five

The room was dark and unfamiliar. As the soft cushions held my weight on the couch, I heard nothing other than the rush of blood in my ears. For the first time all day, I felt relaxed. I closed my eyes. Before I knew it, they shot open again at the sound of a key scratching inside a lock somewhere in the room. I froze in terror, suddenly forgetting where I was and who I was supposed to be with. I couldn't gather my thoughts in time before I saw a tall, stalking shadow approaching me from the far gloom at the opposite end of the space I was in. I tried to scream; I tried to move, but nothing happened. My body wouldn't cooperate with the messages from my brain. I felt glued to the surface and my eyes fixated on the figure ahead of me. It approached quickly and, just as a large hand reached for my throat, I sat up so quickly I almost knocked my attacker off balance.

'What?' Ellie stepped back, shocked by my sudden outburst.

I was breathing heavily, panicked by my nightmare.

'I thought you were Jimmy.'

'Thanks,' she said, taking a seat next to me.

'This is what my life is going to be like now, isn't it? I'm going to be waking up in terror and looking over my shoulder for the rest of my life, wondering if he's one step behind me.'

Ellie hugged me tight. 'Not necessarily. I've had a long chat with Louise and another woman downstairs. They've helped me to come up with a plan that will keep us safe and get us as far away from here as possible, but you have to talk to them first.'

I took in Ellie's words. 'Why do I have to talk to them first?'

'Because, you're the one who has fled domestic abuse, and you're pregnant. They want to make sure that the plan in place is what you need and what is right for you.'

I nodded in agreement. I would do anything to get as far away from Jimmy as possible. I just couldn't imagine where that would be. Nowhere on earth would be far enough away.

'You need to get some rest though. It's been a long day for you and baby and you need your strength to be able to understand everything that's going to be discussed later.'

My eyes wept for sleep but my mind fought against it. I didn't want to close my eyes for fear of seeing him. Sixteen years' worth of being strong, battling against his abuse, and keeping myself alive, doing anything I had to, to keep him on side had finally released the person I had become; a fearful, quivering, pathetic mess.

–

I was sitting on the same couch that I had tried desperately to sleep on earlier in the evening. I had drifted in and out of sleep for a few hours with Ellie by my side, but I just couldn't settle. Every time my body had begun to relax,

Jimmy's face crept its way into my unconscious and I was instantly awake.

'You didn't get much sleep earlier?' Louise's voice was soft.

I shook my head, too tired to speak.

'Did Ellie explain everything to you?'

I nodded. 'Not in great detail, but enough that I know you've put a plan in place to get us away from here.'

Louise smiled at me. 'That about covers it, yes. How are you?'

How was I? Was she serious? How the bloody hell did she think I was feeling? Just fine and fucking dandy? 'I'm fine, thank you.'

Ellie may have heard my tone. She smiled and bowed her head and I was glad my initial reaction was in my head and I hadn't said it out loud. Louise and Ellie are trying to help me, I remind myself. I don't want to lash out at anyone who doesn't deserve my wrath. I can't help but get angry at my situation, but I suppose that is something which will ease with time.

'Why don't you tell me what you want, how can we help?' Louise asked, as she sipped on a mug of black tea.

So, I told her everything; from the rape, to the beatings, my pregnancy, and my desire to lead a normal life. I felt like I was spilling my blood. I released everything that had built up within me over the past sixteen years. I explained how I had tried to leave before but had been firmly put in my place. Ellie had gone on to say how Jimmy had raped her too and threatened to rape Mandy. Everything had come pouring out. I hadn't realised I was crying.

'We will do everything we can to help get you back on your feet, Kat. And you, Ellie,' Louise said.

I couldn't imagine a point in time where I would feel safe. Everything I thought of involved Jimmy creeping around in the back of my mind, leering over me and letting me know he would be with me every step of the way, no matter where I was living, who I was with. Yes, the women's refuge might be able to get me back on my feet, but they would never be able to stop me from feeling like this. And what if Jimmy did find me? The police wouldn't be able to do anything because they would never find him. As soon as he found me, the site would pack up and move on, or at least the Dentons would. This wasn't going to go away just because we'd managed to escape the site. I would have to change my name, my identity, although Jimmy made sure I didn't have much of an identity. He had stripped me of... well, *me*. I wasn't allowed to choose what I ate, what I wore, what I said, or who I said it to. So, I suppose in a way, I would be starting from scratch.

'Did you bring any personal belongings, Kat?' I heard Louise ask. My thoughts were still at the forefront of my mind; her voice was distant.

'I didn't bring anything other than myself and a photograph of my parents. It's the only possession I have of my own. Jimmy never knew about it, he'd have destroyed it otherwise. It's the only thing I'd managed to save.' Ellie gripped my hand as my voice cracked again.

Louise nodded and wrote something in a small book.

'We didn't bring anything at all. We thought that if we left all of our belongings back at the site, it would take Jimmy and the rest of them a while to figure out that we had left. We wanted as much time as possible to get away.'

Louise smiled briefly. 'That's understandable. Are you happy for us to go ahead and sort things out for you to be rehomed?'

I nodded. 'So long as we can be rehomed together. I need Ellie with me. I can't do this by myself.'

'You will be rehomed together if that is what you want.'

'Where?' Ellie asks.

'Anywhere we can, far enough away that he won't find us, but not too far that I won't be able to travel back to find my roots again. I want to start again, I want to have a completely new identity. Not that I had one to begin with. But the harder it is for Jimmy to find me, the better.'

Ellie nodded. 'Fair enough.'

Louise wrote something else in her book. I looked at Ellie, wondering if she was thinking the same thing as I was. Would Louise be able to do everything I needed her to? Would she really be able to help us to move forward?

'The other workers and I will do everything we can to help you both start your new lives. No matter how long it takes. You'll both stay here until we are able to rehome you.'

I shot Louise a look. 'Stay here?'

Louise nodded.

'But, he'll find us.' I began to panic. My heart began to thump inside my chest and my palms were clammy.

'Kat, he will not find you here. Our front office does not give out any information about people who stay here. You will be completely safe. Is there any way that he could know that you have come here?'

It was Jimmy we were talking about. He could have followed us here for all we knew. What if he had seen us on that bus? He could be allowing me to think that I had been successful in my escape, and he could be waiting until I least expected him to turn up.

'There is no way on this earth that he would know we're here. There are plenty of women's refuge centres in Scotland. We could be at any of them; and who's to say that he will even have thought of that, Kat? He may not even have realised that we've gone yet. I know my brother, he's a thug, but he's not that clever. Please, try to not worry,' Ellie said.

. I knew she was probably right, but was shocked at the state I had got myself into. He was nowhere near me, and yet he was still controlling my thoughts. The bastard that he was.

I stood up and went to the window. Our refuge flat was four floors up and we had a good view of the street. It had just turned nine o'clock in the evening. The nightlife had begun, and the women were all walking around in tiny skirts and huge-heeled shoes. If Jimmy had seen me walking around like that, he'd have slapped me. I was only to dress like that if he said so, and even then it was only ever for his benefit. I shivered at the thought. How could one human be so vile, so violent, and cruel?

'I know, but I just can't help but think he's out there looking for me, or worse, that he's already found me and is waiting for the right moment to drag me back to that shit-hole.'

I felt Ellie's hand on my shoulder. 'Well, he'll have a fucking fight on his hands if he does turn up, do you understand me?'

I sighed. I was exhausted from it all. I heard Louise say something about leaving us for a while and coming back later. The door closed quietly and I went to put the chain on. I imagined him standing at the other side, with that sadistic smile on his face, knowing that I would be cowering from him if he really was there.

'I just want this to be over, so I can try to build a life for this baby coming.'

'And it will be, we just have to lay low here. We'll do everything we have to with the help of the refuge and we will start again. New names and everything. He won't be able to find us if we start afresh.'

I shook my head. 'Never say never.'

I felt like we'd been in the refuge longer than we had. The place was lovely, clean, and comfortable, far better than the trailer I was used to. But the feeling was similar to that of when I was in our trailer, it was like being in prison. I didn't feel like I could leave for fear of being seen by Jimmy or one of his cronies, even though I knew it was unlikely. I stared out at Hope Street and watched the bustle of the city's nightlife begin. He could be down there, in the bustle, hiding within the crowd. He could be looking up here, straight at me. Smiling, watching me squirm as he lay in wait.

'Let's listen to some music. The silence in here is killing me,' Ellie said.

She switched on the radio and the music which flooded my ears made my stomach leap and churn. It instantly transported me back to a time I didn't wish to be reminded of.

'Turn it off,' I said, rushing over to the radio.

'What?' Ellie was confused.

'I can't listen to that,' I said, reaching for the off switch.

The familiar sound of Oasis's 'Don't Look Back in Anger', filled me with dread. Suddenly, I was back in that trailer the night I had tried to leave the second time. That song was on repeat, either that or the CD had stuck. I remembered how he had manipulated me, using soft tones as he spoke. Telling me that I hadn't really wanted to leave. He had asked me what he would do without me and had been soft in his touch. That was just moments before he had forced his way inside me. I hadn't been able to stop him. That song had been playing in the background.

'Why not?' Ellie said, as I slammed my fist down on the radio.

'I just don't like that song. Is that all right with you?'

Ellie held her hands up in defeat.

'I'm sorry, just any song but that.'

'Is it something to do with him?'

I didn't want to tell her. I didn't want to think about it, I just wanted to forget.

'No, I just don't want to hear that song, ok?'

We put on the television and watched *BBC News 24* for the remainder of the evening. All the while, I continued to look out of the window. As Hope Street became busier, I imagined Jimmy out there; it would be easier for him to blend in with the crowd now that there were more people filling the street. This was my life now. This would be my life forever, or at least until he found me. And he would, he most certainly would. Jimmy Denton wouldn't let me go this easily.

Chapter Six

The heat consumed me. My face felt like it would melt if I didn't get out of the trailer quickly. I pulled my shirt up over my face and tried as much as I could not to breathe in any smoke. I tried calling out for my dad, hoping he would help me, but I couldn't speak. My voice was hoarse and I couldn't see a thing. My head began to spin as I fought my way to the bedroom door. A hand pulled at my arm and before I knew it, I was outside. I couldn't open my eyes and I couldn't hear anything. I couldn't stop coughing and I vomited in between breaths. The sound of the roaring flames surrounded me, and all I could see as I crouched down were several pairs of shoes. I looked up and as I saw my home turn to ash, I began to scream.

The tears ran down my cheeks as I opened my eyes, horrified that I had experienced the same nightmare that terrorised me for three years after the fire that had killed my parents.

'What's the matter?' Ellie asked. I hadn't noticed she was still in the room.

'It's nothing,' I replied, reluctant to talk about it. The nightmare was bad enough. I couldn't get the images out of my head.

Ellie accepted my words and left me on my own. I sat up and decided that, as hard as it would be, today would be the first day of the rest of my life. I wasn't going to let Jimmy control me anymore, especially now that I had managed to escape him. The only way my past was going to get to me was through the dreams I wouldn't be able to control as I slept. I just wished my parents were still alive to help me through this. Come to think of it, I wondered if I would even be in this mess had they survived that fire.

I could feel rising panic in my chest. I swallowed it down, hoping that if I just breathed through it, the feeling would pass. Looking back at my life, it seemed like one big disaster. I'd transitioned from one traumatic event to the next without even really understanding the true extent of the situation. Now I was thirty, parentless, and with nothing to call my own. Jimmy was the only person I had left in the whole world and as much as I hated him, even leaving him felt like a loss in the sense that he was the only constant I had had in my life from my early teens. The feeling confused me even now. I had never been on my own before. Never.

Thinking about Jimmy looking for me and that I had finally escaped him made my stomach roll, and I remembered that I was carrying another life. It felt strange. I would never have thought that I would have wanted to keep a baby that had been partly created by the scum that was Jimmy Denton, but the more I thought about it, the more I came to realise this was because I had always thought I would have to stay with him. How could I bring up a baby around him? The poor little thing would have been at risk of abuse any time it cried for too long or craved attention at the wrong time.

I put my hands to my abdomen and imagined how different life was going to become. I would have someone else to put first, someone to care for and nurture. I stood up and walked over to the window. Staring out at Hope Street, I watched as people made their way to work and the road was filled with buses and taxis. Jimmy could be out there right now. But I was beginning to relax and knew that it was unlikely he would find us, especially since I had left everything behind, except for one photograph of my parents. It was the only thing I had managed to salvage from the fire. I kept it close to me at all times as I knew that Jimmy would have used it in one of his torrents of abuse.

The photograph had a single name and an address on the back. I was always curious as to whom the name and number belonged, but I hadn't tried to contact them. I never really knew why. Maybe now that I had left Jimmy, I would be able to, although I imagined the number would no longer exist.

'Tea?' Ellie's voice came from behind me. I turned towards her and she was holding a mug with steam swirling up and around her face.

'Yes, please,' I replied.

She handed me the mug, and we sat down together. I sipped at the hot black tea and slumped back on the sofa.

'How are you?'

'I'm ok, I think.'

'And how is the little one this morning?' Ellie placed a hand on my belly.

'She's fine.'

Ellie's brow furrowed. 'She?'

I nodded and smiled. 'I don't know why, but I have a feeling it'll be a girl.'

I hadn't thought about it before now; in fact, I hadn't even really noticed I had referred to the baby as 'she'. It just felt natural.

'And if she comes out a he?' Ellie laughed.

'Then I'll give him a boy's name.' I smiled back. 'But I can tell you something right now. No matter what, my baby will never know anything about Jimmy. And I mean, never.'

Ellie nodded. 'Agreed.'

'From now on, Jimmy's name will not pass my lips. He will never be mentioned and his name will not go on the birth certificate. I will change my name but I'll change it to something other than my maiden name. If I don't, then there's a chance he'll find us.'

I felt stronger as the words poured out of my mouth. I was beginning to believe that I would find myself now I had escaped his clutches. I hoped he was suffering now, wondering where I was, and I hoped he was tormented. He would be planning how to punish me when he found me. And if I knew Jimmy, it would be a lifetime of punishment. How dared I leave him? How dared I find the courage to try to live my life without him? That's what he would be thinking. I wondered when he would have realised I had left.

I knew what his reaction would be. He would go absolutely mad, smashing things up and putting his fist through the paper-thin walls in the trailer. He would shout at his friends and family, saying that if anyone knew where I was and was keeping quiet, they would suffer for it. Jimmy viewed me as his property. Always had and always would.

Well, no more. I would rather die than spend the rest of my life with him. There was a fine line between love and hate, and I had finally crossed it.

'I think that's the best thing you can do. And I think I'll have to change my name, too. As much as your protection is at the forefront of all this, I have to make sure that Jimmy, or my dad, doesn't find me. Because if they find me, Jimmy finds you and that little bundle of yours,' Ellie said as she gently patted my belly.

I couldn't bear to think of what would happen if he found us and realised that I had taken away his child. He would kill me, simple as that.

'I'm still terrified, Ellie. I'm terrified at the prospect of starting this new life. The life I have always wanted to live, the normal everyday get-up-for-work life that I never had. I'm terrified of starting again and failing.'

'And why do you think you'll fail?'

'Because I have never relied on myself or made my own decisions. I have had everything in my life decided for me. Jimmy told me what to wear, what to eat, and even what I should or shouldn't say in others' company. Not only do I need to make decisions for myself, I need to make the absolute correct decisions for my daughter, or son. And I just can't get those decisions wrong.'

'And you won't get them wrong. Why do you think you would?'

I sighed. 'Well, I've never had the freedom to decide things for myself, have I? It's pathetic.'

Ellie put her arm around me and I tried to balance the mug of steaming hot tea on my lap, fearful I would spill it and scald myself. 'You are far from pathetic; you're a strong lady trying to take control of your life.'

I smiled and took another sip. 'Do you think I'll ever be able to look back at this day and feel anything other than anger and resentment?'

'I think you're already on the right path.'

I stood up and pulled the photograph of my parents out of my jeans pocket and handed it to Ellie.

Happiness shone out from the image, the sun in the background and my dad staring down at my mother, who appeared to be laughing. They were young, happy. They were yet to become a family, still unmarried, going by how young they seemed. My mother wore a light blue blouse and a high-waisted pencil skirt. My dad wore a white shirt, sleeves rolled up past his elbows.

The way he looked at her made my heart ache. Everyone deserved to have someone look at them like that.

My mother was barefoot on the grass in what looked like a garden at the end of a small house. I imagined how they were feeling that day. What they'd spoken of; future plans, children, jobs perhaps? I liked to think of them sitting at the end of that garden, soaking up the sun and chatting about what they were going to do together, how they would spend their lives. It broke my heart that their life together was cut short in such tragic circumstances. How they came to live in the campsite of hell I may never know.

Ellie looked at it and smiled. 'You still think of them all the time?'

'Every minute,' I said, swallowing the growing lump in my throat.

'Can I ask, how did you manage to save this picture? I mean, there was nothing left of your trailer.'

I breathe, blocking out the image in my mind. Ellie was right, my life had literally been turned to ashes.

'My dad had given me his wallet, asked me to go to the shop in the morning to get Mam a bunch of flowers. It was coming up for their wedding anniversary. There wasn't much in it, some coins and this picture. I'd put it in my housecoat pocket when I'd got up to go to bed and had fallen asleep with it on.'

Ellie looked at me through sympathetic eyes. I didn't want to make contact, I was barely holding it together as I recalled the memory.

'Look on the back,' I say, trying to steer the conversation in another direction.

Ellie turned the picture over and stared at it for a moment. 'Who's Oscar?'

I shook my head. 'I don't know.'

'Are you going to visit the address?'

Again, I shook my head. 'Not now. Maybe once I'm settled. Although, I don't know what I would say. "Hi, you knew my dad or my mum but they're dead, can you help me?"'

'Sounds like a good start to me.'

When I tried to think of who Oscar might be, my mind went blank. Why would my parents have a name and address on the back of a photograph of themselves? 'For all I know, this person might not live there anymore. Going by the photo and my own age, the photograph has to be at least thirty years old.'

I would think about it at another time. First, I had to get my head together and make a start with pulling my life back together.

'You're being so brave, Kat. I admire you.'

I rolled my eyes, trying to play down Ellie's words.

'I do, you're one of the bravest women I know. My mam went through the same thing you have with Jimmy and she never had the guts to leave. I always questioned her about it. You know what her answer was?'

I shook my head. *Fear, deep fear which is embedded in the depths of your soul?*

'She said leaving would be disloyal to the family and to the fact that my dad provided for her and her kids.'

I breathed a sigh of relief. That could've been me had I not had Ellie for support.

We were both silent for a moment, allowing the enormity of our situation to sink in.

'Let's go down and speak to Louise. I want to get the ball rolling with whatever we need to do next. We have new lives waiting for us.'

I smiled as Ellie held her hand out for me to go with her. I cleared my throat, not wanting to cry any more.

'Ellie, you said that you admire me for my bravery through all this. But if it wasn't for you, I wouldn't be here right now. You're the one who got us out,' I said.

She pretended not to, but I could tell she was trying not to cry.

Chapter Seven

One year later

As we stepped inside, I looked around the three-bedroomed flat and just couldn't believe how far we had come. Having fled to a refuge, being supported in what had happened and what was to come, and standing in what could possibly be my own home for the first time in my life, felt like a dream. It had been a tough year. Ellie and I had moved from the refuge to a homeless unit until they could find us permanent accommodation. The homeless unit wasn't as bad as it sounded, it was a proper flat in the city, provided by the council on a short-term basis. But there was nothing homely about it, it had been bare, unloved. But it was still better than the life I had been living in the trailer. Now, Louise had finally found us somewhere, a place we could call home, not long after I'd had the baby.

I held my beautiful girl in my arms and watched Ellie familiarise herself with what could be our new surroundings. The place was a decent size for a family of three, and relatively clean. The area itself didn't seem too bad either. We seemed to have landed ourselves our very own goldmine. Not literally, of course. I would never have imagined myself here, with my own life, own home, and a lovely, perfect daughter.

'So, what do you both think?' Louise asked. She was standing at the living room window.

I looked at Ellie, who had said that I could have the final say. I smiled and nodded. 'It's exactly what we need. We'll take it.'

Louise smiled and left the room to make a call.

'Ellie, can you believe we're actually here?'

'I know, it's bloody fantastic. And what do you think little Lucia will make of it all?'

I looked down at my baby girl, to whom I'd given my mother's middle name, and felt my heart swell. 'If she's happy, then that's all that matters.'

Of course she was happy. She was fast asleep in the safest place she could ever be. Lucia had been born almost three months ago, and she had come into the world screaming her head off. I went into labour close to my due date and she didn't come for two days, the stubborn little thing. But I hadn't cared how long I had to put up with that pain. I'd just wanted to get her here safe and well.

Holding her in my arms for the first time after I'd given birth made all the bad things in my life seem worth it. If going through them meant leading me to the point where I got to raise my daughter the way I wanted to, in the safest environment possible, then I would do it all over again.

–

I thought of Jimmy again for the first time in months when Lucia was born. Would he still be looking for us? Would he still be angry, or had he realised that what he had done was wrong and was now punishing himself? I wouldn't bet on it. Little Lucia was all that mattered to me at that moment, and as soon as I held her for the first time in my arms, I wanted to protect her more than I wanted to protect myself. Ellie had been my birthing partner, of course. However, she had been absolutely useless. As soon as I began to push, she had passed out and was nowhere to be seen until after Lucia actually arrived. I hadn't let her live it down.

'I thought you were made of stronger stuff than that, Ellie.' I laughed at her as she appeared in the ward.

'I can't believe I fainted. I'm so sorry you had to go through that by yourself.' Ellie was scarlet with embarrassment.

'The midwives did a good job. I survived.'

Ellie had been so worked up about her episode that she hadn't even really noticed that I was feeding Lucia as she was standing in front of me. 'This is Lucia, by the way.'

Her eyes filled with tears.

'She's the reason you fainted, just so you know.' I laughed again.

'She's tiny,' Ellie replied, a tear falling down her cheek.

'Trust me, she didn't feel tiny when she was coming out of me.'

Pulling up a chair, Ellie sat down beside me. Lucia continued to feed, and I suddenly couldn't remember what life was like before I had my daughter.

'Was it really that bad?'

I looked down at Lucia and remembered how horrific childbirth had been. 'It was worth every minute.'

As I lay in the hospital bed, feeding my new daughter and feeling like my heart would burst, my mind started to tick, knowing that if Jimmy began searching the hospitals, he would probably find us since I hadn't changed my name yet. With all the moving around and getting things organised for the baby coming, I just hadn't got around to it. I knew it was unlikely that he would begin searching hospitals again nine months after I had disappeared, but it would be just my luck that he would and he would find me.

–

I went to the bedroom and pictured what the place would look like as a little girl's room. I didn't want it to be the traditional pink and cream colour scheme. I wanted to go for colours which no one would think of. I supposed a little part of me wanted to rebel against the traditional pink girly room because everyone went for pink when there was a baby girl on the way. I wasn't going to do it just because everyone else did. No, my girl would have neutral colours and, as she got older, she would choose what she wanted. She would have control of her likes and dislikes and I would give her all the freedom she would need to grow and become the person she wanted to become.

'Hi, baby girl. Your Auntie Helen and I are going to take such good care of you here,' I continued to whisper to Lucia as she slept in my arms. 'We had to change our names to keep you safe. I won't even say his name because I don't want you to have anything in that innocent little mind of yours that would cause any kind of pain. I've carried enough of that for the both of us to last a lifetime.'

I saw Ellie's reflection in the window of the room which I had decided would be Lucia's when she was old enough.

'You know, she has no idea what you're saying to her, so even if you did talk about him, it wouldn't matter.'

'It would matter to me.' Lucia stirred in my arms but remained asleep. 'I mean it; I will never mention him or even think about him when she is around. I can't risk her knowing about him when she's older. I want her to have the freedom to choose which paths to go down, and I will never stop her from doing the things in life that she wants.'

Ellie interrupted, 'Within reason.'

'Obviously, but if she comes to know about him when she's older and decides she wants to meet him, I would have to go back on my word and stop that from happening, and I don't ever want to stand in her way. So if she doesn't know about him, then I won't have to control that part of her life. I will not ever become what he was.'

Ellie shook her head. 'Kat.'

'Katelyn from now on. We have to get used to it for when we meet new people and for when Lucia gets older.'

She nodded. 'Ok. Katelyn, you will never be anything like him. If anyone was going to mirror him in any way, it would be me. I'm linked by blood, remember?'

'You are nothing like him. If you were, we wouldn't be together now.'

We fell silent. I had promised myself that I would never speak of him again and here I was, doing it. Even after a year away from the scumbag, I was still affected by him.

'I can't believe he can still do this to me. I swear, if I ever see him again…'

'Then you will turn on your heels and run. You will not take him on and you will not try to be brave. You don't have to prove anything.'

I knew she was right but feeling this way was embedded in me. I looked at Ellie, (I need to get used to calling her Helen) her eyes were full of sadness.

'What's wrong?' I asked.

'I can't stop thinking about Mandy. Do you think she will be ok?'

I nod. Was anyone ever ok around Jimmy? 'I'm sure she will. She's his sister.'

'So was I.'

We both stayed silent, unsure how to carry on our conversation. I decided to break the silence with a change of subject. The guilt of leaving Mandy behind was killing me as much as I'm sure it was killing Helen too.

'So, have you picked your bedroom yet?' I smiled at Helen as we walked through to another room that was bigger than Lucia's bedroom. In fact, most of the rooms in the flat were bigger than any other room I had ever been used to. I had been resigned to living in a trailer my whole life but I had never truly felt like I belonged there. It had never felt like home. Even when my parents were alive, and I'd lived with them, it just hadn't felt right. There had always been something missing inside me and I could never understand it. But right here, in this flat with Ellie (who would now be forever known as Helen) and Lucia; this was home. Today was the first day of the rest of our lives.

We entered the room that would be Helen's and she stood in the middle and gave a twirl. 'Do you like?'

'I do. It's very spacious. Do you think you'll be comfortable here?'

Helen nodded. 'How could I not be?'

I walked through the door and into the bedroom that would be mine. Somewhere that would be mine and only mine. I had never owned anything before. Of course, I didn't own this flat; it had been offered to us by the local housing association. But this was the first time that I would be able to choose everything by myself.

'I can't wait to decorate it. I can have any colour I want.'

Helen laughed. 'You're excited about decorating?'

'Well, I have never had the choice before. I know it might not be important to you but it's a big deal to me.'

The room was rectangular, with a medium-sized window set in the middle of the far wall. The building seemed fairly new, and the place looked as though it had been freshly painted. It was almost like I had been given a blank canvas. The bedroom I had picked was what Louise referred to as 'en suite,' basically meaning I had my own bathroom. I was beginning to picture where the bed would go when I was interrupted by Louise.

'So, you're happy with it?'

'Definitely,' I reply.

'Great, then I will get the paperwork sorted today for you both to sign. You've both come so far. You can look forward now.'

Louise left and I stood in the middle of the room, not quite believing that I am finally here. Helen had disappeared again. I found her in the kitchen, opening cupboards and drawers.

'What are you doing?' I asked.

'I just can't believe this is all ours. It feels so strange.'

She was right, it did feel strange. It all felt strange. We had new identities. I went by the name of Katelyn Phillips and Ellie was now Helen Benham. The surnames were so random that we were confident Jimmy would never find us. Louise had suggested some names for us to choose from during the rehoming process, and we looked up others on the internet.

I chose Katelyn because it was similar to the name my parents had given me, and I wanted to keep the connection as close as I could. My new surname was chosen at random. There was no meaning there. No way it could be traced back to the old me.

Ellie had chosen Helen Benham because she wanted something she had chosen herself, with no connection to the Denton name. She laughed when she picked it, saying, 'Ms Benham... I sound like a teacher or something.'

Our new flat was in the Gorbals. From what I had seen of it, it seemed ok, quiet enough. But I suppose I had been through worse things than noisy neighbours, so if we did encounter any problems, I wouldn't be bothered with having to deal with it. We were up two flights of stairs, which was another new experience. Yes, we had lived at the refuge which was, of course, higher up than the flat, but that was temporary. This was the first fixed home I would live in and I would have all the privacy I had ever dreamt of. I had everything I ever needed and, for the first time in what seemed like a lifetime, I felt happy.

The kitchen was long with a window at the end above the sink. The flat looked out to a car park, nothing too exciting but better than the site. The hallway was relatively big and had been fitted with a new carpet. The walls were blindingly white and already I knew that I wanted to add purple. Jimmy hated that colour. In fact, I had come to realise that anything I liked, Jimmy hated. But from now on, I could do whatever I wanted because he would never be here to kick me into his way of thinking. Jimmy Denton could take a flying fuck; I was back, and I was going to do things my way.

Chapter Eight

I put the paintbrush back in the tray and stood back to admire my work. I had never painted anything in my life, so I had anticipated that it would be an absolute mess. However, as I looked up at the purple wall, I was pleasantly surprised. I hadn't made much of a mess at all. In fact, it looked bloody brilliant.

I gave a sigh of relief and decided that I was done for the day. The hallway was finished. And it wasn't a disaster. Now I could really focus on Lucia's room.

'Helen, come and look at this,' I called out. I could hear Lucia babbling away in the living room as she lay under her mobile. Helen was by my side and looking up at the wall I had painted. 'So, what do you think?'

She smiled, placing her hands on her hips. 'I think it's purple.'

My face fell. 'You don't like it? I can change it.'

'And why would you do that?'

I suddenly heard what I had said and shook my head. 'Sorry, natural reaction.'

'Nothing natural about it.'

I was so used to receiving a slap if I voiced my opinion that when Helen had said what she did, I had automatically tried to please her.

'Sorry.' There I went again.

Helen shook her head and laughed. 'I'll run you a bath.' She turned to go into the bathroom, and I heard Lucia beginning to cry. She was due her bottle. I went into the living room, noticing I was covered in purple paint. If I picked Lucia up, she would end up looking like a giant grape. Helen came back into the room and I told her that she would have to feed Lucia while I cleaned myself up.

I lit some candles on the unit next to the mirror, turned the light out, and slid into the bath which Helen had filled with bubbles. Lying back, I closed my eyes. In my previous existence with Jimmy, this kind of relaxation was never possible. Anytime I was naked, he saw it as an opportunity, so all I ever got to do was jump in the shower when he wasn't around and I would be in and out in seconds. I suppose this was the most relaxed I had ever been. My eyes were closed, but I was still aware of everything around me. The gentle swish of the water filled my ears and I could hear the wick of the candle popping under the small flame. I began to relax, surrendering to the sleep that crept upon me. The warm water lapped around my neck. I was asleep within seconds.

–

'You will not see him, do you understand me, Katrina?' my dad said. His tone was kind, but I knew he meant business.

'But, Dad, he really is nice once you get to know him.' I knew I was pushing my luck by forcing the issue but I just couldn't help myself.

My dad kept his temper. 'I said you're not to see him again, and that is my final word on the matter.'

I looked at Mam and she had her eyes on me as she nodded in agreement with my dad. 'Your dad is right, Katrina. He's bad news, this Jimmy character.'

Being a private person, I didn't want to declare that I couldn't stay away from Jimmy because I was head over heels in love with him. But I had so much love and respect for my parents that I couldn't betray their wishes. 'Ok, I'll end it.'

My mam seemed shocked, like she had expected me to protest. 'Good girl. Now, go and get these from the shop and if you see him, make it clear and simple.' She handed me a list and, without a word, I left our trailer and began walking up the hill towards the site exit. The sun was splitting the sky, and all I could really think about was how I was torn between my parents and the first boy I had ever been in love with. They didn't see the Jimmy that I saw. He was kind, gentle, and very complimentary of me. Yes, I'll admit he was rough around the edges and sometimes a little unpredictable, but what boy wasn't at his age?

I kept my head down and walked quickly to the shop at the top of the site. I didn't want to be faced with Jimmy and have to tell him that we couldn't see each other anymore. But what I wanted and what I got were two very different things.

'Kat, where are you going?' Jimmy's voice came from behind me.

Shit! Now what?

'Getting stuff for my mam and dad. What are you doing?'

Jimmy grabbed me and pulled me close. 'What if we go to my wagon before you head back to yours and we can have a quickie?' He smiled. Those bright white teeth sparkled along with his eyes and I just melted. But I had to be strong.

'I can't.'

Jimmy's face fell. 'Why not?'

How the hell was I supposed to tell him? What would I even say? He looked into my eyes expectantly and I just didn't have the heart to break his. 'What about later?'

He smiled then, relief filling his expression. 'I'll come to yours and we can tell your mam and dad we're going down to the burn for a walk.'

I just nodded. I knew it was never going to happen, and I tried desperately to stop the tears from flowing. My chest began to ache, and I kissed him gently. 'See you later, then.'

Jimmy let go of me and I turned in the direction of the exit. My eyes filled up and I couldn't stop the tears from spilling over. I was consumed with the pain of giving him up. My dad wouldn't make me do it if he didn't have a good reason. Yes, I may be a daddy's girl, but I trusted him with my life and if he was doing this in my best interests, then that was good enough for me.

On my way back from the shop, I turned around the bend towards my trailer which was around a hundred and fifty yards down the hill. I could see Jimmy standing at the front door talking to my dad, smiling and looking up at him. What was going on?

I slid behind one of the large oak trees and waited until they were both gone. I wondered why Jimmy was smiling. Had my dad changed his mind? I doubted it. I peered out from the large trunk that had completely hidden me from view and watched as Jimmy walked away, seemingly happy.

–

I opened my eyes. The only light was the flickering flame from the scented candle. The water was still warm although the bubbles had dispersed. Why had I dreamt of that day? I hadn't thought of Jimmy like that in a very long time. It's strange how dreams can transport you back to not only a day or a moment in your past, but they can also make you feel the way you did at that moment. I remembered loving Jimmy like that, but I certainly didn't now. I wondered why my brain had taken me there. Maybe now that I was feeling a little more in control of my life, my mind had taken down some of the barriers it had put up over the years to protect me. Either way, it was still strange to me that I had dreamt of him that way. But it was nice to have dreamt of my parents. I missed them dearly.

'Katelyn, have you fallen asleep in there?' Helen knocked on the door.

'No, well, yes. But I'm awake now.'

'Do you want me to put the dinner on?'

I smiled. 'Yes, please.'

I sat up and realised that the water had turned to a prune shade of purple. I had fallen asleep before scrubbing myself. I let out the plug and switched the shower on. I let the hot water run over my head and face and thought of my parents. They would have loved to have met Lucia.

Chapter Nine

The waiting room was clinical, like a doctor's office. The walls were white, without as much as a speck of dust anywhere to be seen. Pictures hung in the centre of each wall and the sunlight flooded in through the window, creating a pool of light on the wooden floor under our feet.

Louise had helped Helen apply for jobs and prepared her for interviews, one of the many things the refuge helped us with. We'd agreed I wouldn't work until Lucia was older, until things were more settled.

'Are you nervous?' I asked Helen as I noticed her picking at the skin around her thumb nails.

'No, it's only a cleaning job, for Christ's sake.'

'Then why so tetchy?' I teased.

'Katelyn, don't wind me up. I need to be calm.' Helen shook her head and picked up a magazine which was lying on a small table to the side of her seat. She flicked through it aimlessly and then placed it back on the table before being called into the room where she would be interviewed.

'Ms Benham?'

We were greeted by a man in a pristine suit. He had dark hair, which was styled to the side slightly, hazel eyes and clear skin with a pinch of pink to his cheeks.

Helen shook his hand a little awkwardly. I couldn't help but smile. As she followed him through to his office, she glanced back at me and winked. I looked down at Lucia and shook my head, although the smile remained. 'What *are* we going to do with Aunty Helen, Lucia?'

I stood up, pushed the pram out to the hallway and went into the lift. I pressed the ground floor button and waited for the lift to come to a stop. As the doors opened, I noticed that the reception area was filled with people. I became nervous suddenly. I couldn't fathom why. I pushed Lucia out of the lift and headed towards the door. I had planned to go to the supermarket just down on Crown Street next to our flat and then head back to meet Helen after the interview. I manoeuvred Lucia's pram through the ever-growing crowd of people and vaguely heard them discussing a training course. I kept my head down and made my way towards the double doors at the front of the building.

That was when I heard it. That name; the name that sent a chill up my spine. I thought my heart would stop. The voice was male, which made it worse.

'Jimmy, Jimmy, calm down!' The voice sounded panicked. I knew the feeling. I didn't know what to do, where to go. I was trembling. I continued walking and just prayed that it was a coincidence.

'Jimmy, what are you going to do?' The voice was getting closer and my heart was beating so fast I thought I was going to have a heart attack. I began to speed up, keeping my head down and my eyes on the direction I was heading. Then I realised that I had to go somewhere other than the flat. I didn't want him to know where I lived. My breath quickened and I could feel sweat building on the palms of my hands.

'Jimmy, you'll end up in the jail!' The voice was almost on me, and now I could hear heavy footsteps syncing in time with my own.

Something made me stop. I was ready to turn around, ready to brave it out and face him. I had to protect Lucia. He couldn't do anything to me that I hadn't dealt with in the past. He had already done his worst. I took a deep breath and turned to be faced with a man in dark blue overalls with an oversized belly. His face was bright red and the man chasing after him appeared ready to keel over.

'I don't give a fuck if I end up in the jail. You don't steal my tools and get away with it.' The man almost knocked me off my feet as he opened the back doors of a van that had the words 'J&S Plumbing Services' printed across them.

The relief that washed over me must have been apparent because both men were staring at me.

'You a'right, hen? Ye look like you've seen a ghost.'

'Fine.' I turned away and began pushing Lucia in the wrong direction, keen to get as far away from my flat as possible so that my place of safety remained unknown. My whole body was tingling with fear. My salivary glands had erupted like a pair of volcanoes and as I turned the corner, I leaned over a wall to my left and threw up my breakfast. I gulped in as much air as I could in between retches and even though I had emptied my stomach, my gut continued to attempt to reject whatever evil it regarded was inside me.

God, if this was what I was like when I thought he was near, what would I be like if I really did come across him again? I stood up and steadied myself. My head was spinning and I felt like I could throw up again. I jumped when I felt a hand on my shoulder. I spun around and saw a little old lady smiling at me.

'Are you okay, dear?' Her voice was kind, but frail.

I nodded. 'I'm fine.' There was that word again. The word I used to describe how I felt when I was anything but fine.

'It's not easy having one of these wee ones to look after when you're ill.' She looked into the pram and I noticed that Lucia had fallen asleep.

'I'll be ok.'

'Take care of yourself, young lady. That wee one will need her mummy,' she said, handing me a tissue. I watched as she hobbled away, gripping onto her walking stick with one hand and clutching at her bag with the other.

'Come on, Lucia, let's go home.' I turned the pram around and made my way back to the flat. Helen would know just to head back home when I wasn't outside the office to meet her. I couldn't face going back into that building with all those people and reliving the last five minutes. It wouldn't matter how far down the line I progressed; I would hear that name and most likely have the same reaction every time.

The rational part of my brain knew that even if Jimmy did come looking for me, he really wouldn't know where to start. Helen and I had changed our appearances since taking on our new identities. Helen now sporting a short bob hairstyle, dark brown as opposed to blonde. I no longer had long curly red locks, but instead straight brown hair that sat on my shoulder. I was sad to see my hair go, it was the one thing that I liked about myself but it was also the one thing that made me stand out from the crowd. So at a glance in a heavily populated area, he wouldn't see us, surely?

Once inside the flat, I decided to leave Lucia sleeping in her pram while I made a cup of tea. I wanted to put something stronger in it but I decided against the idea, at least until Helen came back. I boiled the kettle and found the tea bags in the cupboard above the toaster. I poured the boiling water into the mug and squeezed the tea bag to the point where it almost burst. The stronger the better.

As I sank down onto the couch, I fell into a daze. My own mind was tormenting to me. First, I had dreamt about Jimmy as he had been at the beginning of our relationship. Remembering what it was like when I was young and completely oblivious to his brutality wasn't how I wanted to think of him. I didn't want to remember my naivety. Then, my mind had made me believe that he was behind me today. I didn't think I would be able to cope if that happened again, especially if I was on my own.

I sipped at my tea and stared at the television, seeing my own, pathetic reflection in the screen. I could barely look at myself. I had to get a grip. I thought I had, but clearly I was still a mess. What a mind-fuck Jimmy Denton was. He had stripped me of my self-esteem a long time ago and even though I was no longer with him, he still had that control over me.

The key in the lock made me jump and I almost spilled my tea. I was beginning to make a habit of that. I stood up to meet Helen in the hallway. She had a grin on her face.

'I got the job,' she said. Just as the words were out of her mouth, the smile fell from her face. 'What's wrong?'

Was I that obvious? 'That's fantastic. Well done, when do you start?'

'No chance, don't dodge my question. What's wrong?'

I shook my head and burst into tears. They came in floods and I couldn't stop the sobs from coming along with them. Again; pathetic. 'I thought I saw Jimmy.'

Helen hugged me and led us into the kitchen. She opened the cupboard under the sink and pulled out a bottle of whisky. 'But it wasn't him?'

I shook my head while using the back of my hand to wipe away the tears, most likely creating mascara smears across my cheeks. 'No, but I really did think it was. I thought I'd had it, Helen. I thought he had found me and he was either going to drag me back to the site with Lucia or just kill me on the spot.' I went on to tell Helen how I had heard someone call his name and say that he would 'end up in the jail.' Helen poured the whisky and gave me a glass.

'Here, get that down you.'

The warm liquid calmed me. I needed more than one but I wasn't going to allow myself, not with Lucia to think of.

'Better?' Helen queried.

'Yes. I'm sorry; I've totally taken away from the fact that you got the job.'

'Och, don't be daft. It's just a cleaning job.'

I nodded. 'Yes, but you've achieved something on your own. You should be proud of that.'

Helen smiled, knocking back one more whisky shot. 'I am. And you know the best part? The boss is hot.'

That was the best part? Helen seemed to be thriving in our new environment. I wished I could have said the same for myself. I couldn't seem to move on from living in fear of Jimmy finding me. Had I made the wrong choice in moving to a flat that was dangerously close to where the site was situated? Something inside me said yes. But something also said no, that no matter where I went, I would always have that fear.

'You do know you can't act on it? He's your boss.' I tried to keep my mind off Jimmy.

'He's just a bit of eye candy, it's harmless.'

I hoped it would be harmless. The last thing we needed right now was man drama, of any sort.

'Are you ok?' Helen asked.

'Yeah, I will be when Jimmy gets the hell out of my head.'

'He will. You're doing great. Look at you now, compared to this time last year.'

I tried to take Helen's positivity on board. But right now, all I could do was take each day a step at a time, hoping that I would forget about Jimmy a little more. But I knew that his memory would never leave me, and that his face would be forever stuck in my mind.

There were two Jimmy Dentons. The one I fell in love with when I was a teenager, and the one I eventually left. Jimmy had tried to hide his aggression. But it was as if once I had married him, he no longer felt the need to try. As the months and years had passed, his vulgar behaviour had become worse. Not that I ever did this, but if I had had the chance to say, 'This is my husband, Jimmy,' his response could have been, 'And this is my property, Kat.'

I wondered how differently things would have turned out had my parents survived the fire.

Chapter Ten

They say that in a fire, you're most likely to die of smoke inhalation. I don't know if that's better or worse than being burned alive. My parents were asleep when the trailer was engulfed in flames. They didn't stand a chance of getting out.

The fire brigade was able to put the fire out quickly, but it was too late for my parents, who were found, still in bed, scorched and blackened. It was strange to think that I hadn't heard their screams or pleas for help. Perhaps my brain had blocked that memory to save me from the miserable flashbacks that I would have possibly endured. The smell of the smoke, the sound of the crackling frames all locked safely away somewhere in the back of my mind.

After I was dragged from the trailer and laid on the ground and coughing to the point where I thought my lungs would explode, I vaguely remember there being a lot of people around me. Screeching sirens, people screaming, and the sound of crackling flames invaded my ears. All I wanted to do was to get up and save my parents, but I couldn't move. I couldn't speak and could barely see.

I remembered going to bed that night, and the next thing I knew I was flat on my back, watching my home burn to the ground. From that point that my memory dips in and out of the rest of that day. Waking up in a hospital bed is the first thing I remember clearly. My vision was blurred and there was an oxygen mask over my face. Jimmy was sitting beside me and I could feel his hand wrapped around mine. He smiled at me, but it wasn't a smile that said he was happy to see me alive; it was a sympathy smile. I ripped the mask off and tried to sit up. Jimmy stood up and put a hand on my shoulder.

'Where are they?' I asked, in breathless panic.

Jimmy didn't say anything. He just shook his head as he gripped my shoulder. I fought to push away the crisp white sheet that covered me, as if it was crawling with spiders. I tried to stand, but Jimmy was by my side trying to force me back into bed. I fought him off but fell into a heap on the floor. I wanted to scream as the uncontrollable sobs tried to break through my chest, but my lungs wouldn't allow it. Instead, I wept silently. I felt Jimmy's hand slowly stroke my hair after he helped me back into the bed. I had no idea where I had planned to go once out of the bed, but I just couldn't lie there after finding out that my parents had died in that fire.

'What am I going to do now?' I said. I noted that my voice was hoarse and my words came out as a whisper.

'I'll look after you now. You'll come and live with me.'

I drifted in and out of sleep for the rest of the evening. Every time I woke up, Jimmy was right there, by my bedside, ready to take away my pain and grief. Over the next few days in hospital, tears stung my eyes whenever I woke. And in that first split second of being awake, I would forget it all. Then it would come to me. All I saw each time I closed my eyes were the flames that killed my mum and dad.

I dreamt of my parents that night as I lay in hospital. They had wanted me to be happy in life and tried to look after me the best way they knew how. I still had so many questions for them. I remembered Dad talking to me when I was younger about the home he had grown up in and the family he had. He had never mentioned names or places, but he did talk about his parents and how the house he had lived in was huge with a big back garden and all his friends used to play football with him in that garden in the summer time. I remembered asking why he didn't stay there anymore, but he would never answer me. I never understood why he had become a traveller or why he and my mam never discussed their past, but I told myself that I would find out. One day.

I had taken a photograph from my dad's keepsake box when I was about eight years old. It showed him and my mam holding me when I was a baby. It was the photograph that I had on me the day I walked into the refuge. Everything else had been lost in the fire.

I always said that I would visit Oscar, whose address was scrawled on the back, one day. But I never did. I had never told anyone about that photograph either. I wanted it to be just mine, something only I would know about, since I had nothing left after the fire. I always kept it on me, in my pocket. I had managed to keep it from Jimmy for all those years. I never knew who Oscar was or how he knew my parents, but I was still intent on finding out.

A few days after the fire, Jimmy and his parents had taken me back to the site to live with them. I suppose I had no choice really, with no other family or friends who would be able to help. I was happy to be with Jimmy, even though my dad had disliked him and told me to stay away.

I felt guilty for betraying him, but what else was I supposed to do? I had nowhere else to go. I remember getting out of the car and looking over at where my parents' trailer should have been. The ground was saturated with water and the grass was blackened. The trailer was gone.

'Oh my God,' I said under my breath, as I collapsed.

Jimmy caught me and lifted me in his strong arms before carrying me into his home. I clung to him like a baby orangutan clings to its mother. I didn't want to let go.

'You'll be safe here,' he said, as he lay me down on his bed. 'Get some sleep. I'll make you some food when you wake up.'

I couldn't sleep. All I kept thinking about was the fire and how I should have died with my parents. The pain in my heart was too much to bear, so I pushed their faces to the back of my mind and got out of bed. I went out to the living area and saw that Jimmy was sorting through a pile of clothes.

'Ah, you're up. I have something for you.'

'What?' I asked.

Jimmy approached me with a chirpy grin on his face and held an item of clothing up in front of me. It was a long-sleeved black shirt. 'Perfect,' he said.

Glancing at the couch, I saw there were three black bags with clothes in them. 'Are those all for me?'

Jimmy's grin widened. 'Yes, I picked them out for you.'

I didn't know what to say. I could see he expected a thank you. I opened my mouth to speak but before I could, he surprised me with a full-on kiss. 'Why don't you go and try on your new wardrobe?'

Before I could answer, he was gently pushing me into the bedroom with one hand and holding a black bag bulging with clothes in the other. It was that day our relationship changed. That was the day when I was no longer his girlfriend but his property. I didn't fully see it until it was too late. Jimmy Denton would strip me of my personality piece by piece, every day for the next sixteen years.

Chapter Eleven

As I lay awake listening to Lucia breathing softly in the cot beside me, I began thinking about the photograph I had saved from the fire that night. Who was this Oscar character, and how did he know my parents?

Maybe he would be able to give me some insight into my parents' lives before they became travellers. And why hadn't my mam or dad ever mentioned him before?

Lucia stirred but stayed asleep. I watched as her little chest rose and fell and wondered how my messed-up past would affect her, if at all. She would never know her dad, so I suppose in that sense she would never know what I had to endure to get away from him. But I was beginning to ask myself the questions that she may eventually ask.

She would want to know where she came from, who her dad and other family were. How was I going to answer those questions? I sat up and pushed the duvet off, swinging my legs around so they were dangling off the bed. The night-time breeze gushed through the open window and I got up to close it so that Lucia wouldn't get cold.

Had I known back then what I know now, that by the time I was thirty I would have no parents and no real family to call my own, I would have strived to find out more about my family history, where my bloodline led, my origins.

Lucia was safe with me, with Helen. But what if something happened to me as she was growing up? I believed she would need more than just a mother and an auntie as her family. It was the one thing I missed now because I think if I had any family, I would have left Jimmy a lot sooner than I did. Perhaps I wouldn't have married him at all? Perhaps if I had family other than my parents, then I would've gone to live with them after they died?

Wrapping my dressing gown around me, I tiptoed out of the bedroom and into the kitchen. I filled the kettle, not bothering to put the light on. I didn't want to wake Helen since she was due to start her new job in the morning. My mind wandered to the fire again. The more I had the freedom to think about it, the more it was beginning to tear me up inside. I should have died in that fire, but I didn't. I had never been able to remember in full what had actually happened. All I could remember was what was replayed to me in my dreams. My mind would transport me back to those moments as I escaped, the smoke taking full residence in my lungs as I fought to breathe. Nothing in the world could make me forget.

'Come on, you need to move,' the voice had said, as hands pulled me out of the trailer. I instantly recognised it as Jimmy's. 'Stay here, I'm going back for your mam and dad.'

He disappeared as I vomited. I gasped for air and, opening my eyes, all I could see were several pairs of legs. I couldn't lift my head. I tried to stand but nothing happened. Before I knew it, Jimmy was by my side, apologising. But I don't remember much else after that.

I suppose in a way that was why I had become so dependent on Jimmy. He saved my life, had tried to save my parents. He was all I had had left, down to the simplest of things like clothes. I believed I owed my life to Jimmy, I really did. Jimmy was a good person, for doing what he did, wasn't he? I had to trust in him.

–

I was brought back to present day by artificial light filling the kitchen. I turned to find Helen standing in the doorway. 'One of those going for me?'

'Jesus, Helen. I'm sure you're trying to kill me.'

She smiled. 'I still can't get used to you calling me Helen. It sounds weird.'

'Well, you'd better get used to it, and fast. We can't afford to slip up.'

Helen shook her head.

'What?' I asked, as I sipped my tea, realising as it hit my lips that I hadn't removed the tea bag.

'You need to stop obsessing about him. He is not going to find us.'

'You think I'm obsessing?' I replied.

'Just a tad.'

Maybe she was right, but I could never be too careful. 'Ok, maybe he won't find us, but what if someone else does?'

'Like who?'

'Well, anyone from the site. That idiot Rab for one. If he sees us, then we've had it.'

Helen burst out laughing. 'Big Rab Brannigan, that goon? The only reason he'd be in this neck of the woods was if he got lost.'

I wasn't laughing. Rab Brannigan may have been what some would describe as slow, but he was a sixteen-stone powerhouse and I wouldn't doubt that if I ever did bump into him, he'd throw me over his shoulder and carry me back to Jimmy himself. He was a big fan of Jimmy and did anything Jimmy ever told him to even though he treated Rab like a piece of shit every time. There were times where I was more scared of Rab than Jimmy, and for the most part I felt like I had been married to both of them.

'Katelyn, don't worry about this. You have to start moving on and put that lot to the back of your head. Neither Jimmy, nor Rab Brannigan, is going to find us. Do you hear me?'

I nodded, not taking in one word. I was as terrified now as I had been the day I left the site. I didn't think anything would change that.

'I'm heading back to bed. I have work in the morning,' Helen winked at me.

I went back to bed too. But I couldn't sleep. I lay awake, thinking about my life then and now. I pulled the photograph out of the bedside drawer and stared at my parents' faces. I turned it over, revealing the name and address on the back. *Oscar, 23 Keltrom Cottages, Killearn.*

I had no idea where this place was, but I was absolutely certain of one thing: I was going to find out. This Oscar person must have known something that could help me find out more about my parents' history before they became travellers. A part of me worried that Oscar would have moved house, and I would knock on the door and be faced with someone who would have no clue what the photograph meant, and I would never find the answers I was looking for. Or worse, what if he was dead? Then where would I be?

I had a lot of questions for Oscar. I just hoped he would have the answers I needed for closure.

–

As I looked into his eyes, I could see how angry he was that I was fighting back. I had no other choice; it was fight or… I dreaded to think what he would do to me.

'I'm not your property, Rab. You can't tell me what to do,' I said, adding as much force to my tone as I could muster.

'You don't want to upset Jimmy now, do you?' Rab sneered. He was right; I didn't want to upset Jimmy, I loved him and I wanted him to love me. But I also didn't want to stash drugs in my bedroom.

'My dad will kill me if he finds it.'

'If your dad finds it, *I'll* kill you.' He smiled, but deep down I knew he wasn't kidding. 'Don't make me have to go back to Jimmy and tell him his precious little girlfriend wouldn't do what she was told. You know what he's like, it would really upset him. And if he's upset, we'll both be on the receiving end of it.'

I snatched the small bag from Rab's hand, but before I stuffed it down my top, he grabbed my wrist and squeezed it tight. His eyes burned into mine, his breath heavy as he leaned in closer.

'Rab, let go of me. That hurts,' I whimpered.

'This is *nothing* compared to what I'll do to you if you ever breathe a word of this to anyone. You'd better not let us down, Kat.'

'Jimmy would never let you away with speaking to me like this,' I spat. His grip became tighter still.

He leaned in closer again. I drew back, but he held me so close I thought his lips would touch mine. I turned my head, and he whispered in my ear, 'Who do you think sent me here?'

I knew Jimmy had his flaws, but I wouldn't believe he would ever intentionally send one of his heavies to hurt me. 'No, he didn't.'

Rab let go of my wrist then and laughed. 'Just goes to show, you never really know a person.'

I rubbed furiously at my wrist as he walked away. Putting the bag down my top, I turned to face the opposite direction. I was stunned to see Jimmy standing at the window of his wagon. Had he watched what had just happened? Surely he wasn't going to allow this kind of behaviour from his so-called friend? I felt anger in my stomach but an ache in my heart. I thought Jimmy liked me. How could he stand by and watch his friend treat me like a piece of dirt? Come to think of it, how could I have let it happen?

I stopped. Jimmy hadn't taken his eyes off me as I approached his wagon. I didn't know what to do or where to look. And why was he staring at me like that? His face was expressionless as he moved away from the window. I remained frozen to the spot. Jimmy appeared in the doorway of the wagon and swaggered towards me, the corners of his mouth lifting slightly as he did so. He stood close enough that I could feel his breath on my face. My heart thudding in my chest and my breath quickening, I opened my mouth to speak. Just as my lips parted, he kissed me. His tongue slid in gently and swirled around mine. He pulled away and wrapped my hand in his. I looked into his eyes, awaiting another kiss, almost forgetting what had just happened. The pain in my wrist kept the memory close by.

'I hope he was clear.' Jimmy said, raising one eyebrow.

'What?' I stammered, not sure what he meant.

'I said, I hope Rab was clear in his instructions?'

My heart sank. Rab wasn't lying when he said it was Jimmy who had sent him. I nodded, fearful of what he would do if I disagreed. I didn't want him to tell me things were finished if I didn't do what he wanted.

'Good girl,' he said softly. 'No one would ever suspect you. You understand, don't you?'

My head was swirling. What the hell had just happened? Was I overreacting? Maybe this was normal. I had never had a boyfriend before Jimmy. Maybe this was the kind of thing girls did when they went out with boys. I really liked Jimmy and I wanted things to go well between us. I certainly didn't want to do anything to upset him. I made a promise to myself that I would do anything to make him happy.

I smiled at him. Relief flooded through me when he returned my smile. His eyes glistened and his whole face lit up when he flashed those beautiful white teeth.

There was a commotion behind me, and Jimmy's eyes flared before he began running in the direction of Rab's trailer. 'Oi, get the fuck off him!'

I turned just in time to see old Robert Brannigan uppercut Rab, sending him to the ground. He lay in a heap. He was still. Jimmy crouched down and gave him a shake. I watched from afar, not daring to move any closer to the madness unfolding in front of me.

'What the fuck was that all about?' Jimmy was getting to his feet. He was the same size as Old Robert Brannigan, but not nearly as sturdy. It was hardly surprising, considering Jimmy was only sixteen and Old Robert was closer to fifty and much fitter.

'What's it to you, wee boy?' Old Robert sneered.

Jimmy balled his fist and took a swing at Rab's dad but missed. Before I could stop myself, my legs carried me across the gravel towards them. I forced myself between them, an overwhelming need to protect Jimmy washing over me. It was the stupidest thing I could have done. Jimmy swung for Old Robert a second time and caught me on the side of the head with his fist before he realised I was in front of him. My legs buckled and I fell to my knees before losing consciousness. I could only have been out a few seconds. I vaguely remember Jimmy picking me up. Old Robert was laughing like a hyena behind him. Jimmy was angry. At me, of all people.

'You idiot, what were you thinking?' Jimmy hissed, dragging me towards his trailer.

'Are you being serious? I was trying to stop you from getting knocked out.' I concentrated my eyes on the path in front, feeling dizzy. 'You haven't even asked me if I'm ok.'

'You're fine, you can walk and talk. Could've been a lot worse.'

'What do you mean?' I stopped. I pulled away, but he gripped me tight. He stared dead into my eyes before turning and walking away towards the wagon. I was left, standing alone, in the middle of the site, wondering what the hell had just happened to me.

'Oi,' I heard Jimmy call. 'If you want us to be together, I'd suggest you get your backside in here.' He smiled, but it didn't reach his eyes.

Something in my gut told me he wasn't kidding. I moved quickly, so as not to upset him anymore, even though I wasn't that sure I had done anything wrong at all. I forced a smile, hoping to soften his mood. My smile wasn't returned. Instead, he went inside. He didn't speak. When I was inside, I made him a cup of coffee. I tiptoed back to him. He was sitting on the sofa, feet resting on the coffee table.

'I've made you a coffee,' I said, my voice more timid than I intended. I placed it down in front of him, waiting for him to respond. My stomach was churning so much I wanted to be sick. I hated the thought of him being angry at me.

Suddenly, Jimmy got up, making me jump. 'You'd better go and see if Rab's okay.'

I frowned. 'Me? Why?'

'I had to leave him lying on the ground because you got in my way.' I had almost forgotten about the knock to my head. Remembering made the pain return. 'On you go. And bring him back here. Don't let him go back into his dad's trailer. He'll get another tanking if he does.'

I looked on in shock. How the hell was I supposed to do this? Jimmy sat back down and lifted his coffee. 'Cheers, by the way,' he said, raising the mug in thanks.

'How am I supposed to stop him from going back to the trailer? That's if he's even still out there.'

'Well, you seemed to think getting between me and Old Robert was going to make a difference. So if you can do that, you can do this.'

Later, standing outside, I looked across at Rab's trailer and wondered what would happen to me if I knocked on the door. I knew Rab wouldn't be in there, so I turned right and began walking along the eastern part of the site. Rab and Jimmy's friends mostly lived along the eastern part so if Rab was going to be anywhere, it would most likely be there. I walked along, subtly peering in the windows of the wagons and trailers, but there was no sign of him. I started to panic, having irrational thoughts that he was dead and it was my fault. Jimmy would lose the plot with me in that case. After a half hour of searching, I gave up and decided to go home and tell Jimmy I couldn't find Rab.

I opened the door and, to my surprise, Rab was sitting on the couch next to Jimmy. They were playing the Xbox, and both of them looked up when I entered the living area. 'Oh, there she is, the fuck-up,' Rab commented.

'Oi, that's my missus you're talking about.' Jimmy nudged Rab. 'So, you never found him then?'

'Obviously not,' I said, before I could stop myself. 'Are you ok, Rab?'

'Nah, my old man fair packs a punch.' Rab rubbed at his jawline.

'Do us a favour, eh?' Jimmy said. 'There's a couple of cool packs in the belly box. Jump out and grab one for Rab.'

Not wanting to cause any more hassle, I rushed out to the belly box, grabbing the Allen key on the way past the door. I lifted the plank of wood at the base of the wagon to jam the belly box door open so as not to get trapped inside. I could see the cool box at the back end of the trailer. I hauled myself in and crawled to the back, reaching for the box. I imagined the amount of dust and dirt I would be covered in when I came out. I spun round on my stomach and started for the door when Rab appeared in the space leading to outside. He smiled.

'Hope you like the dark,' he said.

Suddenly, I knew what was coming. He stood up and kicked the plank out, allowing the door to slam shut. I was plunged into darkness.

Chapter Twelve

I sat at the computer desk in the local library and asked the librarian to help me with the computer. It was like looking into the black tunnel of the unknown; I had never used a computer before and had no idea what I was doing. Even if computers had been around properly during my time at school, I'm quite sure I'd still have been none the wiser due to moving around so much.

'What can I help you with?' the librarian asked, as she sat down on a chair beside me. All the while Lucia was sitting in her pram chewing on her fingers.

'I want to find out where Killearn is, and I wondered if you could help me.'

The woman smiled. 'My sister lives out in Killearn. It's a lovely place. I'd say it takes around an hour in the car from here. Or on the bus it would take about two.'

My expression must have shown that wasn't the answer I had expected.

'You thought it was further out?'

'Yes, I did. Do you know this address?' I handed her the piece of paper I had noted the address on.

She nodded. 'I've heard of it. It's a private estate in the east of the village. A very wealthy area. You'll be able to get a bus from Buchanan Bus Station. Just check the timetables as they can sometimes be few and far between.'

The woman kindly printed off some information, and I left the library. As I pushed Lucia along the road in her pram, I thought about what would come of me visiting Oscar. I didn't know how he knew my mam and dad, I didn't know how he would react to me turning up, and I didn't know what I was expecting from him. I didn't even know what I was going to say when I got there. I supposed I would just let the words flow out and hope that he would be able to give me some insight into my parents' past before they became travellers. What scared me was what I would find out. Were the reasons they left their home bad reasons? Did my parents do something they couldn't come back from? And if so, would this person accept my presence once he found out who I was?

It dawned on me that the photograph I had in my possession was so old that perhaps Oscar no longer lived there. He could be dead for all I knew. That scared me. It would mean no link to my parents at all. A dead end.

I slowed my pace on the approach to the crossing at the park. The traffic whizzed by, creating a gentle rush of cool air. Lucia was smiling up at me as I began to cross the road and I couldn't resist her little face. She just melted my heart. It was a good thing she looked nothing like Jimmy. That wouldn't have been easy; looking down at the most amazing thing to come out of my life and seeing him staring back at me.

'Will we go and feed the ducks, baby girl?' I cooed into the pram.

Lucia's response was to stick her fingers in her mouth and babble. I took this to mean yes. I headed in the direction of the duck pond, strolling at my leisure. I looked around at the families who had gathered in the park. I watched young boys kicking a ball about with their dads. I watched women push their daughters on the swings and I watched couples walk their dogs.

I felt a pang in my chest as I realised I was alone with Lucia. Yes, of course we had Helen, but it wasn't the same as Lucia having a loving dad. Jimmy had made sure that wouldn't happen even if he hadn't realised it.

We reached the duck pond and I turned Lucia to face it, so she could see everything that was going on. I took the few pieces of stale bread left over from the loaf at home out from the bottom of the pram and broke a piece off.

'Are you ready, Lucia?' I said, before chucking it in. The ducks began quacking and swimming over to the single piece of soggy bread and Lucia let out a giggle. I smiled and clapped my hands as she watched the ducks fight over their treat. I threw the rest of the bread in, and we stood beside the pond for a while. My mind had been working overtime, and it was nice to be able to relax and get away from the flat, even if it was just to the park.

'Watch out!' I heard a male voice shout out from my right. I turned, only to see a football heading straight for my face. I put my hands out and was surprised when I was able to deflect it. I was horrified to see it land smack bang in the middle of a family picnic about five metres behind me.

'Oh my God, I'm so sorry.' My cheeks felt like they were on fire with embarrassment.

'It's ok, my dad's sandwiches are rubbish, anyway.'

A man around my age was walking towards me, looking apologetic. 'Are you ok?'

I smiled. 'Not sure about those sandwiches, though.'

He laughed. 'That was our picnic. I suppose I deserved that after I almost took you out with my son's football.'

The boy approached us, with a grin on his face. He was around eight years old and looked just like the man whose football had almost killed me. 'Are you ok? My dad is rubbish at football too.'

The man ruffled the boy's hair, and the boy ran back to the trashed picnic. 'Seriously though, are you ok?'

'I'm fine. And so is she.' I gestured to Lucia, who was none the wiser and still hugely entertained by the quacking ducks.

'Michael,' he held his hand out.

I was surprised by his gentlemanly manner. I wasn't used to it. I took his hand and he shook it gently. 'Katelyn; and this is Lucia.'

I noticed Michael glance down at my left hand, presumably looking for a wedding ring. After years of wearing it the dent in my finger remained slightly. He didn't comment.

'And that cheeky wee scamp is Scott, my nine-year-old.' I had been close in guessing his age.

The heat was burning in my cheeks but I tried to hide it. 'We should be off. Try not to kill anyone with your lovely football skills.'

I turned back to Lucia's pram. She protested by letting out a squawk which was similar to the ducks'. Making my way towards the swing park, I wanted so much to look back, but I didn't. I couldn't afford to like anyone right now. And for all I knew, it could have just been an excited flutter that I had discovered a man who could not only apologise but be nice at the same time. What a sad day it had become when I got excited over a guy saying sorry and asking if I was ok.

'Maybe we'll meet again?' I heard Michael call out.

I turned back, not knowing how to respond. I smiled when I saw his son rolling his eyes. Then I realised, where was Scott's mum? I simply wave at Michael to acknowledge his suggestion.

As I reached the swing park, I looked at my watch. It was almost time for Lucia's bottle, so I made my way back to the flat.

As I crossed the road, I saw a familiar car parked outside the sandwich shop next to the library, just a few doors down from my building. My stomach lurched and I could feel the blood drain from my face. Rab Brannigan's car.

I was convinced that one of two things was about to happen. Either Jimmy was about appear and drag me into the car before I had a chance to scream, or I was going to somehow get past him, but never find the courage to leave the flat again.

*Why the fuck is he here? *

I lowered my head, keeping my eyes on the car. Rab wasn't in it, which was actually worse than if he had been. That way I would know where he was and if I had been seen. As it was, I had no way of knowing if he was watching me from an unknown corner or alley.

Helen was right when she said he was a goon; he certainly was slow in all manners of the word. But he was dangerous and would do anything Jimmy told him to do. My heart created a thunderous rumble in my chest, and my hands were so sweaty that I didn't have a proper grip of the pram. I was sure I was done for; the stupid git would just lift me over his shoulder, throw me in the back of his car, and I'd never be seen again.

I kept my eyes on Lucia the whole time and refused to lift my head until we passed the car and were out of sight. I waited for the inevitable as I kept walking, for Rab to appear before us and snatch us away. The more I thought of this, the more my eyes filled with tears. As though she could sense my fear and misery, Lucia looked at me through sad eyes and my heart, although still creating merry hell in my chest, melted at the look on her face. Rab walked past us, without as much as a breath in our direction. Lucky for us, I had changed the most defining feature about me, and he looked right past us. Rab appeared to look exactly the same now as he did when I last saw him.

I lifted my hair out of my face and smiled with relief at Lucia. The tears were now beginning to spill over and flow down my cheeks. Lucia smiled and began to giggle and I increased my speed to take cover in the flat as quickly as possible.

–

'What do you mean, you saw Rab Brannigan?' Helen blurted out on her arrival home from her first cleaning shift.

I shook my head. 'His car was parked outside that sandwich shop next to the library when I was bringing Lucia home. He was walking straight towards me, as plain as you are in front of me right now.'

'Fucking hell, did he see you?'

'Do you think I'd be standing here right now if he had?'

Helen hugged me. 'It'll be ok.'

I pulled away. 'How will it be ok?'

Helen couldn't answer me; she knew her words held no truth.

'What the hell was he even doing here? The site is miles away,' I said, through gritted teeth.

'He was probably picking up some dodgy gear or working the street market up in Argyle Street.'

I wondered what the chances were that I would see him again after today. It wasn't a chance I was willing to take.

'I'm phoning Louise. I want us moved. I can't risk him seeing me. It would be different if I didn't have Lucia to think about, but I do. She is my priority and I'm not risking her getting caught up in all of this shit.'

Helen nodded. 'I'll do it. Just you sit down and chill out.'

I went into the living room and slumped down on the couch. All I wanted was a quiet life. Why couldn't I have that?

Chapter Thirteen

Leaving the flat after staying cooped up for a week wasn't easy. It took me all that time to muster up the courage to go outside after my heart almost gave up on me on seeing Rab Brannigan. The only reason I had decided to venture outside was to allow Lucia some fresh air. So, I thought I would kill two birds with one stone and make the journey to Killearn. I worried that I was putting Lucia in danger by having her with me. But as much as I trusted Helen, I just couldn't leave Lucia behind. Helen had offered to come with me, but I felt like I had to do this on my own. I knew it was a long shot, but I had to try to find Oscar. I had to know how and what he knew about my parents.

I managed to get to the bus station and get Lucia and me onto the correct bus without having a panic attack about being so exposed in public.

I looked out of the window as the bus left the station and made its way along the busy street away from the city. Lucia looked out of the window and up at the sky, happily babbling away without a care in the world. I wondered what it would feel like to have nothing to worry or care about. I realised that I would most likely never have that feeling, so long as Jimmy still had air in his lungs and blood pumping through his veins. As the bus left the city and reached the open road, I sat back and took in the scenery.

For the first time in a long time, I felt relaxed. The hum of the engine and the gentle chatter which surrounded us allowed me to enjoy the journey. I looked down at Lucia, who was beginning to fall asleep in her pram. I leaned down to lay her seat back. When I sat back up, an older woman was sitting beside me. I smiled politely but didn't say anything. I could feel her eyes burning into the side of my face and she was beginning to make me feel nervous. I turned to face her, ready to ask what her problem was, but when her eyes met mine, I couldn't bring myself to be rude.

'Is something wrong dear, you look troubled?' She spoke softly.

'What do you mean?'

'We all have troubles in life, and you look particularly troubled.' Her eyes searched my face, like she was looking for the answer to her question.

'That's an understatement,' I heard myself say.

'You're going somewhere nice today?'

I nodded. There was a short silence before I decided to introduce myself. 'I'm Katelyn.'

'I'm Elsa.' She smiled.

'And this sleeping beauty is Lucia.'

Elsa smiled down at Lucia and then looked into my eyes. 'Whatever it is, my dear, you will get past it. Life throws us some unexpected challenges at times; embracing them is the best way to deal with them.'

I had no idea who this woman was, but I knew she was right. I had allowed Jimmy to control me, the whole of my adult life, through fear of violence. Not only was I terrified of being attacked by him, but I was afraid of being alone. Jimmy was the only person I'd had until a year ago. I didn't have friends or family. My life was a sad, pathetic mess until Helen took me under her wing. Then Lucia came along, and I certainly didn't want her growing up like me.

'That's exactly what I'm doing,' I replied. As I turned, I saw that Elsa was reading a book.

'You'll be just fine then,' she said, without lifting her eyes.

The rest of the journey was quiet and peaceful, Lucia slept the entire time and Elsa read. I had wondered if she was going to the same place as me but I refrained from asking. The journey was made all the more pleasant because of the sun shining through the windows and warming my skin. I felt its heat through the glass and allowed it to wash over me.

'Dear, are you going into Killearn?'

I turned to see that Elsa had put her book away. 'Yes, I am.'

'It's the next stop.'

I managed to get Lucia ready to leave the bus without waking her and, as the driver pulled into the terminus, I realised that it was the last stop. So, Elsa was going to the same place I was. The driver got out of his cab and helped me off with the pram.

'Thank you,' I said.

He nodded in reply and climbed back into the bus. 'Last bus leaves tonight at six, if you're not staying, that is.'

Facing the village of Killearn, I realised I had absolutely no idea where I was going.

'It was nice meeting you,' Elsa said as she placed her bag over her shoulder.

'Elsa, before you go, I wonder if you could help me with something.'

I pulled the photograph out of my pocket, address side up, and handed it to Elsa. 'I wondered if you would be able to tell me where I can find this house.'

She looked down at the address for what seemed like forever. When she met my gaze, her brow furrowed. 'Who do you know here?'

I sighed. 'I don't, yet. It's a long story, but basically I think the person named on the picture was a friend of my mam or dad. I have questions that nobody else can answer. This person is my last hope.'

Elsa handed back the photo and was quiet. She hadn't turned it over to view the picture.

'Are you ok?' I asked.

The church bells began chiming loudly. I jumped and so did Lucia.

'Dear, what were your parents' names?' Elsa replied.

'Michelle and David Murdoch,' I replied.

Elsa's face fell and she stepped closer to me. I was inclined to step back but I stood firm. 'What?'

'Katrina?' she whispered, eyes glistening in the light.

My heart stopped. My hearing became muffled and my palms began to sweat. I hadn't heard anyone call me that in years. Only my parents ever called me by that name. I tried to remain calm. I couldn't speak.

'Katrina Murdoch?'

I was reluctant to answer that question. I didn't want any comeback from that name. I took the picture out of my pocket and handed it back to Elsa, picture side up this time. She looked at it and tears filled her eyes. She let out a little sob. 'Oh, it really is you.'

'Who are you?' I asked, hoping she didn't hear the panic in my voice.

'I'm Elsa Murdoch. I'm your father's sister.'

I'm stunned by what she says.

'You're my aunt?' I ask.

Nausea rises to my chest as I hear her words. The way she says it makes me think she doesn't know that he's dead. I can't speak.

'There's a café across the road there, we could go inside, have a chat?' She suggests. I follow her, trying to work out in my head how I'm going to tell her that her brother died a long time ago.

—

I sat at the table in the café which was just across the road from the bus terminus and watched the steam rise from my coffee. Lucia was still asleep. The chiming of the church bells had only created a stir, and she went straight back to sleep.

Elsa was a lot older than my dad would have been now, but she seemed fit and healthy. She admired Lucia as she slept and hadn't let go of the photograph since she realised who I was.

'I can't believe you're here. How are you? How have you been?' Elsa smiled and shook her head. 'I'm sorry, it's just that after my brother,' she glanced at me, '*your parents*, passed away, I really didn't expect to see you.'

I'm flooded with relief that she already knows. This sudden find was hard enough to deal with without having to break that sort of news.

I just stare at her, unsure how to respond, even though the question in the back of my mind lingers, *Why didn't you come and find me?* But I don't ask, not yet.

'I didn't even know you existed until now,' I say.

'What brings you all the way out here after all this time?'

I sighed. Where the hell could I start? Should I be honest and reveal the whole story, or leave out the parts I couldn't bear to go over?

'It's a long story, Elsa.' I stared out of the window, looking into the past at everything that had gone wrong in my life. There was barely anything I could say that would resemble a happy memory in the last sixteen years, with the exception of Lucia, of course.

Elsa smiled. Her eyes glistened as she looked into mine. She shook her head. 'Sweetheart, I have all the time in the world.'

'Well in that case, I had better start from the beginning.'

I told Elsa everything.

Chapter Fourteen

We finished our drinks before Elsa took me to her house, 23 Keltrom Cottages, Killearn. Neither of us mentioned Oscar. I still didn't know who he was. Maybe Elsa's husband? Either way, I was one step closer to finding out more about my parents' past. Elsa led us down Balfron Road towards the church. I prayed the bells wouldn't ring again; poor Lucia would get the fright of her life.

As we passed the church on the right-hand side, the road swung to the left, and we began the descent of the hill. I had to hold back on the pram as the gradient of the hill pulled us down. Elsa was quiet.

'Elsa, where is the cottage?' I asked, trying to fill the silence.

A sudden nervousness crept over me. I was trusting a complete stranger, without question until this point. I swallowed the feeling because I had to know everything I could about my parents. Lucia needed family as much as I did even if it was just stories to tell her.

'It's at the bottom of the road. On the right-hand side is a country path. It's very secluded and private. Perfect for children like young Lucia here. Would have been perfect for you and your mam and dad all those years ago.'

I wondered why my parents had decided against this beautiful setting and instead had chosen that godawful site.

'So, why did they leave then?' I asked, cautiously.

Elsa shook her head, still leading the way. 'It wasn't a choice, my love.'

She guided us down the country path she had told me about. At the end of the path stood a lovely little house with bay windows and flower boxes hanging on their ledges. The grounds were lined with sand coloured pebbles and perfectly cut grass.

'Is this all yours?' I asked.

Elsa nodded. 'I live here on my own.'

No Oscar then? I wondered.

Elsa opened the heavyset door to the front of the cottage and gestured for me and Lucia to enter first. I hesitated, wondering if I was ready to know everything I had come here to find out. 'Please, if you don't mind removing your shoes. Father never did like shoes in the house.' 'Never *did*?' I emphasised. 'He passed away last year.' I nodded in acknowledgement as I removed my shoes. I placed them neatly by the door and waited before entering another room. I didn't want to seem pushy in any way. 'Let's go through to the dining room. We can have a cup of tea and discuss everything in there.' Elsa had already started for the dining room before finishing her sentence. She really did seem assertive. I liked that about her already. It made me realise she would be able to give me the answers I needed to be able to make sense of my life as a traveller. 'Tea or coffee, my love?' Else's gentle voice interrupted my thoughts. 'Tea please, black, no sugar.' Elsa busied herself by the kettle and I took a seat at the huge dining table. I counted and found that there were ten seats around the oak table. How many people had actually lived here at one time for the need for ten chairs? 'I've never seen a dining table like this,' I remarked. 'Shame really, not a lot of people have dined around it.'

I drank in my surroundings as Lucia continued to sleep in the pram. The decor was dated but still had a warm feel to it. The curtains hung heavily on the large bay window, and when I looked closely I saw that the material was velvet. They would surely keep out the daylight if they were closed. To the right of the window was a tall free-standing lamp with a floral fabric shade. It was not particularly pretty. The dining table itself was empty of decoration except for a single runner, made of the same material as the curtains. I found myself twirling my hair with my index finger before a cup of hot tea was placed in front of me at the table. 'Where to begin?' Elsa said, as she sat down opposite me. She seemed so far away at the other end of the table. 'To be honest, I'm not too sure where to start.'

She smiled. 'How about the beginning?' 'The beginning of what?' I asked, unsure of what she meant. 'Time, dear. The beginning of your time, or at least as far back as you can remember.' I took a deep breath. *Here goes nothing*, I thought, or in my case, everything. 'Well, I've always felt lost, like I never belonged as a traveller. When my parents were alive, my dad would tell me things about his past. Just little things, like playing in the garden with his dad or helping him to dig up the vegetable patch. He would never divulge further details like where the house was or who his dad was. I was never given a name and I never had the confidence to ask. Dad would always become a little sad when he spoke of his time before becoming a traveller. He never said why and like I say, I never asked. Mam never hung around when he spoke about it. Again,

I don't know why.' I paused and waited patiently to see what Elsa's response would be. She just nodded as though she understood what I was saying. 'Does any of this make sense to you?' I asked. 'Yes, it does, unfortunately.' 'Unfortunately?' Elsa looked down at her mug of tea and sighed. 'Carry on, dear, with your story and mine. Everything will make sense eventually.'

I wasn't sure if I liked the sound of that. Lucia caught my attention as she began to stir in her pram and as I peered in, she opened her little eyes and stared up at me. 'She's due her feed,' I said. 'I have all the time in the world.' And then I began to think, of course we wouldn't be able to talk everything out in just one day. Would she want me to come back and ask more questions? Elsa allowed me to heat Lucia's bottle and feed her at the table. She cooed over my lovely daughter and was perfectly hospitable towards us. It was nice knowing that Elsa only knew me as I was and not as Jimmy's punch bag. 'The daddy?' Elsa asked. I shot her a look before I could stop myself. She didn't notice. 'He's not around.' 'Poor wee thing.' 'She's better off without him, we both are.' Elsa shook her head. 'Your dad would disagree.' Was she serious? She barely knew me and she was lecturing me about a scumbag she knew nothing about? 'And I can tell you, my dad would have strongly disagreed with you. If you knew what he did...' Elsa stood up and walked to the window. She was quiet for a moment before turning to face me. 'I think we've strayed from the track we were on. Let's start from the beginning and this time I'll talk.' I was taken aback by the strength in her words. I felt like a little girl scared of the school teacher. Maybe if I had been more assertive, the way she was, Jimmy wouldn't have had such a hold over me. Maybe I should send Elsa to see him; maybe she would be able to sort him out. 'Your dad, my brother, he was very strong-willed. He would never be told what he could or couldn't do; well, not unless he agreed with what he was being told.'

I had no idea what Elsa meant but I let her go on, assuming she would get to the point. 'Oscar, our father.' She smiled at his memory. 'He was a little controlling at times, but only when he thought it was in the best interests of the person in question.' 'I assume you mean my dad?' I asked. Elsa nodded. 'Your grandad, Oscar, was a wealthy man who built up his own business as a groundsman. He would care for the gardens of the wealthiest people in Killearn and the surrounding areas. It took a long time, a lot of hard work, and little money. But in the end he became wealthy himself. He then expanded and began selling equipment to other groundsmen from further out. It was at that point your dad began working for the business. He was just nineteen at the time and had a natural gift for it. He worked hard and the books were looking healthy. Dad was pleased with him. It wasn't long after that your dad met your mum. She was working at the local fair, collecting money for the attractions, I was led to believe. The fairground was due to be in town for a few weeks. Your dad and a few of his friends went on the first day they arrived...'

'They?' I questioned.

'The travelling community.'

'Anyway, you know what teenage boys are like. Messing around, going on the rides, playing the games. Your dad, when he came home on that first day, he was... different.'

'What do you mean?'

Elsa smiled. 'It was like he had been put under a spell. He floated around the house that evening, in a trance-like state.'

'What was wrong with him?'

Elsa laughed gently. 'He was smitten.'

I found myself smiling now, thinking of my parents like this. Anything was better than picturing them in a furnace.

'He returned to the fair every day for three weeks after that.' Elsa approached the table and resumed her place at the head. 'There was a twinkle in his eye which grew bigger every day.'

'So what happened? How did my dad come to be a traveller?' I felt myself becoming impatient. I wasn't sure why.

'David brought her home one evening for dinner. He introduced her to my dad and me and showed her around the village. Dad kept quiet, but I knew all too well that he wasn't happy about the situation.'

I pictured my parents as teenagers, smitten with each other and without a care in the world. How did they get to where they were as I knew them?

'Why wasn't he happy?'

'He thought that Michelle wouldn't be good for David's head, what with the business going so well and all. He thought she would cause him a lot of distraction.'

I wasn't stupid; I knew Oscar wouldn't have been happy because of where Mam came from. For the first time, I felt myself defending the fact that she was a traveller. 'You mean he didn't want her class mixing with the likes of my dad.'

Elsa frowned. 'I didn't say that.'

'But I bet Oscar was thinking that,' I replied. I wasn't bitter about it. Let's face it, I had never felt like I belonged as a traveller. But I wasn't open to hearing negativity about my mam just because of her background. She was a good person and had nothing but love and admiration for my dad. Surely that could only have been a good thing?

'David brought Michelle back to the house after showing her around. We had dinner together. She chatted about, well, everything really. She seemed to be oblivious to the fact that our dad was dead silent at the table as we ate. Either that or she was ignoring it. Anyway, your dad walked her back to her site and when he came back, things turned.'

I could imagine how my dad would have reacted to Oscar's attitude towards my mam, likely similar to the way he told me never to see Jimmy again; calm and quiet.

'In what way?' I asked.

Elsa sighed before turning her attention to a framed photograph on the wall. She stood up and retrieved it. Bringing it back to the table, she placed it in front of me. 'This is your grandad Oscar.'

I stared at his face and felt a lump in my throat. It was like looking at my own dad. The hair colour was of a slightly different tone but other than that, the resemblance was uncanny. My heart began to swell. I sincerely wished that Lucia could have met her grandad. She would have loved him so much. 'So, you said things turned. In what way?'

'Your dad came home, smiling from ear to ear. I hadn't ever seen him smile like that before. Then, out of the blue, your grandad Oscar said David wasn't to see her again.'

The words sounded familiar. 'What was Dad's response?'

Elsa hung the frame back on the wall and stared out of the window. 'David laughed at first. He didn't believe Dad. Why would he? Michelle had been nothing but pleasant in our company. When your grandad didn't respond, it was then that David began to react.'

'What did he do?'

'He was honest. He said that he had fallen in love with Michelle and there was nothing anyone could do about that. Oscar turned nasty then, saying he would cut David out of the business if his affair were to continue. He said he didn't want a filthy traveller getting their hands on his money.'

I was shocked. How could anyone be so brass? Yes, I would admit that Jimmy and the rest of the Denton's were scum, but Mam should have been given a chance to prove him wrong at least. 'My mam wasn't like that.'

Elsa nodded. 'I knew that just by the way she carried herself. And of course, your dad knew it too. But not Oscar. He jumped to the conclusion that all travellers were thieves, and he wasn't having his son risk everything the family had built up over the years for some travelling love interest.'

I could picture my dad and how he would have reacted. Anger wouldn't have been one of the emotions he would have shown. Instead, he would have most likely nodded in acknowledgement of his dad's words and said nothing more on the matter. I expressed this thought to Elsa, who was impressed at how correct I was.

'The only difference was, David put it plain and simple; Oscar had to accept the fact that he was in love with a traveller and allow him to make his own mistakes, or interfere with his life and risk losing his only son.'

That sounded exactly like my dad. There was no getting around the fact that if he knew what he wanted, there was no stopping him. But he would always conduct himself with grace and dignity. I supposed that was where I got it from.

'I assume he left?'

Elsa nodded. This time, her eyes filled with tears, threatening to spill over and reveal years of pain and anguish that her family had been ripped apart. I feared she would blame my mam for her pain. 'Oscar screamed and shouted. He even threw something as your dad walked out. Of course, I was in tears and hysterical about how quickly everything had happened. Just three weeks previously, everything had been fine. Now, my brother and best friend was walking out of the family home, and all because my dad was a stubborn old sod.'

'You were close with my dad, then?' I asked.

'We were.' She wiped a lone tear from her cheek. 'I was so surprised at how calm he was about everything. He wasn't taking any of Oscar's nonsense. David knew what he wanted and he wasn't about to let anyone stand in his way.'

Elsa stopped talking and glanced up at the clock. I watched her for a moment, wondering what she was thinking when she said, 'Time's getting on a bit, you must be hungry. I'll make us some sandwiches.'

I looked at the clock and already three hours had passed. It hadn't felt like I'd been sitting here that long. I could tell she wanted a break from the memories. It must've been hard for her to recall those days. However, now conscious of the time, I wanted to make sure we caught the last bus back to Buchanan Street Station.

'Elsa, can I come back?'

'Come back?'

'Yes, I mean, we have a lot of years to cover. We won't get through them all in a day.'

'Katrina, my love, I haven't seen your dad since that day, I'm not sure there is much more I can tell you about his time between leaving and having you. We wrote to each other. But he never returned to the village, and I never knew where he was from one month to the next. Oscar knew nothing of the letters and if he had, he would have burned them. It was as if he had disowned David. It was so sad, to see our family break down like that.'

I couldn't believe that Oscar and my dad had just stopped speaking. There had to be more to it.

'So, you have nothing more to tell me?' Surely not? I hadn't come all this way just for this.

'Not about what happened when David left, not really. Though, I do have something that may be of interest to you. It may settle the many questions you have. I'll be back in a moment.'

Elsa left the room. What could she have for me that would help me understand who my parents had been?

'There's more where that came from,' she said, returning to the room. She handed me an envelope. 'I had this one out just the other day, was going through some bits in the back room and came across it. I'll leave it with you while I go to find the item I want you to have.'

'What is this?' I say, looking from the letter to Elsa.

'It's one of the first letters your dad sent to me after he left,' Elsa said, before disappearing again. I stare down at it, my heart swelling in my chest as I open the envelope carefully.

Chapter Fifteen

Dear Elsa,

These last few months have been hard since we haven't been in contact. I hope you understand why I had to leave and why I have chosen my new way of life. It hasn't been plain sailing, I can assure you. Settling into the travelling community has had its difficulties, especially with the locals. Michelle has been wonderful and introduced me to everyone in her community. Most of the people have been welcoming and pleasant enough, but not everyone is as forthcoming. It's funny how you think you understand a way of life, or a different culture, but then you're faced with it and you realise you are ignorant and unequipped to deal with it. In the travelling community, I'm known as a 'flatty', which is someone who is a non-traveller. Michelle's family took a little time to accept that I was moving into the trailer with her and taking on this whole new life. They weren't happy that I had 'come into' their community all of a sudden with no traveller ties of my own. But after a good month or so, they came to accept that Michelle and I are for keeps. I don't know how you feel about Michelle, or how you really feel about my departure from the house, or the business.

I know Dad well enough to know that he probably hasn't mentioned me, and if he has, his words would have been harsh and most likely uncalled for. We parted on extremely bad terms, as you know. I wonder if he'll ever accept this. He was so against my relationship with Michelle, for reasons we both know are completely ridiculous and untrue. She is the kindest, loveliest woman I have ever met and I will not allow anything to stop me from being with her. If that means I have to give up my side of the business and my inheritance once Dad is no longer around, then so be it. I know you're probably thinking that my decision is irrational, but when you love someone, all rational decision-making goes out the window.

None of that means to say that I don't care. Of course I do. I miss you both every day and I wish things could have been different, I wish he could have accepted my choice. There are so many stereotypical opinions out there about travellers and their way of life. They're not bad people, they're just like anyone else, except they live in trailers and travel the country in order to make a living. I'm sure there are worse people out there who aren't travellers. I'm not sure if you agree, maybe you do? Like I say, none of it matters to me because I know Michelle and I know that she is a good person. She is a decent, hard-working woman and I will embrace my new life alongside her. There is nothing wrong with it, despite what Dad thinks.

I would like to see you, maybe meet up with you from time to time. I couldn't bear to lose contact with my only sister. I will try to patch things up with Dad, but of all people, you know how stubborn he can be. He rejected me when I made my life decision and I don't see him going back on his choice anytime soon, no matter how much it might hurt him.

The site we are currently living on is relatively big. We've been moving around a lot doing carnivals and fayres. It's definitely different from what I'm used to. The trailers aren't too bad either, a little small for a family but we'll get our own eventually. Michelle told me that sometimes the community will organise fund-raisers to help people with money towards a new trailer or chalet. It would be helpful since we don't have a lot of money, just enough to get by. Obviously, living with Michelle's family helps because they provide food and a roof over our heads, but we don't have a lot of privacy.

My plan is that, one day, we will have our own trailer or chalet, we will have a family of our own and we will get married. I really hope that you can be a part of that, Elsa.

I will try to write to you as often as possible. Please keep in touch. I have enclosed our site address.

All my love

Your brother, David.

Chapter Sixteen

I smiled as I read the letter and found that as soon as I had finished I read it again. I felt so lucky to be able to see a little into my parents' past by reading this letter and I was already craving more. I folded the letter and placed it carefully back in the envelope.

While Elsa was gone, I couldn't resist the opportunity to have a look around. The house was a cottage. It should have been small, but was actually quite large. There was a hallway of doors outside the dining room, all of which were closed. Natural curiosity made me wonder which room had previously been my dad's, and if it had been left untouched. I had just reached out for a door handle when I heard Lucia call out. I headed back down the hallway towards the dining room and lifted her out of the pram. She had been asleep for such a long time, there would be no way that she would go down early tonight.

'Here we are then,' I heard Elsa's voice behind me. I looked around to see her carrying a shoebox.

'What's that?' I asked.

'More of what you've just read. Everything you want to know is in this box.' Her voice shook in her throat and it set something off in me which I wasn't expecting. How could everything I wanted to know be inside a shoebox?

The lump in my throat ached but I didn't allow the tears to come.

'Seriously? Everything I want to know about my parents' past is in that tiny box?' I said.

'That and possibly more. I know more about you than you think, young lady,' Elsa said.

There was so much to know, I wondered how far her knowledge stretched. 'I'll take your word for it.'

'I'm gifting you with this; it's yours to keep. I only have one condition,' Elsa said softly.

'And what would that be?'

'You can keep this box and its contents, so long as I can see you again. Every so often, I would like you to come and visit me, or for me to be able to visit you, see what your life is like.'

I couldn't argue with that, finding Elsa wasn't something I'd even thought of this morning. I had a family connected to my parents, Lucia now had extended family, this was what my dad would have wanted. Of course I would want to see her again.

'Then I accept your condition,' I replied.

Elsa placed her hand on my wrist and gave it a gentle squeeze and when I looked into her eyes, I saw my dad.

We cried together and Elsa hugged me the way I imagined I would hug my parents if I ever got the chance again.

–

We ate sandwiches and drank more tea before I had to leave in order to make the last bus back to Buchanan Street Station. I packed the shoebox of revelations into the bottom of the pram and made Lucia comfortable. I felt bad that she had been stuck in there all day. Maybe I'd leave her with Helen the next time I visited Elsa.

'When will I see you again?' Elsa asked. 'It has been lovely to have a connection to David again after all this time.'

'I'll phone ahead so that you know I'm coming,' I replied, as I slid my arms into my coat. 'Elsa, you have no idea how much this has meant to me. So much has happened to me since my parents died. Now that Lucia and I have you, and I have a chance to learn about my parents, I think it will help me to move on with my life.'

Elsa took my hand in hers. 'Anything for my brother, my love.'

As I left the cottage and made my way to the bus stop, I wondered what village life would be like in Killearn. Everything seemed so quiet and peaceful; nothing like my life had ever been.

I looked ahead and could see the bus pulling into the small terminus. I picked up speed, and the same driver came out of his cab to help me onto the bus. Lucia and I were the only passengers. Bless her, she had been so good today. It was almost like she knew what I was doing and had allowed me to do it. Her little eyes stared up at me from the pram and she was so contented in the comfort of her blanket.

The bus pulled out from the terminus a few moments later and I resisted the urge to open the shoebox resting under Lucia. I was so curious about what was inside. Obviously, it was enough for Elsa to comment that she knew more about me than I thought. Then I recalled she had mentioned writing back and forth to my dad. That was it; it was the letters from all those years ago, inside that box. I didn't know how to feel about that. I was anxious about what I would read. But at the same time, I was relieved. I would find out about my parents and the short life they'd led together before I came along.

The journey to Buchanan Street Station felt longer than the journey out to Killearn, but we eventually made it back to Glasgow. By this time, the sky had become hazy as the sun was setting. I decided to take a taxi back to the flat and get Lucia her night-time feed and bath before settling her for the night. That way, I could settle myself with a glass of wine and the letters in the shoebox.

A pang of anxiety gripped my chest as I walked to the nearest taxi rank. I had become exposed to the crowds once more, and irrational thoughts of Jimmy watching us from a car or nearby building filled my head. I decided to breathe my way through it and keep my eyes on Lucia. I approached the cinema on Renfrew Street and looked up to see the gathering crowds awaiting entry to see the newest release.

Shit, shit, shit, I thought, as my mind raced to find a pathway through them. Before I could stop myself, I had rammed one of the wheels of the pram into someone's foot. 'Oh, sorry.'

The man turned and I recognised him instantly. 'Katelyn?'

My brain went into slow motion as I tried to place him. Then I remembered. 'Michael?' The man who had almost taken me out with his son's football in the park.

'Nice to see you again.' He smiled. 'Where are you off to at this hour?' His eyes sparkled in the sunset and his bright smile filled his face.

'I'm heading home. We've been out…' I hesitated, '…
visiting family.' Why had I hesitated? He didn't actually
care where I had been at all; he was just being polite.

'We've just been to see the latest superhero film. He's
daft about them.'

I looked down to see Michael's son dressed up in full
hero costume. 'Hi again.'

'Hi,' he replied.

'I should get going, I really need to get this one into
her bath and get her settled.'

Michael nodded and peered into the pram. 'Night
night, wee girly.' He looked up at me and our eyes met.
'Maybe we'll bump into each other again?'

I smiled a little. 'Maybe.'

We parted ways and I got into the first taxi I saw. I
pushed Michael out of my head. This was not the time.
My mind was all over the place, and even if I did like
him, or anyone else for that matter, I had serious trust
issues when it came to men. How could I be sure they
weren't all like Jimmy Denton? Michael came across as
lovely, but how could I know for sure he wasn't of the
same mind? The thoughts raced through my head so much
that I hadn't noticed the taxi had pulled up outside my
building.

I got Lucia upstairs and inside where I found Helen
lying on the couch.

'Where have you been all day? I was getting worried.'

'You seem worried,' I laughed. 'I was out at Killearn,
visiting my dad's sister.'

'Your dad had a sister?'

I nodded, still barely able to believe that I had just made
the first connection to the family I hadn't known existed.

Helen frowned. 'And how was it?'

I lay Lucia under her play mobile and took off my coat. 'It was… informative.'

'Informative, how?'

I showed Helen the shoebox.

'What's in it?'

'Letters between my dad and Elsa, his sister.'

Helen saw to Lucia while I got her bath ready. I was on autopilot; I couldn't stop thinking about that box. Would there be anything of use to me contained in those letters? And if so, what would I find? I had been dreaming of this day for sixteen years and all of a sudden I felt guilty, like I was delving into a part of my parents' lives that I wasn't supposed to. Maybe I wasn't supposed to know any more than I already did. Or perhaps I was destined to find out about what happened after my dad left Killearn.

'My dad hadn't always been a traveller,' I said, as I watched Helen bathe Lucia.

'What do you mean?' she asked, not lifting her head.

'He left a wealthy family and lifestyle to be with my mam.'

Helen lifted Lucia out of the bath and wrapped her in a snug, pink hooded towel. 'Are you serious?'

I nodded. 'I mean, I knew that one of them had family somewhere, and I knew they hadn't always been travellers because of the stories they told me. But I never for one minute thought that he had changed his whole life so he could be with my mam.'

Helen looked as shocked as I felt. Her life had changed so much in the past year too, it was likely that she could relate to my dad, in some way or another.

'You're quiet,' I remarked as Helen put Lucia down to bed for the night. I was grateful for the help if I was honest. I loved Lucia with every breath in my body, but being a mum wasn't easy, especially not under my circumstances.

'I'm thinking.'

I was scared to ask what about. 'Are you regretting leaving the site?'

Helen shot me a look. 'Oh God, no. If anything I'm regretting not leaving sooner. I was thinking about you and how you're finding yourself. It's… admirable.'

I wasn't sure I agreed with her. I wouldn't say it was admirable, more that I had been desperate to find myself and where I had come from for so long. Now that I had the chance, I was scared.

'I don't think so.'

'Are you kidding? You've bounced back from years of torment and unimaginable abuse from the one person who promised to love you no matter what. And here you are, a baby in one arm and a box of the past in the other, ready to find out where you've come from. All the while mending yourself from your own past and raising a child, while living in fear of Jimmy coming back to get you. If that's not admirable, I don't know what is.'

I had never looked at it like that before. Was I being too modest, was I too full of self-doubt? Exactly what was I so scared of finding inside that box? Or, maybe it wasn't really the box and its contents I was scared of? Maybe I had lived a life where being scared on a constant basis was just normality. A pathetic way to exist.

'Well, thank you for your confidence. It means a lot that you think of me that way.'

Helen smiled. 'You don't have to thank me. It's all your work that's got you to this point. Give yourself some credit.'

'Well, in that case then, thank you for being with me during this past year. I definitely couldn't have done this without you. You have given up so much to be with Lucia and me. Not everyone would be willing to do that.'

Helen laughed. 'What exactly have I given up? A fucked-up family with a scumbag brother and a drunk for a dad? My youngest sister will either turn out just like them or fall prey to them, and that lifestyle. I gave up nothing when I left that site, except for my sister.' Helen fell silent for a few moments. Jimmy Denton had so much to answer for. Not only did he marry me and slowly strip me of my personality piece by piece, forcing me into becoming a recluse for the whole of my adult life, but he tore his own family apart too. That scum must have been conceived through venom and hate. He couldn't possibly have been created by love. No one could turn out that evil otherwise. Then I thought of Helen, who shared the same blood as Stan and Jimmy. How could she turn out so differently? A pang of guilt hit me in the stomach when I thought of her. She had lived with them her entire life, her upbringing was surrounded by aggression and violence. I'd only had to live with it since I was a young adult.

'I'll go back for her one day,' Helen whispered, her voice cracking with emotion.

'Would you really?'

'I don't think I could go through life with that thought in my head. I wouldn't forgive myself if I didn't try.'

She must have seen the look on my face; the look I always had on my face. Fear.

147

'Oh, don't you worry. I will make sure he never finds out about you if I ever do go back. I wouldn't just waltz in there, I would be sure to plan it properly. If I knew I could get away with it, I'd kill the bastard and leave him to rot in his own shit.' I could see the hatred trailing across her face. 'No, I'll be sure to watch him for a while before I go in and persuade Mandy to leave with me.'

I worried that with Helen leaving the site, Mandy would refuse to go with her if she ever did go back for her. Maybe Mandy would view Helen's behaviour as deceitful, like she'd betrayed the family. Or maybe Mandy wouldn't want to leave the site, leave her family, because she thought it was the right thing to do by staying.

'Don't think about that right now, you'll end up having nightmares,' I said. 'I'm going to call it a night, it's been a long day and I just want to sleep.'

Wracked with guilt because Helen wouldn't have left Mandy had she not helped me, I hugged Helen goodnight and retired to my bedroom. I closed the door quietly and sat down on the bed. I had laid the box on my pillow when I had come home earlier. I stared at it. Should I open it now? Should I begin to read? If I began now, would I be able to stop?

I fell back onto the pillow next to the box. I turned to face it. I couldn't resist the urge. My mam and dad's lives as travellers could potentially be in there. I sat up and rested the box on my knee. I took a deep breath and opened the lid. There they were, staring up at me; a picture of my parents, young, fresh-faced, and loving life. Loving each other. This time, they were on what looked like a pier. There was a note on the other side of the photograph. Blackpool, July 1980. I recognised the

148

handwriting straight away. Cursive, little flicks at the end of each word. Each letter perfectly formed, just like my mother was herself.

She looked as beautiful in that picture as she had the last day I saw her.

I imagined what she would look like now. Would her red hair still flow in ringlets like it did all those years ago? Would her blue eyes have aged much?

My eyes scanned over the picture to Dad, laughing, Mam's hair swirling around his head in the wind.

I blinked away tears which threatened to spill. I missed them so much.

–

I was wide awake as I lay on my bed, staring at the ceiling. Yet, I could hear the roar of the flames as if my bedroom was on fire. I opened my mouth to scream, but my voice was silenced by the shock of what was unfolding in front of my eyes. This wasn't happening, I knew it wasn't real. Yet the heat against my face told me otherwise.

I clawed at the duvet, gripping handfuls of it and trying to pull it apart, as if I was trying to escape from somewhere. I couldn't breathe, yet there was nothing to stop me from taking a breath.

I sat up, gulping in air, searching the room wildly. Nothing out of the ordinary.

I ran my fingers through my hair and felt the beads of sweat which had formed on my head. I'd heard of night terrors. Some people experience them but remember nothing, others are fully aware of what is happening, that things seem normal, yet they cannot escape the rising panic which the terror creates.

Was I losing my mind over this? Having never had the chance to grieve properly, to talk about how being abandoned to death by fire had really affected me, I suppose I was deeply traumatised by that event.

I threw the covers off and got up to check on Lucia. She was, as always, sound asleep. I had managed to get her into a good bedtime routine even though she still slept through the day. I had made Lucia my main focus after leaving the site. She was the one who helped me get through the day. I wanted to pick her up and hug her tight, but I resisted the urge.

I sat down on the bed again and took a sip from the glass of water on my bedside table. I couldn't stop thinking about the shoe box. I had placed the photograph of my parents which I had taken out of the box on first opening it on my bedside table.

They looked happy, like they didn't have a care in the world. They were free and in love. I had never known either of those emotions. I had decided not to read any letters tonight from fear of not being able to stop. I *wanted* to read all of those letters, but I had to space them out. If I read them all at once, then soon my discovery would be over and I would no longer have new information about my parents. I wanted the new feeling to last. That box was the very last link to my parents, to Lucia's grandparents. My heart lay inside it, in the dark and safe space that held the life of Mam and Dad.

I stopped myself from opening the box and lay back down on the bed. Taking a deep breath, I closed my eyes and hoped that I wouldn't be subjected to another terror.

Jimmy was always on the periphery, floating in on clouds of smoke which plagued every waking minute.

I didn't know why, but Michael had crept into my thoughts. I found it strange that I had bumped into him again. I hadn't allowed myself to think about another man since I'd married Jimmy. Even thinking of or imagining another man had been enough to set him off. Michael, in contrast, had been very polite on the two occasions I had met him. I wondered if I would ever bump into him again.

'Morning,' Helen said chirpily, as she appeared in the doorway.

'Morning,' I replied.

'So, what do you want to do today?' she asked, trying to distract me as she stole a piece of toast off my plate. 'It's my day off, so I thought we could go for some lunch and take Lucia to the park?'

I liked the sound of that. Getting out for some fresh air and taking my mind off everything was just what I needed.

I finished my toast and got Lucia ready. We decided to walk as it was such a lovely day, I wasted enough time worrying about running into Rab and Jimmy, I looked different enough now that even if they were to appear, they wouldn't recognise me. Deep in the pit of my stomach, something churned because my head and my stomach were thinking differently but I couldn't keep Lucia cooped up.

We walked along Norfolk Street and crossed the bridge into Glasgow Green. Lucia looked up at the full trees and listened as the birds chirped happily under the sunshine. This was the kind of thing that she would be missing had I stayed with Jimmy. He would never have let me take Lucia too far in case I left him completely. I had previous form, and he wouldn't have trusted me. I would have been kept under close scrutiny to make sure I stayed put. It was so much safer for us both that I had left in silence when I did.

I often wondered if he ever found out that Helen had bought a pregnancy test, and if he had, would he believe that it was his sister who was pregnant? As far as Jimmy was concerned, his sister and I had never really got on. But surely he wasn't so stupid that he wouldn't have realised we had left together?

We took the long way round the park and past The People's Palace. It must have been extremely warm inside, considering the sun was shining and it was mostly made from glass.

'Even after all this time, I still feel so exposed when I'm in a public place,' I said quietly as we walked along.

Helen nodded. 'I know what you mean, it's like everywhere we look, he's there, watching us, waiting for the right moment.'

My eyes widened. 'Bloody hell, Helen. Way to make me feel better.'

'Sorry. But that's just the way I feel. You said yourself that you feel exposed.'

Helen knew how to set the scene. Unlikely as it was that Jimmy would jump out from behind a tree and drag me back to eternal torture, I still couldn't help picturing it.

We wandered out of the park and up onto Trongate, looking for somewhere to have lunch. We went into an Italian restaurant and a waiter found a table for us. He offered a high chair for Lucia but I kept her in the pram.

The restaurant was bright and spacious. The smell of garlic and wine filled the room, and I was taken aback by how magnificent the place looked. I hadn't ever eaten in a proper restaurant before. It was something we just didn't do when I was growing up. I looked at Helen, who seemed to be feeling the same as me, judging by the embarrassed expression on her face.

We sat down at the table and I watched Helen run her hands over the white table linen. The wine glasses sparkled under the light and the soft music playing in the background filled my ears. I was both entranced by the beauty of my surroundings and worried that I looked like I didn't belong.

'This place is...' Helen started.

'I know.'

We sat down and I began browsing the menu. There was so much to choose from and everything sounded so delicious. Just as I was about to settle on my choice, I was interrupted by a familiar voice.

'If I didn't know any better, I'd say you're following me!'

I looked up to find Michael standing at our table, that wide grin spread across his face again. My shock must have been apparent because Helen had to jump in and fill the silence.

'Hi, I'm Helen, Katelyn's friend.'

Helen and Michael shook hands as I tried to restart my tongue. I stood up to greet him. 'Hi. What are you doing here?'

His grin lessened but smile remained. 'I own this restaurant.'

Helen's eyes sparked. I knew what she was thinking, and if I was honest with myself, I was thinking it too. He was so handsome and his smile alone had a certain charm to it. I felt something stir inside me that I hadn't felt since I was fourteen and had first laid eyes on Jimmy. This worried me; that relationship hadn't turned out to be the best, yet Jimmy had still managed to draw me in. I wasn't going to allow myself to be captivated by an idiot ever again. I would always have my guard up.

'Are you a chef?' I asked, not knowing what else to say.

'No, just a businessman. Actually, my dad died a few years ago and I took over.'

'I'm sorry to hear that,' Helen said softly.

Michael caught my gaze and I found myself studying his face. He was the opposite of Jimmy, with fair skin, dark hair which was greying at the sides, and soft green eyes.

'This place has kept me going.'

There was silence for a few moments before a waiter arrived at our table and took our drinks order. Michael hung around until the waiter had finished. I didn't know what it was but something made me will him to hold my gaze. I always remembered my dad and how he was with my mam. They would speak to each other with respect and he always kept his eyes on her. She was his queen and I was his princess.

'These are on the house,' Michael said, jolting me from my thoughts.

'There's really no need, honestly,' I said.

'I'd be offended if you didn't accept,' Michael replied.

Helen thanked both Michael and the waiter and they left us to look over the menu before taking our order. I felt confused by the situation. I had only met Michael three times, including today. Why would he offer us drinks for free? Why was he being so nice to me?

'Katelyn, he really likes you,' Helen said as she picked up a breadstick from a basket on the table.

I eyed her suspiciously. 'No, he doesn't, he's just being polite.'

Helen nodded as she took a bite of the breadstick. 'If he was this *polite* to all his customers, his bar takings would take a serious hit.'

I watched Michael behind the bar and wondered why we had bumped into each other three times in such a short space of time. After everything I had been through, I wasn't a big believer in fate. But what if this was something that was supposed to happen for me? What if Michael and I had crossed paths for a reason? I wasn't sure if I was willing to find out. I lost my train of thought when Michael suddenly appeared at our table again.

'I don't usually do this, but here,' he said, handing me a small card. 'It's my number.'

I was speechless. What was I supposed to say?

'You don't have to get in touch but seeing as we've run into each other three times now, I imagine it isn't likely to happen again. So, this way, if you want to see me again you can give me a call.'

I glanced at Helen, who was busying herself with Lucia.

'Thanks, I will.' The words were out of my mouth before I could stop them.

Michael smiled and left us alone. I felt Helen's eyes burning into the top of my skull as I peered down at the business card. I looked up to be faced with the biggest grin I had ever seen.

'Nicely played, Katelyn.'

Nicely played? How had this even just happened? I didn't have time to be getting involved with a stranger when I had a million other things to be doing. My head wasn't in the right place for it, let alone my heart. I put the business card into my handbag and pushed what had just happened to the back of my head.

The only thing that should be at the forefront of my mind right now was Lucia and finding out about my parents' past. And I fully intended to find out everything I could to help me move on from that part of my life. Of course, I would never forget my parents; how could I? But something inside me wouldn't allow me to move on until I had read every single last word on every letter inside the box that Elsa had given me when I had gone to Killearn.

'It's not the right time for me to get involved with someone,' I replied, smiling as Lucia blew raspberries at me.

'Who said anything about getting involved? All I meant was he likes you, so why not go on a date and have a bit of fun? You deserve that.'

I thought about that word, fun. I had no idea how to have fun. I hadn't had fun for over sixteen years. Before Lucia came along, I couldn't remember the last time I had even smiled.

–

I lay on the sofa flicking through the channels on the television, but nothing grabbed my attention. Helen had already gone to bed and Lucia was down for the night. I switched off the lights and the television and went to bed.

Resting my head on the pillow, my mind began to wander, and thoughts of Michael filled my head. I had put his card in my handbag and said I would phone him. Why had I said that when I wasn't sure if I would? I supposed that I had never been able to say no to Jimmy, so maybe it was just habit? And if that were true, then would I ever be able to say no to any man? From an outside perspective, this would sound weak and ridiculous, but I was certain I would never be able to shake the worry that all men were like Jimmy.

'You will never leave me! Get that into your thick skull!' Such were the pleasantries often shared by my husband, along with a slap across the cheek or a kick to the back of the knee.

Jimmy was the leader of a small group of other male travellers back at the site, and they would often keep an eye on me if I was out and about, but that was mostly down to Rab. Out and about meant hanging out the washing or doing the shopping. I was never actually out socially, for two reasons: one, I was never allowed; and two, I actually had no friends to socialise with. Through choice, I would never touch alcohol, anyway. Jimmy already had enough control over me, and I refused to allow more while I was under the influence. There had been many a time where I would have happily downed a bottle of vodka to make me numb to the attacks and help me to forget them the next day. However, I knew that in time it would only make things worse.

I had seen how much Helen was drinking before we escaped the clutches of the site, never knowing why, and thinking she was just a hard-faced cow. I knew so little about her back then, knew nothing of the abuse she had suffered at the hands of Jimmy to protect Mandy.

Of course, Helen wasn't drinking now. She was a solid rock for Lucia and me, and I couldn't imagine where we would have ended up without her. I thought about what my life would be like if I hadn't left the site; if I had stayed with Jimmy. I whole-heartedly believed I would be dead. Would I have had Lucia before that? I tried not to torture myself with what might have been. My life had been bad enough up until now. There was no need to make it worse by imagining what-ifs.

I sat up and, as I ran my hand through my hair, I turned to see Lucia asleep. I did not ask the universe for her, but I got her. She was the only good thing to come from Jimmy. How could something so evil have produced something so beautiful?

I swung my legs off the bed and crept over to Lucia's cot. I watched her little chest rise and fall as she filled her lungs with clean air. When I imagined her in the trailer, I pictured her breathing in filthy air. Everything back at that site was tainted, even the oxygen. Here, she could breathe clean, pure air and I would never have to worry about her becoming infected by Jimmy's evil. I stroked her short, fluffy hair gently so as not to wake her. She stirred slightly but remained sleeping.

'You're nothing like him and never will be. And you will *never* know him. I will keep running if I have to, just to keep you safe,' I whispered.

I would run around the world twice over if I had to, but I knew deep down that one day, Jimmy would cross my path somehow. I just had to make sure that Lucia would never be involved. But how could I make that possible if

I didn't know when that day would come? It was then, staring at my beautiful daughter, that it hit me. I would never be able to keep her one hundred percent safe. That thought terrified me more than the anticipation of any beating Jimmy could ever put me through.

The only way I could be sure we would never fall prey to him again was if he was dead.

Chapter Seventeen

Dear Elsa,

We have been travelling all over Scotland for the past few months doing fairs. I'm exhausted, but I have loved it. Well, I say I have loved it, what I mean is I have loved being with Michelle. Of course, she is so busy during the day and late into the evening, so we don't get a lot of private time together. But just being with her, standing by her side every single day, is enough. I never believed in all that mushy love guff before I met Michelle. If I hadn't met her, I still wouldn't believe it.

I think about home a lot. I don't particularly fit in with the travellers here. They're nice enough when I chat to them, of course. However, I don't think they like that I'm an outsider. It's not entirely acceptable here. Some of them are fine with it, but there is one family in particular who make it clear that they are not happy with my presence. Michelle deals well with it. She just tells them to back off. The family is a heavy bunch. Michelle's dad has had a few run-ins with the head of the family, Stan. I personally would love to punch him in the face but that wouldn't get me anywhere other than in hospital. He's a brutal man, a tad handy with his fists, especially if his wife steps out of line. Of course, nobody will speak about it because as far as he is concerned, nobody knows about it. Michelle's dad does try to stay clear of him, but it's impossible when we are all travelling together and living as a community. His wagon is thankfully at the other end of the site, but that doesn't stop him from causing chaos. He drinks like a fish and most nights he stumbles about the site, shouting and bawling about a load of nonsense; things like, 'I'll call the shots on this site,' and 'Nobody messes with my family.'

Michelle's dad is the only man on site who is brave enough to stand up and tell him to rein it in, which of course he doesn't like. So most nights there are fights between the two of them. But the next day, when Stan is sober, he acts like nothing has happened. I'm beginning to think he doesn't remember his behaviour when he's been on a bender. Although just the other night, he was outside our trailer, drunk as per usual and he was shouting something about being a traitor. I instantly knew he was talking about me. Michelle's dad, Steven, went outside to tell him to keep his mouth shut. Michelle and I listened from the window in the kitchenette and I heard him slurring something about Steven and the family being traitors to the travelling community by bringing a 'flatty' into their lives. He went on to say how I was the scum who would take stories back to his friends and give 'us travellers' a bad name. He used some choice words in amongst all that, I must add. I got up and went outside to confront him. Michelle was pulling at my arm, trying to stop me.

I got into his face, told him to shut up, he knew nothing about me or my life before I had arrived. He wasn't happy I had confronted him. I had never seen him up close before, but I realised he was the same age as me. How could he stand there and act the big tough guy when he was only nineteen or twenty? There were other men on this site who were older, just like Steven, who were just sitting back and allowing him to behave this way. Anyway, to cut a long story short, we ended up in a scuffle. He came off worse, I broke his nose. I'm not proud of it, but it did shut him up for a while. It was only last week, but since then, he has backed down a little. He still gets drunk every night and rambles on about a load of rubbish. But he has backed off from us, which I am glad of.

I was surprised that I reacted at all. Maybe all of Dad's nastiness about my relationship with Michelle and his bad attitude towards her lifestyle was what pushed me to breaking point, and I took it out on Stan. And maybe the fact that I broke his nose has made him realise I am not one to be messed with. Although I think you and I both know that is not entirely true. If I can avoid confrontation, then I will. However, avoiding confrontation is completely different to allowing someone to walk all over you. And no matter what, I never allow someone to walk all over me. I think I have already proved that to Dad.

Has he mentioned us at all? I don't suppose he has. And I believe that if he knew about my scuffle, he would be quite happy about it. In fact, I can just see him now, smiling from ear to ear, saying 'What did I tell you?'

Our life here is going well, with the exception of our problems with the particular family I have mentioned. But please don't worry about me. I think living as a traveller is actually helping to strengthen my backbone. I do sometimes wish things could have been different and that we could have been part of the family in Killearn. I know Michelle would have loved it. But wishes never come true, do they?

I miss you every day, Elsa. I miss the house. I even miss him at times. But I miss the dad he used to be, not the dad he became in the end. That's what hurts the most. I'm grieving for a man who is still there but is hiding behind a hardened exterior. It is his loss as well as mine, but I have also gained the love of my life. I just wish he would have allowed me to share that with him.

I'll write to you again soon.

All my love,

David

Chapter Eighteen

The sun shone through the crack in the blinds, and sunlight trailed across the carpet towards the door.

I had read my dad's letter to his sister last night before falling asleep. I couldn't comprehend how I had drifted off so quickly after reading the words on the page. I wasn't a believer in coincidence, especially when it came to this. After everything I had wished for, everything I wanted to know about my parents, it all came back to the one family I didn't want anything more to do with. The man in my dad's letter was Stan Denton. It had to be. I looked into Lucia's cot but found it was empty. I got up and wrapped myself in my dressing gown. I opened the door and made my way down the hall towards the living room. Helen must have come into my room to get Lucia when I was still asleep.

Something stopped me in my tracks. I felt a chill, deep within me. A fear I had never felt before. Something wasn't right. The flat was quiet. Too still. Then, a sudden giggle from Lucia filtered through from the living room. I relaxed. I opened the living room door and to my horror, Jimmy was standing by the window, holding my daughter in his arms. He looked up as I froze on the spot.

'Ah, there you are.' His twisted smile slithered across his face. 'I have been looking all over for you. Now, be a good little wife and get your gear together. We're going home.'

My throat was constricted by fear. I clutched at my chest and my legs gave way. I let out a scream. He was by my side, hand under my arm, yanking me to my feet. Lucia reached out, but he refused to pass her to me. I tried to speak, tried to plead, but the words would not leave my throat.

'Are you going to do what I told you, or do I have to make you?' His lips barely moved as he spoke.

My eyes stung with tears. Through them, I could see Lucia's little face, trying to make sense of the situation. I couldn't turn my back. I had to keep my eyes on her.

'No, I won't.' My voice was small and weak.

Jimmy's brow furrowed. He put Lucia down on her play mat. 'I will not tell you again, Kat, get your stuff together. We're going home.'

I shook my head, in utter disbelief that this was actually happening and in defiance of his request. I couldn't care less what he would do to me. I just couldn't allow him to take Lucia.

He grabbed my wrist. 'Don't fuck with me, not in front of the wean.'

'Like you care about her. All you care about is getting your own way. Well, fuck you, Jimmy, I will not do what you tell me.'

'You're right, I don't give a shit. Have it your way.'

He lifted his hand, the sun glinting off his wedding ring as he balled it into a fist. It connected with the side of my head.

An electric shock shot up my spine and lifted me off the sofa where I was sitting. There was no Jimmy, no Lucia.

My eyes searched the room frantically for my daughter. I jumped up and ran to the cot in her bedroom. No Lucia. I threw the bedroom door open and roared my daughter's name.

'She's in here. What's wrong?' I heard Helen's worried tone.

They appeared in my line of sight as I approached the kitchen. Helen was giving Lucia some breakfast. I slid down the frame of the door and sobbed.

Helen was by my side. 'What's the matter?'

Through sobs, I told her about the letter and about the clear-as-day vision I had just had. Night terrors were now becoming day terrors.

'It's never going to stop, is it? He's always going to be there, no matter what I do, no matter where we go.'

Helen hugged me tight. 'I think you need a trip to the doctor. If I'm honest, I don't think those letters are going to do you any good. If that last one is anything to go by, you're only going to feel worse.'

I shook my head. 'No, I have to read them all. It's the only way I can move on from their deaths. It'll be like reading the last chapter in a book. It might help me move on from everything.'

Helen was right, I did have to see a doctor. My fear was that I would drive myself crazy if I didn't deal with my trauma.

Chapter Nineteen

Flashbacks of Jimmy Denton were one thing. Flashbacks of the fire which killed my parents were another entirely. Dreaming of my past was almost as bad as actually living it at the time, like I couldn't escape it. Waking up in the middle of the night in a cold sweat, trembling with fear after reliving a beating, or watching my parents perish in a trailer fire was getting me down. Helen was right; I couldn't cope with this on my own. I made an appointment with my GP, who turned out to be lovely and very understanding. She suggested counselling.

I wasn't entirely convinced that raking over the past was something I wanted to do, and when I really thought about it, I didn't believe it would help. How was I supposed to get past the traumas in my life if I had to sit down and relive them on a weekly basis? Yes, I longed to find out more about my parents' lives before me, but I wasn't keen on the idea of reliving the reason for their demise.

'Counselling is a tool you can use to help you explore the real reasons behind your anxieties,' she had said.

–

I was sitting opposite my new therapist. A male therapist. At first, I hadn't really considered my feelings on the matter of having a man listen to my problems.

'How comfortable do you feel with the fact that I'm a male therapist?' he asked, as if reading my thoughts. He had introduced himself as Seb, short for Sebastian, I assumed.

I paused before answering. 'I haven't really thought about it, if I'm honest.'

Seb nodded. 'From your notes, I can see that you left an abusive relationship over a year ago. Do you think that you will feel uncomfortable talking about your issues with me because I'm male?'

I shook my head, not in disagreement but in uncertainty. I was the first to admit that I had trust issues when it came to building new relationships with men. But would that be the same with Seb? He was a professional therapist, someone who had trained to help people deal with their traumas. Surely the fact that he was male wouldn't affect my ability to deal with everything?

'I don't think so,' was all I managed as a reply.

'I need to go through this set of statements,' he held up a sheet of paper, 'before we can begin. Are you comfortable to go through them now?'

I nodded in agreement.

'Ok, I'll read out the statements and you can answer with "always", "often" or "not at all". Is this ok?'

'Yes,' I croaked. Why was I so terrified about what was going to come next? I had no clue what to expect.

'I feel alone,' Seb read the first statement.

What was my answer to that? This time two years ago, I had become numb to the pain of loneliness. I did feel alone at times now, but I wasn't alone in terms of having Helen and Lucia with me. Physically, I was surrounded. Mentally, I was trapped inside my own mind, memories of the past playing over and over like a torture film on repeat.

'Often,' I replied.

Seb ticked a box and moved on to the next statement. 'I feel desperate and afraid.'

Desperate, no, not any more. Not since I had escaped Jimmy's clutches, anyway. Afraid? I was afraid of Lucia finding out who Jimmy was. I was afraid she would find out what happened to me before she was brought into this world. I was afraid that Jimmy would find me and kill me, leaving Lucia without a mum to protect her from the evil in the world, from him. I was afraid that the feeling would never go away.

'Always.' I looked down at my hands as I said the word. I studied the lines on my palms to distract me from breaking down. How had my life come to this? Sitting in a chair in front of a stranger, discussing my mental state.

'I have had suicidal thoughts,' Seb said. He hadn't looked up from his page.

'Not since I fell pregnant with Lucia,' I said, with urgency. He looked up then.

'How would you grade that statement right now?'

'Not at all,' I replied.

How could I possibly feel suicidal with Lucia around? She was my reason for living now; the only thing that kept me going and gave me a reason to smile.

'I have had disturbing thoughts about harming another human being.' Seb moved on.

It disturbed me that I *wanted* to harm Jimmy, and that I wasn't fazed when I pictured how he would die. I had played out the scene in my head, holding a gun to his head, holding a knife to his throat, running him over with a car. It worried me that I wanted him to die and I wanted to be the one to stop his lungs from filling with air, the one to stop his blood. I felt a release when I imagined him dead. I felt safe.

When I was Kat – battered wife and slave to a thug – I was too scared to even breathe in the wrong direction. Was it any wonder I was having thoughts like this now?

'Often,' I replied. I watched Seb's eyes. They didn't flicker, he didn't blink.

I took a deep breath. I was only four statements in and I was already exhausted. We had another ten to get through. I pushed on and at the end, I cried.

'How do you feel?' Seb asked.

'Exhausted,' I said, dabbing my eyes with a tissue and clearing my throat.

'Those were just the statements. Maybe that was enough for this session?'

I noticed that Seb had the most calming voice I had ever heard. It reminded me of my dad's voice. I took comfort from that.

I looked at the clock. There were still fifteen minutes left of the session.

'No, I'm ok to go on.'

Now, I was Katelyn, a new mother who was going to be strong and keep getting stronger for her daughter. I was well aware that I had far to go in terms of forgetting about Jimmy and moving forwards, forming new relationships, and trusting new people. But I was proud to allow people to see Katelyn, the person I was becoming. I wasn't sure though if I was ready to let my guard down and bare Kat's soul to the world. Only two people knew the old Kat: Jimmy and Helen. Helen had also given up her old identity to escape the clutches of the site, so on some level she would understand why I would want to keep Kat buried. Looking at Seb, I hoped he would too.

'Why don't you tell me a little bit about what you would like to gain from your sessions with me?'

'Well, if I'm honest, I don't know yet. It took some convincing to come here at all.'

I expected him to preach to me about how he would be able to help. But he didn't. Clearing my throat, I continued, 'I don't want to feel scared any more, or to have to look over my shoulder every second of the day. I have a daughter, and she is the most important thing in my life. If it wasn't for her, I don't think I would have bothered to fight.'

Seb's expression didn't change. I was beginning to feel more comfortable in his presence.

'I would like to address my parents' deaths. I don't think I grieved for them properly. I wasn't allowed to, now I think about it.'

'You would like to be free to be you?' Seb asked.

I nodded, a small smile lifting the corners of my mouth. 'Exactly. I have never been free to be me. Never been free to do anything.'

'Then we have some work to do,' Seb said, his eyes lighting up as he smiled.

We agreed on fortnightly sessions.

As I walked home, I reflected on all the things I wanted to achieve, all the things I wanted to make happen and have as a normal everyday occurrence for Lucia and myself. I could make them happen. I would work hard and build myself up to be the person I wanted to be. The only thing that would stop me was the one thing I couldn't control, and that was Jimmy. He would always be the one thing that would linger in my subconscious. He would always be there, unless I found out that he was dead. I wasn't that lucky.

I got home and climbed into bed. Helen had put Lucia down for the night and had fallen asleep on the couch, the television talking quietly to itself. I pulled out a photograph of my parents from the box my aunt Elsa gave to me. I stared at it. I fell asleep with their faces in my mind.

But not even a session of therapy could blank out the memories of that fire. I still woke up in a cold sweat, coughing hard as though I had inhaled thick, black smoke, and screaming out for them to be saved. I wasn't ready to let them go. I feared I would never be ready. I feared the image of that fire would swallow me up and I would never be able to move on. I hugged my pillow and sobbed the way I had sobbed on the night they died. Their smiling faces stared up at me from my quilt as the photo lay on the bed. As much as I was suffering the nightmares of my past, it seemed my first session with Seb had opened the flood gates wider than they already were.

I gathered myself together and wiped away my tears. I took a long, deep breath and wriggled my fingers and toes as I lay on my back. I was in for a long journey of self-discovery, tears and, most likely, heartbreak as I talked about my past with Seb. My past had sculpted the person I had become. Now it was time *I* sculpted the person I wanted to be.

Chapter Twenty

Inside six weeks of therapy sessions with Seb, I learned so much about myself that I hadn't known. I explored my existence on the site and my relationship with Jimmy until I was exhausted. Seb was brilliant, never filling silences, never filling in for me when I couldn't find the right words.

'Katelyn, you mentioned that your sister-in-law suggested seeing your GP to help you come to terms with what has happened with your husband and parents. Do you think therapy is something you would have sought out on your own if Helen hadn't mentioned it?'

'To be honest, probably not. I've never contemplated therapy. No offence, but before now, I never believed it worked.'

Seb raised a brow and smiled. 'You're not the first person to say that.'

'Don't get me wrong, I'm glad I came to see you. I can't imagine where I would be if I hadn't.'

'And think where you will be, come the end of our sessions.'

I wasn't sure I was ready to think that far ahead. 'I'm still taking things one day at a time.'

Seb asked me to talk about my marriage and how Jimmy had behaved towards me. Saying it all out loud had opened a door to the deepest and darkest parts of my mind.

'Things were fine in the very beginning. After the fire, Jimmy asked me to marry him. I was delighted. Our wedding was small, and he picked my dress, which wasn't what I'd have chosen. But it kept me covered up, just the way he liked it when I was in public.'

I felt like Kat was watching me as I spoke of her ordeal. The sessions had created a distance between myself and the old me, Katelyn and Kat. I felt stronger than she ever had. I liked the fact that I viewed us as two different people now, it was like part of the healing process, although I was nervous of what I would reveal.

'How did it feel to let him pick your wedding dress for you?'

'I actually didn't care at the time. All I cared about was that my dad wouldn't be walking me down the aisle. It wasn't even an aisle.' I sigh at the memory. 'We got married in the local pub, so I basically walked between two rows of chairs.'

'Who gave you away?'

'Jimmy's best friend, Rab. He was the person Jimmy put in charge of me when he wasn't around.'

'Your husband put someone in charge of you?' Seb repeated, calmly.

'Yep. I didn't realise it at the time. But that was why Rab was around us so often. I felt like I was married to both of them.'

I took a breath, allowing my heart rate to slow. 'I was suppressed by Jimmy, and Rab. At least I had a break from Rab every now and again. But I lived and breathed most of my days with Jimmy. I relied on his affection. But the more I needed it, the less he gave it. He was the only thing I had in my life that was mine. He was the only person I had who could offer any sort of affection. I no longer had my parents to lean on. My mam's parents died when I was too young to remember, or I would have lived with them. So I suppose that's why I depended on him so much. He must have loved it, knowing that I had no one else and that without him, I was nothing.'

'Do you really believe you're nothing without him?' Seb's expression was straight.

'Not now, no. But back then, I *was* nothing without him. I had nothing.' I felt the lump in my throat grow. 'My parents would never have wanted this for me. He took advantage of the fact that I loved him and twisted it into something poisonous. After I married him, that's when the beatings began.'

Seb wrote in his notepad. 'What would cause the beatings?'

I shook my head as I remembered. 'Anything. Smiling, not smiling enough. Not doing what I was told, the dinner being too hot or too cold. If punters spoke to me at the machines for too long, he would get annoyed. But he had a way of making me suffer.'

'How so?'

'He would be nice to me. I mean, overly nice. Then, out of nowhere I'd get a bang in the mouth or a slap.'

Seb pursed his lips. He looked genuinely sorry for me. I felt sorry for the old me.

'At what point did you decide you'd had enough, Katelyn?'

Thinking about that day made me shiver. 'Nothing out of the ordinary, actually. I got a kick in the face, and he left the trailer. Helen came over and we got talking. She told me some things about Jimmy from when she was younger, and together we decided to get out. I found out I was pregnant the next day, and that night we left when Jimmy and the rest of the guys went to work. I remember climbing the hill which led us out the back of the site. I was too terrified to turn back in case I changed my mind.' My heart pounded as the words came out of my mouth. 'I was leaving the only life and home I had ever known. Every memory I had was from that site. But I knew it was the best thing I could do for Lucia.'

Seb nodded. 'You did the right thing.'

'I know, and I'm proud of myself for it. After the rape, I never thought I would have the guts to leave. Just goes to show it can be the little things that push you over the edge.'

Seb had gone over the statements with me again to see how far I had progressed. I was feeling better, more focused. At the end of each session, I wondered if I would have anything more to say at the next. I talked a lot about things I had never felt comfortable saying to anyone. I surprised myself at each session as I continued to talk about my anxieties and traumas. Today was my third session and my focus was my parents.

'I don't think I grieved for them properly.' I pulled a tissue from the box on the table to my left. 'You must buy a new box of these just for our sessions.'

Seb smiled, allowing me time to pull myself together.

'Jimmy was always there, making things all about him. I never thought much of it. If anything, I was probably glad of the distraction. It got to a point where, instead of grieving for my loss, I was too busy trying to please

Jimmy. I felt like I had to prove that I loved him by doing everything he told me to. And the more I did, the less love he showed me. In the end, all I was good for was sex and a slap when he needed to vent his frustrations, whether I had caused them or not.'

I felt my eyes narrow at the thought. I was a good person; I hadn't deserved any of the things he had done to me. 'It's only been in the last year that I've felt the need to revisit my parents' deaths. Jimmy took up valuable time I needed to grieve for them, and now that I'm away from him I feel like I can finally go back and do what I need to get over it.'

'It's all very deep, Katelyn,' Seb said.

I nodded my head, keeping my eyes on the window set in a large frame behind him.

'I can feel the heaviness on your shoulders. I feel quite emotional for you if you don't mind me saying.' Seb placed his hand on his chest as his words filtered across to me.

'I feel that way every day.' My lips had dried up.

Seb returned my smile and reached for his diary, his pen hovering over the page. 'You say you never had the chance to grieve for your parents, that Jimmy distracted you from the process. Tell me, did you ever build a relationship with Jimmy's mother?' Seb asks. The question catches in my throat.

'No, I never did.' I say.

'Can I ask why?'

Mrs Denton, the woman who had spawned the devil himself. I remember the way she used to look at Jimmy when we were teenagers. Like he was her little ray of sunshine, her pride and joy. He could do no wrong.

'After the fire, she took me under her wing. She knew Jimmy and I were an item and I guess she wanted to help me. But Mrs Denton had a severe alcohol problem.'

'You witnessed this first hand?' Seb rests against his chair, his eyes on mine.

'Yes, and I can't say I blamed her. But when she had a drink, she would say things to me, blame me for Jimmy's behaviour. I remember she caught me crying one night. Jimmy and I had had an argument about a dress he wanted me to wear. I said I didn't like it.'

'This was in the beginning? Before things were physical?' Seb enquired.

'Yeah, he said that he'd spent some money on it and we had a row about my selfish ways. Back in those days, I was always trying to stick up for myself, in one way or another. But he was always able to twist things so that I felt guilty. He told me that I mustn't love him at all if I could hurt his feelings like that.'

'For declining the dress?'

'He said that if I was going to hurt him, then maybe we shouldn't be together. Maybe I really did want to be on my own. Why would I push him away when he was the only person I had in the whole world?'

Thinking about this day, I hadn't appreciated how significant it was in the beginnings of my abuse, until now.

'That must have really hit a nerve with you?'

'Actually, it didn't. Not compared to what Mrs Denton said to me when she found me in tears in the bathroom of our trailer.'

'What did she say?'

'That if I wanted our relationship to last, if I wanted to be his wife, then I would have to man up. That if I didn't, I would only end up like her. A sad, pathetic woman whose only option to escape her own car crash of a life was to turn to the bottle.'

Seb raised his brows, a look of shock and sympathy apparent in his expression.

'Yeah, awful isn't it? I really thought that with my own mother dead, maybe I would be able to turn to her. But she was too busy avoiding a beating from her own husband. And as the years went on, the way she looked at Jimmy began to change. It was no longer the "not my boy" expression. Instead, I could see that she regarded Jimmy the same way she regarded Stan. As a bully, a poor result of a son and a man.'

'Katelyn, that's just awful.'

'Mrs Denton became a shell in the end. Helen didn't have a relationship with her, and from what I could gather, nor did Mandy. The thing is, she is Mandy's role model, demonstrating that it's ok to let men behave that way. I suppose Helen and I weren't much help in that sense either.'

Mrs Denton would die in that trailer, having wasted her life drinking to block out the black cloud which hung over her.

'The scary thing is, had I not escaped when I did, that would've been me in thirty years' time. And I was already a shell when I left. I dread to think what would have happened to me by the time I got to her age.'

Seb entered our next date in his diary as I pondered over the events I hadn't realised had had such significance.

'Do you feel like we've covered enough for today?'

'Today?' I smiled sarcastically. 'I think we've covered enough for the year.'

As my shoes touched the concrete outside and my lungs filled up with fresh air, soft, cold droplets of rain fell across my face. I stood still, allowing the rain to wash over me gently as it became heavier. For the first time in six weeks of therapy, I allowed myself to believe that the work I was doing with Seb was beginning to help. Talking through my past and the hardships Jimmy had dealt me over the years was tough. Reliving it all was heart-wrenching, but it was becoming easier the more I talked about it.

The rain became heavier and I visualised the flow of water washing away layers and layers of grief and trauma. I hoped that by the time my therapy came to an end, I would be able to let the lasting effects of the past sixteen years of my life wash away too.

I walked home in the rain, not bothering that I was soaked through to my underwear. My skin felt cold and my hair dripped. But it didn't matter. I had dealt with worse things than getting caught in the rain. I thought about my sessions with Seb so far and how I felt about everything now.

Never in my life had I thought I could survive on my own. I knew Jimmy was a bad soul who would do me nothing but harm, but he was all I had ever known since I had become a teenager. His personality was strong. Charming, yes, but mostly powerful. Before I realised it, he had drawn me into his being and I couldn't get out. At that time, I didn't want to get out. He was the first person I had ever felt passion for. The first experience of butterflies in my stomach was with Jimmy, and he was the first person to make me smile without having to do anything to make it happen.

Jimmy Denton had me in the palm of his hand almost from day one. I knew he wasn't good for me, but I couldn't help myself.

I hated remembering the good feelings I had about Jimmy in the beginning, the fondness. It was like letting my guard down again. But I *had* to remember everything, and I had to make sure I could recall things without falling into a panic attack. Before my sessions with Seb, I couldn't even hear Jimmy's name without my breath catching in my throat. Now, I could think about the past and present and feel less anxiety.

Before I knew it, I was standing outside my front door. I went inside and found Lucia sitting on her play mat with some stacking cups surrounding her. Helen was sitting beside her, singing a nursery rhyme. Lucia became excited when she saw me and put her arms out for me to pick her up. I saw Jimmy in her eyes, just for a second. I wiped his face from my mind, picked her up and gave her a squeeze.

'How was it?' Helen asked.

I kissed my beautiful daughter's face and nodded. 'It was good.'

'You feel it's working?'

I thought about it for a few moments before I answered. 'Yeah, I'd say it's helping me a little more each time I go.'

Helen smiled at me and got up from the floor. 'Good, that's the main thing.'

The main thing would be for it to erase the last sixteen years of my life, with the exception of Lucia. But that was never going to happen. Seb was helping me to accept that. Yes, after three sessions, I was beginning to feel better. But I was also beginning to believe that it would take a lot of

sessions before the rain would wash the last of the bad
memories away.

Chapter Twenty-One

Dear Elsa,

I know it has been a while since I last wrote to you. Things have been a little chaotic at the site recently. With it being the height of summer, the fairs have been non-stop this past eight weeks. There is no easy way to say this, so I'll just come right out with it.

Michelle is having a baby. We're having a baby. I'm going to be a dad. I can't believe it. It was a complete surprise. We most definitely were not planning to become parents anytime soon. We've only been together for a short time. I am over the moon; we both are.

Michelle is roughly six months pregnant. I am sorry I haven't told you sooner, but like I said, it has been full speed ahead this summer. I am still getting used to being a traveller, so all this moving around can be quite exhausting, along with trying to fit in and making a life for ourselves. If I am honest with you, I would like us to become non-travellers, if you know what I mean. I don't think it would be good for the baby, all that moving around. He or she would have to start a new school every time we moved. They would have to make new friends. Let's face it, being a child in a new school is difficult at the best of times. But to be the new child all the time is bound to have an effect on the wee one's confidence, don't you agree?

Anyway, you know me, always making plans. The only plan I have ever properly followed through on is moving away with Michelle, and you know yourself that decision wasn't made lightly. Do you think I will be a good dad? I have never imagined myself as a father figure. But with Michelle at my side, I am sure we will do the best job we can. I would love to raise our child the way I was raised, in a lovely home, made of bricks and cement with a garden to play in on sunny days. But if I want to be with Michelle, this is the only way. I can't take her away from the only life she knows. I can cope with that sort of change. I don't think she could.

However, there are other things I would like to pull Michelle away from in this way of life other than the constant moving around. There is a family which is a part of this community, a big part. I think I have mentioned them in another letter. They are kind of the 'leaders' if there isn't another way to word it. They are not the nicest of families. The head of the family, Stan, and

Michelle's dad are constantly having run-ins about a million different things. Since I came on the scene, Stan hasn't been happy, and that is mainly the reason they are at each other's throats. Stan's wife has a son and a daughter. The son is the eldest, he is around two years old. The daughter is just a baby. I honestly don't know how his wife can stomach even breathing the same air as him. But then, I don't know them personally, so who am I to judge? I know it's a long time before I will have to worry about this, but I don't want our little one mixing with the children of that family. They will turn out just like their dad, and that's not a good way to go. It is people like him that make me realise where Dad's worries and concerns came from.

Stan cornered me recently, asking if I wanted to join his 'team,' which consists of a few of the guys on the site dealing drugs when we are away at the fairs. When I declined, he wasn't happy, spouting about how I thought I was better than him and how I wouldn't last with him around. I'm not scared of him. I'm not scared of anyone here. But I am scared for my child growing up around that family.

I am rambling on as per usual. Elsa, I just wanted to let you know you're going to be an aunty. I wish things were different and Dad could be involved in this, but he just can't see past the traveller's way of life, unfortunately.

I will write again soon.
All my love,
David

The window in Seb's office was open very slightly, and I could hear the hum of traffic passing by outside. I was in a trance as I stared intently at the painting on the wall. It was a Claude Monet print of a riverbank housing small boats with their sails against the breeze. The people in the painting seemed relaxed and peaceful, strolling along the bank at their own pace, taking in their tranquil surroundings. The colours in the painting were autumnal. Looking at the painting made me feel warm.

'You like Claude Monet?' I heard Seb ask.

I shook my head. 'I don't even know who Claude Monet is. I wouldn't know the name of the artist if it wasn't at the bottom.'

'I have several of his prints at home.'

'I haven't ever thought if I even like art or not,' I replied.

I hadn't ever thought if I liked anything before leaving the site. I had never been allowed my own opinion, so what was the point in considering my likes and dislikes?

'Katelyn, it's ok to voice your opinion in here.'

I nodded. I knew Seb wouldn't give me a hard time for saying what I thought of the painting; I just wasn't used to being allowed to do so. The way Jimmy made me feel was that people wouldn't have any interest in what I would have to say about anything. My opinion didn't matter.

'So?' Seb asked.

I looked away from the Monet and found Seb's eyes on me, expectantly. 'What?'

He smiled. 'Do you like the painting?'

I looked back at the riverbank and began to nod, 'Yeah, yeah, I do like it.'

A sense of overwhelming self-worth took hold of me. I felt invigorated. It was then I accepted that I would be able to continue liking or disliking anything of my choice because I was my own person and no one could control that part of me. I was beginning to see the good in visiting Seb, even if it was to discuss my choice of artist rather than Jimmy.

'So, how are you?' Seb asked.

I regarded the question for a moment.

'I'm... ok,' I hesitated.

Seb frowned. 'You're ok?'

I shook my head. 'No, I'm not ok, if I'm honest. I have been searching through my past, trying to figure out where my parents came from before they had me. I found my aunt, who was my dad's sister.'

Seb waited for me to continue.

'She gave something to me which is allowing me to find out the things from the past that I felt I needed to know, in order to move on from their deaths.'

'And do you feel those things you are discovering are helping?'

I shook my head. 'I don't know yet.'

The last letter I read had come as a bit of a shock. My dad had history with the Dentons and I couldn't quite get my head around it. It meant that the Dentons were a bigger part of my past than I had first realised.

'Is there anything in particular you would like to share which may help lighten the load?' Seb asked. He was sitting back in his chair directly across from me. He was always so relaxed. I often wondered if he ever felt burdened by the problems people unloaded in his sessions every day. From his manner, I could see it hadn't affected him. He was a professional, after all.

'Not right now. I have a feeling that I'm going to discover something I don't want to, so it's likely that this isn't the last you'll hear of this matter. But at the moment, I don't feel the need to talk about it.'

'Do you anticipate something bad?' Seb asked.

I shrugged. 'Hopefully nothing sinister.'

Seb gave a nod, accepting that I didn't wish to discuss the matter further. There was nothing to discuss, really. I was overthinking things, as always.

After discovering my dad had been involved with Stan before I had even been born, I dreaded to think what else I would find in his letters. Had there been a feud between my parents and the Dentons since the beginning of their relationship? Was the reason for the fights really the fact that my dad was originally a 'flatty,' as Stan had described him? I could only imagine.

–

As I walked back to the flat after my session with Seb, I thought about Michael. He had seemed genuine enough; his son seemed to be happy whenever I had bumped into them. I found myself smiling as I pictured him. I wasn't ready for a new relationship; I wasn't ready to let another man into my life. The likelihood that he resembled Jimmy in any way was slim, but with everything I had been through, my instinct was to assume that every man on the planet was a violent control freak once they had you in their clutches. I knew I had to stop comparing and assuming the worst. I just didn't know how to. Not that Michael would be interested in getting involved with someone like me, someone with baggage. Would he?

I was glad I had Seb to help me work through my anxieties. I had never understood how talking about a traumatic time could help. Raking over the past in great detail over and over for weeks on end wasn't something I regarded as helpful in moving on. But now, I was beginning to believe that my sessions with Seb would be the making of me. For the first time in I didn't know how long, I felt a little ounce of positivity within me. I failed to stop the smile from lifting the corners of my mouth. I was beginning to believe things were going to be ok.

My sessions with Seb were helping with the night terrors, they were becoming less frequent, less intense. I wouldn't hold my breath that they would disappear entirely, however I was sleeping a little easier at night.

I decided not to go back to the flat straight away but instead take a walk into town. The sun was still shining, giving off a little warmth as it peeked out from behind the infrequent but full greying clouds. Passing by the back of the St Enoch Centre and through the car park, I found myself standing outside Michael's restaurant.

Why am I here? I asked myself. I hadn't planned it, but all of a sudden I was hoping that Michael was in there. I peered through the window. The restaurant was relatively full, with people in business suits mainly. I scanned the bar area; he wasn't there. I wanted to go inside and ask for him but I wasn't sure what to say. I scanned the tables and the bar once more, in the hope that he would come out from the kitchen or the office, or whatever was behind the scenes of a restaurant. He didn't, of course.

Just phone him, I thought. Why hadn't I done that in the first place? But I turned my back on the restaurant and crossed the road.

'Katelyn!' A familiar voice called from across the street. I turned back and there he was. I waved.

'What are you doing here?' he called.

Did I really want to have this conversation across a busy road? I made my way back over to the restaurant to answer him. He had a grin on his face.

'I don't know, really,' I replied.

'You wanted to see me, didn't you?' His grin remained.

'You're a little sure of yourself,' I smiled back.

What was I thinking? Did I really want to get involved with another man this soon after Jimmy? Or was I too quick to think I shouldn't?

'Do you want to come in for a drink?'

'I don't drink alcohol, well, not often.' I was quick to answer.

Michael shrugged. 'No problem. You can have anything you want.'

I could have anything I wanted. I certainly wasn't used to being told that by a man. I chose fresh orange juice.

'Do you want to come back to the office? We'll get a bit of privacy.'

I took a seat in Michael's office, still not entirely sure what I was doing there in the first place. It was a decent size and fairly tidy. A picture of the city at night hung on the far wall. Headlights from the traffic blurred and trailed around the canvas. A large computer resembling a television sat in the centre of his desk. I was impressed.

Michael moved some papers around and closed a drawer. 'You'll have to excuse the mess; I wasn't expecting to have anyone in here today.'

I looked at his desk. Organised stacks of paper, tubs of pens and highlighters sat neatly on the surface. The place was spotless. I shook my head. 'It's fine. I'm used to mess, I have a child, remember?'

'So, what have you been up to?' Michael asked.

What had I been up to? I repeated the question to myself. Now was most certainly not the time to disclose therapy due to domestic violence. 'Not much,' I lied. 'You?'

'Just running this place, along with the nightclub and being a single dad.'

'Scott's mum isn't around?' I asked, without intending to.

Michael shook his head. 'No, she died when he was just a baby.'

There was silence for a few moments before Michael spoke again. 'Do you fancy going out for dinner tonight?'

I was a little taken aback, but my answer was quick. 'Why not?'

Michael was a nice guy. Why shouldn't I go on a date? The foul memory of Jimmy wasn't going to stop me in my tracks any more, and my own limits would only allow me to take it as far as *I* wanted.

'Great, we can eat here, and then if you like I can take you to my nightclub?'

'Nightclub?' I asked.

'Yeah, I own the restaurant and a nightclub.'

I nodded. A businessman who went out to work to make a decent living. It sounded too good to be true.

'Where is it?'

'It's in the Merchant City, it's called The White Room,' he replied.

'Sounds posh,' I teased.

Michael laughed. 'It's not posh, it's classy and stylish.'

'I look forward to seeing it.'

I had a date, for the first time since I could remember. I was excited and terrified all at once.

I'd never set foot in a nightclub in my entire life. I had no idea what to expect.

Chapter Twenty-Two

The photograph of my parents lay by my side on the bed as I slid the comb through my wet hair. I had thought about that last letter ever since I had read it.

Stan. The name lingered in my mind. My dad had had run-ins with the Dentons since before I was born, and I had the strangest feeling I was going to read more of my dad's letters and find out something I wasn't going to like. I hated the Dentons (with Helen being an exception) with every breath in my body. That wasn't a good thing. I knew it wasn't healthy to feel that way. Ultimately, it meant I had unfinished business, that business being that Jimmy was still alive and at large. I knew he wouldn't stop until he found me. But after all the time of being away from the site, I was slowly beginning to believe that maybe he wouldn't find me. That was a big maybe and wasn't to say that he wouldn't stop trying.

'How do you feel?' Helen popped her head around the bedroom door.

'Nervous,' I replied. 'I've no idea what a nightclub even looks like on the inside. What do I do?'

'Erm, dance, drink. Have a good time?' she replied.

I look at her and frown. 'How do you know?'

Helen winked at me and said, 'You really think I didn't sneak out at night on the odd occasion?'

'Seriously? Did you ever get caught?' I ask in shock.

'Do you think I'd still be standing if I did? Stan would have killed me. I only ever did it once or twice when I was a teenager. It was such a rush to know that I was free from that place. But it was always in the back of my mind that I would get caught. After that I thought better of it.' She smiled at me. 'And anyway, there's no need to be nervous. I think this was meant to be.'

'Why do you think that?'

'Oh, come on, you randomly run into each other three times in a row? That is definitely fate.'

I regarded that word, fate. If everything was down to fate, then the universe didn't like me very much.

'I don't believe in fate,' I said, plugging in my hairdryer.

'Why not?'

'Are you kidding? Was it fate that landed me with Jimmy?'

Helen held her hands up. 'Point taken.'

Switching on the hairdryer and bending forward, I blasted the underside of my hair. Already, I was beginning to consider how Michael would criticise my choice of clothing, how I wore my hair, whether I was wearing too little or not enough make-up.

I knew my thoughts were unreasonable and that he would most likely be kind towards me. However, my default setting was to think the worst of men. I couldn't stop my brain from ruling my heart these days. Yes, I liked Michael; he was handsome, charming... everything Jimmy was when I first met him. It hadn't taken Jimmy very long to begin making changes and throwing in little comments without me realising it.

I tossed my head back and combed through my hair before beginning to dry the remaining damp areas. As I looked at my reflection in the mirror, I could still see the scars Jimmy had left behind. They'd healed physically, of course, however he had left behind a trail of destruction which, to this day, was still running riot in my mind, dragging my mental wellbeing behind.

I finished drying my hair and began applying my make-up, which I wasn't very good at because I hadn't been allowed to wear it all that often. I was better now that I had had some practice living with Helen. I slipped into a nice pair of blue floral trousers with a black top and a jacket. I'd picked them myself when I'd gone shopping on my own. Walking around the clothes shop, searching the racks was something I'd never done before. I'd taken my time, browsed a lot and tried on everything I liked. I'd finally settled on an outfit. I looked pretty. I was becoming comfortable in admitting that these days. I took one final look in the mirror and applied a light layer of clear gloss to my lips.

You're not going out looking like that. You look like a slapper, too up for it!

There he was, leering over my shoulder. I could smell him, I could even taste him. I froze.

Get that muck off your face before I take it off for you, do you hear me?

I kept my eyes closed. I knew he wasn't really there; my mind was playing tricks on me.

Get a fucking move on, Kat!

I opened my eyes and turned around. Jimmy was gone. Of course he was gone; he was never there to begin with. This was bound to happen, wasn't it? As soon as I was back on my feet and feeling more confident about myself, his evil which lingered in the depths of my mind would surface just to scare the shit out of me.

'Fuck off, Jimmy,' I whispered into the room. 'You don't own me anymore.'

I turned out the light and made my way through the hall and into the living room. Lucia was playing on her activity mat and failed to notice me.

'Wow,' Helen said. 'You look amazing.'

I looked down at myself and took a deep breath. I was going on a date, with a man. Any normal woman my age would be excited. I on the other hand, was utterly terrified. I wasn't terrified of Michael or any aspect of going on a date with a new man. In fact, it was my first date, ever. Jimmy and I had never dated, we just jumped right into things.

I was terrified of falling for Michael. I became weak under the influence of passion, that's how I ended up with Jimmy in the first place. I fell for his charms and quickly became damaged goods. Would Michael see that in me?

–

Sitting across the table from Michael felt odd, like an out-of-body experience. I pictured myself watching us at the table, like I was keeping an eye on how things were going and I could warn myself if I thought something was going to go wrong.

With Michael, so far things were pleasant and gentle. He was attentive and had one of his staff wait on us personally. I wanted to keep my guard up though. Letting my protective shield down now would be stupid, considering that Michael was the first man I had been able to speak to without Jimmy breathing down my neck. I still couldn't get used to the fact that when I got home, I wouldn't be walking into a fist.

'So,' Michael interrupted my thoughts. 'Tell me about you.'

I watched him sip a glass of wine. 'There's not much to tell, really.'

What the hell was I supposed to say to this man? *I'm an ex-traveller with mental scars from a nutcase ex-husband, who I'm on the run from, by the way.*

'There must be something you can share? To help me to get to know you a little better?'

I paused. 'I'm a stay-at-home mum.'

'You enjoy being a parent?' he asked.

'I love it, she's everything to me.'

We sipped our drinks. It filled the silence just for a moment.

'Can I ask... Lucia's dad?' The question was never going to be anything but awkward and I knew it would come eventually.

'No idea where he is. Disappeared when he found out I was pregnant.' I felt awful for lying. But it was the better than the truth.

Michael smiled. He searched my eyes with his, like he was looking for me to reveal more.

'What about you?' I interjected as quickly as I could, to prevent more unanswerable questions.

'Me?' Michael sat back on his chair. 'I own a restaurant, as you can see.' He gestured with his hands. 'I also own and run The White Room, which has been on the go now for about two years.'

I nodded. 'And that's where we're headed after we've finished up here?'

Michael agreed. 'Yes, you will get to experience behind the scenes too. I can show you around and we can sit down in one of the booths. I would use the office but with it being a busy night, we'd have constant interruptions, staff knocking on the door every two minutes.'

'Can't you just leave it open for them to have access to go in and out as they need?'

Michael shook his head. 'No. The office is strictly my space.'

'That's fair enough. So, tell me again how you got into the food and drink business, then?' I asked, still trying to keep the spotlight from falling on me.

'I've always worked in the business, starting off behind the bar when I was eighteen, then moving up to bar manager, then eventually inheriting this place. No sparkly story, just honest hard work and motivation.' He drank the last of his wine. 'Being a single dad and owning two businesses is hard going, but I survive.'

'Do you have a manager for both businesses, to take the pressure off?' I asked.

'Oh, yeah, of course. However, I keep my nose firmly in the business. I need to know exactly what is happening, when it's happening, and how it's happening. The restaurant pretty much runs itself and all I have to do is take care of the books. But with the club, I'm very much involved in everything.'

I was impressed. He was a man who knew what he wanted. I took inspiration from it. We finished up in the restaurant and moved on to The White Room. First class treatment was an understatement. The club was beautiful and lived up to its name. Almost everything was white; the bar, the walls, the tables; it must have been a nightmare for the cleaners in the morning. Michael showed me around, introduced me to the bar staff and the manager and then led me to the function room. The room was filled with partygoers, so I had a quick peek.

'Seems the place is packed out,' Michael said.

'We could sit in your office. I don't mind,' I replied. He led me through the club by the hand and to his office.

'Take a seat, we'll get a bit of peace and quiet in here to chat,' he said, as he closed the door behind me.

'Drink?'

'Please, non-alcoholic.'

Michael lifted the receiver from the desk. Within a few minutes there was a barman in the office making up some sort of fancy drink in a cocktail glass for me.

'It's called a mocktail,' Michael said.

The barman left and Michael clicked a few buttons on the computer before music from the club was streaming through the speakers I hadn't noticed in the top corners of the room.

I found the whole set-up quite surreal. My life was changing so quickly that I couldn't keep up. Just a year and a half ago, I had made the biggest decision of my life; to escape the clutches of my brutal husband and my horrible existence. I had had a baby, changed my identity and now, I was on a date with a man who owned two businesses.

'So, I'm intrigued to know more about you.' Michael interrupted my thoughts.

'I've never known anyone to be *intrigued* by me.' I laughed nervously.

Michael smiled. 'There's a first time for everything.'

I definitely agreed with that.

'Well, there isn't much to know. Like I said before, I'm a stay-at-home mum to my beautiful Lucia, and that is as exciting as it gets, really.'

My heart pounded. I really wasn't ready to pour out my life history to Michael. After all, he was still ultimately a stranger. I couldn't help but gaze into his eyes even though my head was telling me not to. I was still too vulnerable to get into anything.

'Your mouth says stay-at-home mum but your eyes say something different. I think there's a deeper level to you that you're not willing to let go.'

I laughed. 'Isn't this very heavy for a first date?'

'I'm just interested to know about you and where you come from,' he said, smiling.

You're not the only one.

'All in good time. Let's just have fun,' I said.

I had so much to learn about myself and where I came from that I had no idea where to begin with Michael.

–

I was back home, sipping on a mug of tea, and smiling. The evening went better than I ever imagined it would. He was kind, gentlemanly, and the absolute opposite to Jimmy.

So this is what it should have felt like when I was with my husband. As much as my head was telling me to back off, my heart was telling me to see him again.

Chapter Twenty-Three

'I thought I'd warned you, Kat? You've disobeyed me. You stay away from those Dentons. They are not good people.'

I wanted to throw myself down on the couch in a complete strop, but I knew that would get me nowhere. 'Why do you think that?' I said in my sweetest voice. 'Jimmy has been lovely to me.'

Dad shook his head. 'Of course he has. He wants to show you his nice side, make you think he's a good guy. Well, trust me on this one, Kat. If he is anything like his dad, which I know he is because he knows no other way, then he is bad company.'

I looked across at Mam, who was folding laundry. She kept her head in her task and without looking up, she said, 'Your dad is right, Kat.' She continued to fold pillow cases, bed sheets, and bath towels without looking in my direction. Mam knew fine well that if she looked at me, I would be able to make her feel sorry for me and she would begin to soften up on the subject of Jimmy.

'They own the site, so isn't it a good thing that I'm in with their eldest?'

'Don't push your luck, Kat. You will respect our wishes and when I tell you to do something, I mean it. Not another word on the subject. Understood?' His voice was gentle, but I knew better than to push it any further. I nodded, but it wasn't left there.

'I said, is that understood?'

'Yes, understood. Can I go now?' I asked.

'No, you can stay in until I can trust that you won't see that boy again.'

Perfect. I was now stuck in the wagon until further notice. And I knew that I had no way of convincing Jimmy to stay away from me. Once he knew what he wanted, he wouldn't let anyone or anything get in his way. Did I even want to obey my dad? I knew his heart was in the right place, but I couldn't help the way I felt for Jimmy. I wasn't sure I was strong enough to fight my feelings and stay away from him.

I banished myself to my bedroom for the remainder of the evening, feeling sorry for myself. My problem was I wanted to please everyone. Of course that was an impossible thing to do. I opened my current book of choice and began to scan over the pages. My eyes fell over the script, reading – appropriately – about impossible love, when I heard a small scratch on the outside of the wagon, next to the window. My heart skipped. I knew who it was. I stood up and peeked through the thin curtain which hung over the single glazed window frame. My Jimmy was standing outside with the biggest smile on his face. He was so handsome and, for a sixteen-year-old, he was pretty well built. I mouthed that I couldn't come out to see him but he couldn't make out what I was saying. I panicked when I saw him make his way to the door. I heard a knock and all I wanted was for the ground to open up and swallow me so I wouldn't have to deal with this.

I listened intently as the wagon door was opened. I heard my dad's voice first.

'She's not in.'

'Funny that, since I just saw her at the bedroom window,' Jimmy replied.

There was a moment of silence before I heard my mam interject.

'She's busy and she won't be around for a while.'

'Is that right?' Jimmy asked, sarcastically. 'And I assume you both had something to do with that?'

I wanted to bang my head against the walls of the wagon. My heart was melting and aching all at the same time. I loved Jimmy; everything about him made me go weak. But I also knew that I had orders to obey, and it wasn't in my nature to go against my dad's wishes, no matter how much I wanted to.

'Yes, that's right. Now if you wouldn't mind, my family and I were about to sit down to dinner.'

I imagined Jimmy's face and how angry he would be feeling. I wanted to scream.

'Not at all. Just let Kat know I'll see her later,' Jimmy said.

I felt the wagon shake as my dad slammed the door.

I sat down on my bed and listened to my mam and dad go about their business as if nothing had happened. I realised my heart was no longer my own, it was broken in two. One half lay with my dad and the other half lay with Jimmy.

I looked out at the site to see Jimmy walking away. He didn't look back at the wagon. But I knew it wasn't the last I would see of him. Jimmy wanted me. I knew that Jimmy always got what he wanted in the end.

'Kat!' my dad called.

I went out to the living space of our wagon and stood in front of him. 'What?'

He cleared his throat. 'I presume you heard that?'

I nodded, fighting desperately against the tears which threatened to fall.

'Then you understand that I mean what I said. The Dentons are bad, *bad* news. I'm only doing this for the good of our family. I'm not doing this to hurt you, you do realise that?'

I looked at my mam, who returned my gaze this time. Her expression reflected my sadness. I turned away from her. 'But you *are* hurting me, Dad.'

He walked towards me and hugged me. 'No more than he would hurt you if he had his chance, Kat. This way, I'm protecting you.'

I sighed. 'Protecting me from what?'

My dad held me in front of him and stared into my eyes. 'Just trust me, Kat. Please, just trust me.'

I didn't understand what the problem was. What was so wrong with me wanting a relationship with Jimmy Denton? My dad kept telling me to trust him, like he knew what he was talking about. What was it about the Dentons that my dad wasn't telling me?

I looked at him with pleading eyes. I didn't want to turn my back on Jimmy. But I didn't want to betray my dad's wishes either.

'Please just tell me what the problem is, Dad?'

He shook his head and for the first time, I could see frustration in his eyes. 'Do *not* push me on this, Kat. Now, just leave it at that.'

I looked at my mam, who shook her head in a way that told me I had been warned.

So that was that then; my relationship with Jimmy was over. How the hell was I supposed to break up with him and make it sound like I meant it? I went into my bedroom and sobbed silently.

–

It was late, around midnight. My parents were asleep in the room next door. The paper-thin walls confirmed this because I could hear my dad snoring like a bull. I quickly dressed and crept out of the wagon. The site was silent, everyone asleep. The cold night air stabbed at my lungs as I jogged across the site towards the Dentons' trailer. I could see that Jimmy's room light was on. My heart began thudding against the wall of my chest as I imagined what I would say to him. I was not ready to end things with him and I knew fine well that he would not accept my rejection. I tiptoed around the front of the trailer and tapped on his bedroom window with one finger as gently as I could but enough that he would hear it.

I was startled when Rab pulled back the curtain. He stared at me for a moment, as if he didn't know who I was. A smile spread across his face and he opened the window.

'What're you doing here?' he asked.

'Is Jimmy around? I need to speak to him,' I replied, annoyed that I wouldn't be alone with Jimmy.

'Aye, he's away for another bottle. He'll be back in a minute.'

Another bottle? I wasn't sure alcohol was going to make this process any easier on either of us.

'You coming in?' Rab said, his bellowing voice echoing around the site.

'Sssh!' I hissed. 'Do you want to wake up the whole site?'

Rab shook his head. 'Fine, wait outside then.'

With that, he sat down on the single bed across from the window and I waited, scanning the site grounds for signs that my dad was watching me. There was no one around.

'Hello, gorgeous. I've been dying to see you all day.' Jimmy's voice startled me. I turned and he was beside me. 'I heard you talking to Rab when I was in the kitchen. So, you managed to sneak out then? Your da' won't be too pleased about that.'

His arms enveloped me and I felt my feet leave the ground. 'Jimmy, we need to talk.'

Jimmy's lips were on mine, stifling my words. I melted in his arms.

'What is it?' He pulled away from my lips but I remained encased in his tight hold.

As I stared into his eyes, I wondered how I was going to tell him.

'It's him, your dad?' Jimmy said, his tone lowered.

I nodded. 'He has asked me not to see you anymore.'

Jimmy let go of me and lowered his head. I knew it wasn't an act of sadness; he was furious.

'And I assume you're here to tell me you're doing what you're told by Daddy fucking dearest?'

'Don't do that,' I said. 'Don't speak about him like that. He's still my dad.'

'And what the hell is he saying about me? I bet you don't defend me the way you defend him.'

I shook my head. How could Jimmy think I wouldn't defend him if someone spoke badly of him? Of course, I knew Jimmy was no angel; that was obvious. He was a sixteen-year-old who drank alcohol, smoked, and took shit from no one. I knew Jimmy liked the fact that the Dentons owned the site; it made him feel superior to everyone else, even those who were older than him. But he was different with me. He made me feel special. Maybe Jimmy wasn't the right one for me and maybe my dad knew that. But right at that moment, as I stood there watching him staring down at the ground, as furious as I knew he was, I couldn't help but allow myself to love him.

'Of course I defend you when my dad says I shouldn't be with you. I love you.'

Jimmy raised his head. 'Then tell him that.'

'I have, so many times. But he won't back down.'

'And what about you, are you backing down?'

I didn't want to. But my heart was torn between Jimmy and my dad. I didn't want to hurt either of them, but by choosing one I was hurting the other.

'I don't know what to do. I feel like the rope in a tug of war.'

I could see that Jimmy wanted to go nuts but he was keeping his temper under control. I reached out for his hand. He took it and pulled me towards him.

'You'd better get back before your dad finds your bed empty.'

'But what about us?'

Jimmy shook his head. 'There's nothing either of us can do right now. You'll have to decide what you want to do, and when you do, let me know.'

I was stunned. I had expected a full-scale fight between us. But he was unusually calm. Maybe this was his way of trying to prove he was worth fighting for.

'I do want to be with you, you know that,' I whispered.

'Then maybe we have to be together on the quiet?' he said, before kissing me gently on the nose.

'You mean sneaking around?'

Jimmy smiled. 'It could be fun. Keeping it a secret would keep our relationship alive.'

My brow furrowed. 'You think our relationship is dying?'

He laughed. 'No, I didn't mean that. I meant keeping us a secret and sneaking around would keep things exciting for longer.'

I considered this. 'Or it would make things stressful. You wouldn't be the one lying to people. I would.'

Jimmy kissed me again, his lips pressing firmly but gently on mine. He pulled me in tight. Who was I kidding? There was no way I could let him go. I was in too deep.

'Then don't lie. Just say it like it is. You're in love and that's that.'

He made it sound so easy.

'What is it about you Dentons that so many people are afraid of?' I asked. If my dad couldn't give me answers, then maybe going direct to the source was where I could find them.

Jimmy smiled widely. 'Power.'

I frowned. 'Power over what?'

'Power over them. We own this site, these grounds; without us the residents would have nowhere to live. It's all ours. Well, it's my dad's, but one day it will be all mine. People don't like the way things are run here sometimes.'

'What do you mean?' I asked, not following the direction in which he was taking the conversation.

'All you need to know is that people want more of a say in certain things here, but when all is said and done, we make the final decisions.'

His lips found mine once more before I could say anything else. He knew how to silence me.

'Go home, get some sleep. We will see each other tomorrow. Don't worry, we'll get over this barrier your dad has put up. I can talk to him, make him see that I'm good enough for you.'

I shook my head. 'That's not a good idea. Just leave it.'

He smiled again, letting out a gentle laugh. 'Ok. I won't say anything. But just promise me something?'

I sighed. 'Anything.'

'Never leave me. I can't be without you.'

I nodded. 'Never. I love you.'

Jimmy hugged me close before pushing me away, turning me round to face the site. 'Go home. I'll see you tomorrow.'

I turned to smile at him as I walked away. He waved and went inside his trailer. I stopped to look up at the stars. Each star twinkled brightly. I drank in the beauty of the night sky and took a deep breath. The air was turning colder by the minute. I watched my breath swirl around in front of me as it was expelled from my lungs. I wanted to turn back and spend the night with my Jimmy, but I knew it wasn't possible.

I wished my parents would understand how much I loved Jimmy and how much it hurt to even think about letting him go. They must have been young once. They must have known what it was like to be in love.

I crept back into our wagon and slid under the duvet still fully clothed. I was beginning to feel the cold as the adrenaline from sneaking out wore off. I lay in the darkness and closed my eyes. Something deep inside me didn't sit right with my way of life. It never had. Especially not since the vague stories my dad used to tell me from when he lived with his dad. I had managed to figure out that my dad hadn't always been a traveller, which meant it wasn't in my blood. Maybe that was why I didn't feel entirely at home on the site. As I drifted off, I began dreaming of my future with Jimmy. I wondered what it would be like if we did end up together. Would we still live here as travellers? I would go anywhere to be with him even if that meant living on the site for ever. My love for him came before any of that.

My body relaxed as I fell deeper into sleep. I dreamt of Jimmy all night. Love takes over everything in a person, even the dreams.

Chapter Twenty-Four

Something cold and evil twisted inside me. I pushed the memories of my feelings for Jimmy back into the dark and closed the door on them, wondering how long they would stay hidden.

'Why do you think you remembered him that way?' Seb asked.

I had been staring out of the window behind him, watching the rain clouds race past as the wind caught them in its grasp.

I shrugged my shoulders. 'I don't know.'

'How did it make you feel?'

I drew my eyes away from the window and back to Seb. I really didn't want to answer this question. Seb waited, allowing me time to gather the words.

'Like I did back then.'

'And how did you feel back then?'

I shook my head. I didn't want to remember him this way. I hadn't expected to remember him this way.

'The Jimmy from back then doesn't exist now. He died a long time ago and was replaced by someone evil and nasty. Why would I let myself think of him like that?'

Seb was quiet for a few moments, allowing me to thrash it out with myself.

'Are you angry with yourself for remembering how he was in the beginning?'

I most definitely was angry, frustrated, and even furious with myself. Jimmy hadn't made me feel anything other than dirty in the last few years. So why would I remember him like that now?

'Yes, I'm fucking furious!'

'Good, it's good to get those feelings out.'

I clenched my fists, gritting my teeth at the same time, forcing the tears to remain at bay.

'I loved him so much back then. He made me feel like the only girl he'd ever laid eyes on. Why would he suddenly begin to treat me like a piece of dirt, like someone he hated?'

I knew Seb couldn't answer that question. Jimmy probably wouldn't even be able to answer that question.

'Do you still love him?'

I shot Seb a look. 'Are you serious?'

Seb nodded without surprise at my change in tone. 'You feel something towards him, otherwise you wouldn't be dreaming about him in that way. Maybe when you're asleep, your body surrenders to a happier time, when you were young and things weren't complicated. When love was just love and nothing else. Maybe the younger version of yourself still loves the younger version of him and that's why you were dreaming of that time.'

I hated to admit it, but Seb was making a lot of sense. Everything wasn't as simple as he was suggesting, though.

'Things weren't so complicated before my parents died. My dad, he hated the Dentons. I never understood why. He was forever telling me to stay away from Jimmy. I was torn. I loved and respected my dad, but everything about Jimmy had pulled me to him.'

Seb smiled. 'Sounds like you knew what you wanted.'

'I did. I just didn't want to break my dad's heart by going against him. And I physically couldn't bring myself to be away from Jimmy.'

Tears stung my eyes, threatening to release the pain, but I refused to let them out. It was bad enough that I was thinking of Jimmy like this after so long. I wasn't about to waste my tears on him too.

'Tell me what your relationship with Jimmy was like,' Seb asked, without warning.

'When?' I replied. 'Back then or most recently?'

Did it matter? I thought to myself.

'Whenever you wish to revisit. Talking about it may reaffirm how you feel now.'

–

I lay in his arms, not daring to move. I didn't want this moment to end. I could feel his breath on the top of my head. His scent was strong and overpowering, in a good way. I felt his chest rise with each intake of breath and I listened to his steady heartbeat. I circled his belly button with my index finger, willing him to wake up.

'That tickles,' Jimmy said. I felt the rumble of his voice against my ear.

I smiled. 'Sorry, I just wondered if you were awake.'

It was the first time I had taken in my surroundings. Since my dad forbade me from seeing Jimmy, the only place I could spend any time with him was in Rab's trailer. It felt seedy and sneaky. But what else were we supposed to do?

'I'm always awake when I'm with you. Otherwise I'd miss out on precious time.'

I laughed. 'Nice line, Denton.'

My heart swelled when I was with him, but my stomach churned from the guilt which was beginning to eat away at me.

'Do you think we'll ever be together properly?' I asked.

Jimmy sat up expectantly, lifting me up onto his chest. He looked into my eyes and smiled. 'You mean, Rab's trailer doesn't cut it for you?'

'Oh yeah, I couldn't have wished for anything better,' I replied sarcastically.

'Be careful, you'll hurt Big Rab's feelings.'

Jimmy laughed before he pulled me towards him and kissed me gently. My lips tingled as his kiss silenced my worries. My whole body surrendered to him and even if I wanted to resist, I don't think I would have been able to.

I wondered if things could ever be on an even keel with my dad and Jimmy. My mum was going on about how young I was, how she knew what it was like to think you're in love at such a young age, but how emotions could be triggered by hormones, that it wasn't real love, just excitement. I knew my own mind. I loved Jimmy; of that, there was no doubt.

'Will we be ok?' My tone was serious now.

Jimmy sighed. 'That's not up to me, that's up to you and your dad. He's made it perfectly clear he hates my guts and doesn't want you near me. I can't do anything about that, but you can.'

I shook my head, searching through my jumbled thoughts for the answer. 'I just can't understand why he is so against you and your family.'

Jimmy frowned. 'You say it as though you're accusing us of something.'

'No, that's not what I meant.'

'I've already told you, sometimes people don't like the final say from us and they vent their frustrations in other ways. In your dad's case, he's taking his frustrations out on you through me.'

I sighed, still completely unaware of what could be so bad that it would mean I would have to end my relationship with Jimmy.

'I still don't get it.'

Jimmy stroked my cheek. 'Does it really matter?'

I didn't want to tell Jimmy that I thought it did matter. What if my dad was hiding something important from me? Something that might explain the reason he didn't want me near Jimmy, or the rest of the Dentons, for that matter. I bit my tongue, not wishing to fuel the fire that was the situation we faced.

'Just snuggle under this duvet with me and I can help you to forget it all, just for a while.'

'I would love to, Jimmy, but I can't stay any longer. I have to go before my dad realises I'm gone.'

Jimmy playfully tightened his grip and held me down. 'What if I don't let you go?'

I sighed. 'If I could stay, I would.'

I wriggled free from his grip and pulled on my trainers.

Jimmy propped himself up on his left elbow and faced me. 'Don't stay away from the palace too long.'

I looked around the cramped room Rab had 'lent' us. It was no palace. In fact, there on the wall above the bed was a poster of a female model, naked in all her glory. I shivered at the thought of being naked in front of anyone except Jimmy, and even that made me nervous.

'If it's where we need to be to be together right now, I don't care.'

Jimmy smiled, allowing himself to fall back onto the mattress. 'Scram, before I pull you back in here for real and never let you leave.'

I leaned down and kissed him, before climbing out of the window which faced onto the back of the site. I jumped down, my feet hitting the ground and spraying tiny shards of gravel out from under me. The site was in darkness, save for a few lights glowing in the windows of the trailers and wagons around me. I scanned the grounds quickly, making sure there was no sign of anyone, before making a dash across the site to my trailer. I positioned a palette under my bedroom window before hoicking myself up, using the flimsy window frame as leverage, and toppled through and onto my bed.

The sounds of the television coming from the living room settled my nerves as I slipped into my pyjamas and into bed. I had managed to slip in and out of my trailer without my mam or dad noticing I was gone. That wasn't likely to continue.

My mind and my heart were in a tug of war between doing the sensible thing and following through on my dad's wishes, or following my heart and continuing my relationship with Jimmy. When I really thought about it, I had already made my choice.

–

The clouds had merged together, the wind had picked up speed, and the rain lashed against the window, sending droplets cascading down the glass. The room had become dull, with only a small lamp offering a glow of light from the corner. Seb passed me a tissue from the box sitting on the circular table between us.

We were silent as I wiped away the tears which had won against my fight to keep them from falling. Staring out of the window was pointless. I knew there was nothing I could do to make my feelings go away.

'Do you believe you were cheated?' Seb finally spoke.

'What do you mean?' I asked, blowing loudly into the tissue.

Seb chewed on the end of his pen. 'Your memories of Jimmy make me wonder whether, on some level, maybe you do miss what you had with him all those years ago. Maybe your mind is taking you back to a simpler time, when all you knew of him was love and excitement.'

I blinked the tears away. They had stopped falling.

'Do you think that might be possible?'

I shook my head.

'Why not?'

'I can't let myself remember him like that because that person doesn't exist anymore. If I remember him that way, I will fall back into my old self.'

Seb nodded, as though he understood. But how could he? How could anyone understand?

'Katelyn, what is so bad about your old self?'

I didn't want to go back there; I didn't want to think about the former Kat Denton. She was weak and pathetic and allowed Jimmy to do whatever he wanted for fear of punishment.

'My former self is my biggest weakness.'

Seb sat forward. 'So use your weakness to build on your strengths. Build yourself up to be whatever you want to be. Don't allow your past to define your future, Katelyn.'

But what if I couldn't move on from the past? What if Kat had never left, and after all this time away, I was just pretending? Suddenly, I was more concerned about Kat than I was about Jimmy. I didn't want to become that girl again, pathetic and fearful. I had to be Katelyn. Not Kat. All this time, I had been worried about Jimmy and what would happen if he found me, when in fact he would never really be gone until I finally got rid of Kat as well.

–

I left Seb's office and made my way down the street towards the main stretch of amenities. The clouds hung low and darkened with my every step. I felt the air, cold against my face as I battled my way through the crowd. I slid my hand into my coat pocket and pulled out my mobile. I searched the contact list for Michael's number and hit call. It rang for what seemed like an eternity. My heart thumped in my chest as I waited for him to pick up.

'Hey, how are you?' His voice filtered through the tiny earpiece on my mobile. I took a deep breath before I answered.

'I just wondered what you're doing.' My breath was heavy.

'Now?'

'Yeah, are you free?'

'Erm, yeah, I'm just at the club, but I can put some stuff on hold if you want to come over?'

It wouldn't take me long to get there. I was already headed in that direction before I had realised it.

'I'll head over now, if that's ok? I'm in town already.'

I hung up and fixed my sights on the building to which I was headed. I dodged an array of bodies in the process, not looking anyone in the eye. I saw a gap in the traffic and quickly crossed the road. I caught sight of my reflection in a shop window and stopped. Kat Denton was staring back at me. She was shaking her head, banging on the glass, and shouting something I couldn't hear. Her face was black and blue.

A blow to the shoulder knocked me off balance and I stumbled back.

'Oh, sorry, Mrs. I didn't see you there.' A boy in his late teens looked worried. 'You ok?'

I glanced back at the window, only to be met with my own reflection. 'Yes, I'm fine.'

I walked on, pushing what had just happened to the back of my mind. I reached the door of The White Room and went inside. The place was empty.

'Michael?' I called out.

A door at the back of the room opened and I was met with Michael's gaze. He smiled brightly.

'Hi, everything ok? It sounded urgent on the phone.'

I walked towards him, not taking my eyes from his. When I reached him, his presence felt strong and his appearance was powerful. My height reached his chin level. I tilted my head towards him.

'Everything's fine. Can we go inside?' I asked as I shifted my eyes to the office behind him.

Michael stood to the side and let me through. I heard the door close behind me. In another life not so long ago, being in a room with a man on my own had been enough to bring on an anxiety attack. But not with Michael. There was something different about him.

Or was it something different about me?

I turned to face him. His expression was expectant. I inhaled his scent. This was the first time in a long time I had felt excited. He was dressed in a navy suit, finished off with silver cufflinks and a silver tie.

'So, what's up?' Michael said. He walked towards me, almost with caution.

'Nothing. I just wanted to see you.' I shrugged. 'Can I ask you a question?'

Michael nodded. 'Of course you can.'

'What do you think of me?'

He frowned, running one hand through his hair.

'I mean, when you look at me, do I seem weak?'

'I'm not sure where this is going?' Michael smiled nervously.

'I know it sounds stupid, but I need to know.'

He sat down on the couch which lined the wall. I sat down next to him.

'Erm, ok. No, I don't think you're weak. I think you're mysterious, but not weak.'

Mysterious? I didn't blame him for it.

'There's a lot you don't know about me; a lot of stuff that is hard to comprehend. Things from my past that have led me to where I am now. But for some reason, I feel the need to tell you about it. And when the words start to come out my mouth, I worry you'll see me as a weak person.'

Michael stared straight into my eyes without blinking. He shifted along the couch, bringing himself closer.

'You said it's from your past?'

I nodded, fearful of what was coming next.

'If it's in your past, then why would I judge you?' He smiled. 'All that matters is that you're here, now.'

I looked down at my hands, which were clammy and unable to hold their grip on each other.

'Remember, we're new to each other. There will be stuff about me you don't know yet. The fun thing about it is, we get to find out. Ok, I don't know a lot about you, but I like what I do know.' He leaned forward and kissed me softly. He pulled away and grinned. 'See, I just learned something new about you.'

My brow furrowed. 'What's that?'

'You're a good kisser.'

I laughed before he kissed me again. He was gentle as if he knew I was fragile. I didn't want to be thought of as a piece of china, cracking under the weight of what life had thrown at me. I wanted to be strong, independent. I realised the only one who could create that perception was me. I instantly regretted asking if he saw me as a weak person. Asking that very question showed that I regarded myself that way. I pushed my lips harder on his, but he pulled away.

'What is it?' I asked, catching my breath.

'Like I said when you first came in, you seem… urgent.' He searched my eyes.

It was at that point that I realised what that urgency was. I wanted to be with Michael, in the way I had been with Jimmy at the very beginning, when the excitement was between us, when the lust for each other was so strong it was overpowering.

'I am,' I replied. I began unbuttoning his suit jacket. 'I'm urgent for you.'

Michael placed his hand over mine, stopping my hands from fumbling over the buttons. 'Are you sure?'

I nodded, continuing to fight against the fabric which surrounded him.

This was the urgency I felt. I wanted to move on with my life, I wanted to feel wanted again. The way Michael took control, I began to realise that sex was something I could share again, not something I had to give to the other person. I had forgotten what lust and excitement felt like. Having that memory thrown at me out of the blue had unexpectedly been a blessing. It had reminded me of what a relationship should be like.

Michael pulled me onto his lap and moved his mouth to my neck. I turned my head, my eyes closed. When I opened them, I saw my reflection in the glass cabinet which stood behind the door. The image of Kat Denton stared back at me. She wasn't shouting or waving frantically. She merely stood still, watching me. Her presence began to fade with every second that passed.

Chapter Twenty-Five

We had been lying on the couch for an hour, in silence at first. I reflected on what had just happened. I felt invigorated for the first time. Michael was gentle but didn't treat me like a fragile mess, which was usually the way I felt during sex. It was almost as though he knew what I was thinking, like he knew everything I had gone through and how I wanted to move past it.

'I have to get back. I was supposed to go home straight after...' I stopped. Straight after what? I couldn't exactly finish that sentence without raising an eyebrow.

'Can we have dinner again?' he asked, not mentioning my sudden pause mid-sentence.

I smiled as I pulled on my shoes. 'Yes.'

I watched him in the reflection of the glass cabinet as he pulled his suit jacket back on and straightened himself up. He was smart, sophisticated, with his own business; he was certainly a catch. But that wasn't what drew me to him. Something about his presence made me catch my breath. Even in the beginning, Jimmy didn't make me feel like that. Looking back, the only thing that had taken my breath away was the number of times I almost got caught sneaking out of the trailer window to go and meet him.

'So,' he said, as I turned to face him. 'I'll phone you, make plans to take you out again?'

'Ok,' I said. My throat began to dry up.

He moved towards me before placing a kiss on my cheek. I left the club and went to the taxi rank. Making my way back to the flat, I had to fight the grin which refused to hide. I got back to the flat just in time to put Lucia to bed.

'So, where the hell have you been?' Helen asked, her tone a little more frustrated than usual.

'I'm sorry. The session got a bit too much for me. I decided to walk it off,' I lied.

'For three hours?'

My head nodded vigorously, as if independent from my body, trying desperately to convince Helen of what I was saying. I should have known better than to lie to her.

'You're lying.'

My eyes widened. 'Why would I lie?'

'So you don't have to tell me the truth about where you were?' She frowned. 'Is it something to do with Jimmy?'

'Oh, God, no.' Poor Helen, I had worried her into thinking the worst. 'No, it's not to do with Jimmy. Far from it.'

I tried to halt the conversation by offering to make tea, busying myself around some dirty dishes. The whole time, I felt Helen's eyes burning into the back of my skull. I tried to ignore her until I surrendered to the silence.

'Ok, ok. I did go for a walk. But...'

'But what?'

'I went to see Michael.' I awaited her judgement.

Helen stared at me blankly, eyes darting left and right for a few moments.

'What?' I asked, not sure what she was going to say or do.

'Why didn't you want to tell me that?'

And when I considered her question, I didn't know the answer.

'Katelyn, I'm not Jimmy.'

And there it was. Him again. I hadn't even realised it. I had been worried about telling Helen because she was the closest person to me. I have only ever existed in this world as someone who felt 'owned' by another, someone who could never have secrets or private thoughts. I was worried about telling Helen because I always worried about telling that close person something, in fear that I would end up saying something that would create a situation, ultimately ending up with a fist in my face.

'I know you're not. It's just habit, I suppose.' I looked down.

'So, you went to see Michael? That's a good thing, isn't it?' Helen moved away from the subject of Jimmy.

'Yes, it's a good thing. Or at least I'm hoping it will be.'

I went on to explain what had happened at my session with Seb, and how I had unwillingly remembered my life with Jimmy before he had swallowed the devil and went on to vomit his evil all over our relationship. I told Helen how I had gone to Michael's club, and known I wanted to sleep with him. Michael had been gentle, nothing at all like Jimmy.

'Sounds like a gentleman,' Helen said, without blinking. 'Maybe you've finally found someone you can be with.'

'Not so fast. We barely know each other.'

Helen raised an eyebrow. 'Well enough that you wanted to have sex with him on the couch in his office. After just one date, may I add?'

Shit! She was right. 'Do you think that's bad?'

She laughed loudly. 'Katelyn, you've gone through life with that arsehole making every decision for you. If you want to get some, then that's your choice.'

I gasped. That wasn't what it was about with Michael. 'It's not just sex, Helen.'

Helen pulled a sarcastic expression. 'Then what is it?'

'I want to take control of my life. I've been away from that life for a little under two years now, and that prick still has a certain amount of influence over what I want to do, right down to the little things. I put on this outfit this morning and when I looked in the mirror, do you know what I thought?' I didn't wait for Helen to venture a guess. '*Jimmy won't like it, too much cleavage.* It took me a few seconds to remember that wasn't an actual issue any more. But even when I did, I was still reluctant to leave the house wearing it. So, no, it's not just sex with Michael. It's about my ability to decide if I want to have sex with him. And I did, so I did.'

Helen held her hands up in defeat. 'Bloody hell, nice to see you're finally giving the finger to that life you used to exist in.'

'You make it look so easy,' I said, almost with a sadness to my tone.

'Well, to be fair, Katelyn, you were worse off than I was. I just hated my life in that place. Dad was old school and head of the family, so I was...' Helen paused as she searched for the words, '... restricted in the way I lived my life.'

I waited for her to go on. I had never really asked Helen about her life with that family. I didn't want to ask her, even now. She knew most of the things I had gone through while married to Jimmy. I hadn't held back once we left, and I knew she hated him enough for the both of us. She had carried a lot of my burden in order for me to cope with the escape from the site and into a new life. I doubted she would ever truly understand how grateful I was for that.

'If I was interested in a guy who wasn't from the community, then it was absolutely out of the question.' She shook her head. 'That rule is outdated now, but not in the eyes of Stan. It was just one of his ways of keeping control of me. And Mandy, for that matter, although she was more rebellious than I was.'

'What about your mam?' I found myself asking.

'Ha, she was too fond of the bevvy to know what was going on. To be honest, I don't blame her for taking to the bottle. I would have too, in her situation.'

'What do you mean?' I asked, not quite understanding what Helen meant when she referred to the 'situation.'

'Battered wife, never allowed to go out. Do you ever remember seeing my mam out and about?'

I shook my head.

'Exactly. She did as she was told and that was the end of that. She would drink herself numb. And when I say numb, I mean numb to everything. Numb to the bruises which never healed, numb to the abuse which came out of Stan's mouth on an hourly basis, numb to the fact that it hurt her kids when she didn't fight for them. Soon it got to a stage where she was drunk constantly and wasn't even aware her kids were around.'

I thought about Lucia and how I would have reacted to that situation had I stayed at the site with Jimmy. I would have ended up like Mrs Denton. I would have become her. Fighting for Lucia was all I wanted. That had become the main reason I made a conscious effort in this new life.

'What about Jimmy? Didn't he want to protect his mam?' I asked, in disbelief he could allow that to happen.

'Aye right, all Jimmy was interested in was impressing his precious dad. Jimmy couldn't give a shit for Mam, just like she couldn't give a shit for him. Stan and Jimmy were one and the same, spun from the same web of evil. Absolute scum with the intent to hurt those closest to them in order to remain in full control of the family.' Helen shook her head, a look of disgust spreading across her face, draining the colour from her cheeks. 'And anyway, why would he give a shit about how his mam was being treated when what he did to me was the exact same? I come from a long line of scumbags, Katelyn. I just feel bad that your family was sucked into all of it.'

I lowered my eyes. If I had just listened to my dad, then I wouldn't be in this mess. If the fire hadn't struck our trailer, they would still be alive today and I wouldn't have had to move in with the Dentons. Maybe I had been destined to a life with the Dentons, regardless of my decision.

Chapter Twenty-Six

As I stepped off the bus in Killearn, the first thing that struck me was the smell of freshly cut grass. Aside from the noise of the double-decker pulling away from the kerb, the village was in silence.

I walked down Main Street, past the war memorial and towards Keltrom Cottages. I pictured my dad working the gardens and the grounds of the properties within the village before he had met my mam. I began to imagine what my life would have been like had Oscar allowed my dad to move Mam into the house in Killearn. I would never have met Jimmy, and would never have gone through the hell I had endured for the whole of my adult life. Most likely I would have been happy, living a quiet life in a village setting with my family.

I imagined Aunt Elsa would have been like a second Mam, since she and Dad had seemed so close before he left Killearn. Of course, I'm happy that he did, so he could be with Mam, otherwise I wouldn't have been born and in turn, neither would have Lucia.

It was bittersweet really, considering how much I loved my daughter, and how sweet she was, when she came from such evil. I worried about evil being in the blood. *I mean,* I thought, *look at Stan Denton; Jimmy turned out just like his dad, if not worse.* I feared it could be in Lucia's blood, even if I kept her as far away as physically and financially possible, even if I brought her up as well as I could and kept her from witnessing violence, there would be nothing I could do. I hoped and prayed that she had my genes and that she turned out pure and good. Of course, Helen was nothing like her brother or her dad. I clung to that thought, hoped that Jimmy being kept in the dark about Lucia would influence how she turned out, that and the good upbringing I hoped to provide with Helen. There was nothing I wouldn't do to keep Lucia safe from Jimmy.

I found myself at Elsa's front door. I hadn't noticed the door during my last visit. It was a dark oak colour, with a cast iron knocker in the centre at face level.

'Ah, you made it, then?' Elsa ushered me inside, squinting as the sun hit her face. 'No Lucia today?'

'No, I decided to leave her at home today. It's not fair to bring her all the way out here and expect her to stay in her pram most of the day.'

Elsa nodded in agreement. 'Fair enough, but be sure to bring her next time. I wanted to show you both something that I think you would really like.'

'What is it?'

Elsa shook her head. 'It's nothing really, just some old photographs of your dad and me when we were little.'

I frowned, disappointed that I wasn't going to get to see them today. 'Can't I see them now? Lucia might be a bit young to understand what she's actually looking at, anyway.'

'Yes, I suppose you're right. Come on, then, get your coat off and come through to the sitting room. I have them in a box in my bedroom. Make yourself comfortable, I'll be back in a minute.' Elsa disappeared. I took my coat off and made my way into the sitting room. I was still in awe of this place. An actual house made of bricks and mortar, without wheels or a damned belly box to get thrown into when I had behaved badly.

Of course, I had been used to bricks and mortar for a while now, having lived in the flat with Helen and Lucia for over a year. The cottage was solid, had been standing for years by all accounts. And the history of the place was all around me; in the framed photographs of Oscar and some other people I didn't recognise. It was then that I noticed there were no photographs of my dad. It seemed Oscar had completely wiped away any trace of him. Perhaps if there were no trace, then it would be easier for Oscar to forget all about the son who left.

If the walls could talk, I wondered what they could tell me about the family history. My dad had left his home in Killearn with nothing more than the clothes on his back and a bag with some spares. I always wondered why he hadn't taken anything else. Now I know what I do about Oscar, perhaps it was easier for Dad to do the same. No images to mull over makes it easier to forget? So, when I was growing up, I saw photographs of my mam's family but I had no idea what my dad even looked like as a child. Did I look like him as a baby? Did Lucia? Luckily, she didn't resemble Jimmy, but then, she didn't resemble me either. So maybe she looked like my dad. I would like to think so, and that she would be like him. It would be a lovely trait to have; my dad was such a kind soul.

'Are you ready?' I heard Elsa ask. I was lost in the distance of my imagination.

'Ready for what?'

'To see what your dad's life was like before you came along. Before you were even thought of.' She smiled at me, knowing full well I would bite the hand of anyone willing to show me just that. I beamed inside.

'Of course. What is it?' I asked.

'Old home movies, photographs, school reports; nothing life-changing, but enough to help you learn more about where you have come from.'

I peered down at the large box that Elsa had sat on the table. The box was filled with papers and photographs – a lifetime of memories – far more than the box that she had given me. This would take me a while to go through. And I intended on combing through every bit of information piece by piece.

'Elsa, you have no idea how much this means to me,' I said, choking back tears.

'It's no problem, dear, you're family. We do what we can for family.'

I smiled as I reached out for the box. As I removed the lid, I half expected a beam of light to come pouring out. There were large envelopes bursting at the seams; more photographs from my dad's childhood, and an old videotape with 'eighteenth birthday' written on it. And many more items that I was excited to delve into. 'Can I take it home?'

'That's why I have brought it out to you. It's much more use to you than it is to me. I had my life with my dad; yours was ripped away from you so cruelly. His life was taken prematurely, so if this is the only way you can learn more about him and your own background, then of course I'm going to let you take it. I just ask one thing, same as the last time.'

'That I stay in touch?'

Elsa nodded. Of course I would stay in touch. She was the only living relation to my dad, and I wasn't about to give that up. 'No need to ask, Elsa. I'm going nowhere. And anyway, Lucia has a great aunt to get to know.'

We had some lunch and talked for a while, going through the items in the box. And I didn't feel like I was learning about a stranger. I looked at some photographs of Dad when he was just little and I smiled when I saw how much Lucia did resemble him. I read over some school reports; good at maths, creative in art. However, the more I learned about his life as a traveller, the more I realised that leaving the site had been the right thing to do, regardless of whether I was a battered wife or not.

I was a mix of traveller and non-traveller, but I had made my choice long ago, maybe even before Jimmy came along. I had just tolerated the lifestyle because that was where we had lived as a family and I didn't know another way of life. I admired my dad for making the decision he did to be with my mam. However, I was beginning to resent the fact that it was because of my grandad Oscar's stubbornness that I myself had been born into the travelling lifestyle. I didn't think of this back then, but now I wondered why Dad never tried to set up his own business even though he was living as a traveller. Perhaps it was something that wasn't allowed.

I regarded the decisions I would make in the future, and how they could affect Lucia. I realised that parenting would most likely be one of the hardest things I would ever do. Every big decision I would ever make would affect Lucia in some way or another. I knew that, hard as it was, leaving Jimmy was making its way down that list. Being a parent was something I absolutely had to get right, no matter what.

Chapter Twenty-Seven

I laid awake in bed, listening to Michael snoring gently. It was comforting to know that he was nothing like Jimmy – he was everything Jimmy was not nor ever would be. Michael was considerate, kind and already putting me first. I had revealed a little of my past, the relationship I had with my parents and that they died in a fire but I kept most of the horrendous points to myself. I didn't tell him I was a traveller. I really didn't want to tell him anything that would make me sound like damaged goods. I had already faced that fact myself. As much as Jimmy had regarded me as his property, I knew that wasn't the normal way for anyone to be viewed or treated. I was learning that day by day. Damaged goods could be repaired though, so I truly believed that, in time, I could be fixed, especially with the help with Seb.

The shrill ring of a mobile phone pierced my thoughts and I felt Michael stir beside me. He sat up and reached for his phone. I had no choice but to listen to the conversation.

'A'right, what's the deal?'

There was a pause before I heard Michael speak again.

'How many can you give me?'

Another pause.

'And they're not traceable? I'm not risking my livelihood just for a couple of cheap crates of bevvy.'

I wondered what he was talking about and who he was talking to. I traced his spine with my index finger, watching as each little blond hair stood on end.

'Ok, come to the back entrance at one o'clock and press the buzzer twice so I know it's you. Is that big guy coming again? I don't want him blabbing to my staff like he did the last time. The idiot nearly got me shut down.'

I frowned, continuing to trace the path of his spine with my finger. He sounded firm, forceful even.

'I don't really care if he's your main contact. If he opens his mouth to anyone this time, you won't be getting another order from me, got it?'

Michael hung up the phone and turned to face me. He beamed a huge smile and kissed me on the nose. I wanted to ask him what the call was all about, but I didn't think it was any of my business, so I kept quiet.

'Sorry about that, business call.' He sat up to get dressed.

'It's ok. Is everything good?'

'Yeah, it's all good. Just a business transaction, nothing to worry about. Do you want to come to the club with me? I have a surprise for you.'

I hated surprises, but I couldn't very well tell him that. He seemed so excited. My tummy flipped a little. Surprises in my previous relationship had usually consisted of a smack across the face for something as minor as breathing in the wrong direction.

'Can't you just tell me what it is, Michael?'

Michael glanced at me, a frown spreading across his face. I instantly felt guilty, but I didn't dare show it.

'You don't like surprises, do you?'

My mouth tightened, and I fought against the nervous grin that was forcing its way out. I shook my head.

'It's a good surprise, if that helps?'

I knew it would be a good surprise, but my gut was so used to flipping when I knew something was coming that I wasn't prepared for.

'We could go for lunch afterwards?' He raised a brow as well as the corner of his mouth. His smile was infectious.

'Ok. Sorry, I'm just not good with the unknown.' It sounded ridiculous, I knew that.

We got dressed and made our way to the club. I began to relax again, knowing that Michael would wish me no harm.

He held my hand as we walked to the car, something I wasn't used to. The only human contact I was used to from another man was a slap, not an act of affection.

'Don't worry, it's not a huge surprise, just something that we could do with the kids.'

I relaxed a little more as we travelled through the city centre towards the club. Was it too soon to be introducing our kids to one another? Or was I being too cautious? Lucia was my whole world and I had already done so much to protect her and keep her safe. Introducing her to Michael and his boy at the same time was a big risk if things didn't work out between us. I supposed it was something I could talk to Seb about. I hadn't told Michael that I had been seeing a therapist because I hadn't told him the whole truth about my past. Now, I was suddenly faced with the prospect of bringing our families together.

'After you, lovely.' I snapped back to the present as Michael opened the passenger door for me. We had arrived at the club. I got out and straightened the creases in my coat from sitting in the car. We entered the club via the back entrance, as always (Michael never opened up from the front door, but I never understood why), and headed straight for the office. The cleaner was in and had just finished mopping the floors.

Michael stopped at the office door and quickly tiptoed across and retrieved some mail which was sitting on the bar. I noted the cleaner's look of distaste towards him. 'Sorry, Bev, just grabbing the mail.'

'Aye, don't come crying to me when you fall an' break yer neck.'

I smiled at Bev, who had taken no notice of me, as she lifted her mop bucket and moved to the bathroom area.

'Ah-ha, it's here,' he said, handing me an envelope.

I reached out and took the envelope from him, studying it carefully. 'What's this?'

'Your surprise.'

I opened the envelope, curiosity getting the better of me and banishing any worries I had. I pulled out the contents and my eyes widened at what I was staring at.

'I thought we could do it with the kids, make a day of it?'

My heart began to pound as I continued to stare down at the tickets for the Irn Bru carnival at the SECC in Glasgow. The same carnival at which I had worked year after year with Jimmy and the rest of the Dentons. I couldn't go if I wanted to avoid seeing them. I began to panic, trying to suck air into my lungs. My body wanted to shut down at the very thought of Jimmy seeing me.

'Are you ok?' Michael asked, noting the change in my demeanour.

I choked on my own words, shaking my head in reply. Michael placed a hand on my shoulder, trying to gain eye contact with me.

'Katelyn, what's wrong? You're freaking me out.'

I looked up into Michael's eyes. He peered into the deepest parts of me, looking for an answer to explain the sudden change in my mood. 'I can't go.'

'What? Why not?' Michael frowned.

'I'm… erm…' I raced through the neuropathways in my brain searching for something – anything – to say. 'I have a fear of going on those big machines.'

Michael drew back before smiling cautiously. 'You're scared of going on the waltzers?'

'It's not funny. I saw someone fall out of the twister ride once and they had to have their leg off. I haven't been on one of those stupid things since I was a teenager. Couldn't pay me to go on one now.'

Michael's smile had disappeared. And I wasn't lying when I said I had watched someone fall out of the twister carriage. The safety brace hadn't been secured properly and the poor guy was sent flying across the platform. His leg had shattered when he landed against the safety barrier.

'I'm sorry, I didn't realise. I can get a refund.' Michael hesitated before hugging me, like I was some fragile little girl.

'It's fine, you weren't to know.'

I held onto Michael as if I was holding on for dear life. It was the first time in so long that I had felt genuine fear of Jimmy finding me. Even if he caught a glimpse of me across a crowded carnival, I would be forever hunted, like a mouse hiding in long grass from a bird of prey. Except in this case, I would be hiding in a city, waiting for him to swoop in and take me away from the life I had worked so hard to build. Michael felt my grip and returned the embrace. He knew there was something more to my excuse, but he didn't force the issue.

'Why don't you go into the office, and I'll get us a coffee. Then we can decide what to do instead of the carnival?' Michael said, as he unlocked the office door.

I smiled and followed him inside. I made myself comfortable as he switched on the computer and the lights. He kissed me on the cheek and disappeared behind the door. I sat in silence, feeling like I could finally breathe after the horror of thinking about what could happen if we went to that carnival. I was startled by the shrill ringing of the office phone. I heard Michael call in from the bar asking if I could answer it. I got up and walked over to the desk, sitting down on the swivel chair. I lifted the phone, ready to answer in the best elegant voice I could manage, when I was interrupted by an automated message, explaining how I could claim back compensation for the accident I had had at work. I put the phone down and stared at the screen in front of me. There was a live feed from the CCTV camera outside. I watched as a van pulled up outside the back entrance to the club.

'I think your delivery has just arrived!' I shouted out. Michael didn't reply and his image appeared on the screen. He must have heard the van pulling up. I felt like Big Brother, watching him like this, but for some reason I couldn't pull my eyes away from the screen. I clicked on the microphone icon on the screen before I could stop myself and the speakers came to life, filling the office with the sounds of the back alley and daytime noise.

'You got the right order this time?' Michael's voice filtered through the speakers.

'Aye, it's all there. Check if ye don't believe me,' a rough voice replied.

'I will, if it's all the same to you,' Michael said before peering into the van for several seconds. 'Ok, just put it all in there and I'll do the rest.'

A second body came into sight with the camera, wearing dark trousers and a puffer jacket. The man was tall, with a scruffy appearance, and he was hunched over as he carried a huge box. Just as he placed the box in an area out of view of the camera, another man stepped out of the van and began pulling more boxes from the vehicle.

'Jimmy, how many are there? Ma arms are fucked awready.'

My eyes fixed on the screen.

'Stop fucking greetin' and get the rest of them dumped, we're late fur the next delivery.'

I froze with fear, fully expecting that my heart would come shooting out of my mouth.

'Mick, be sure to give us a shout when you want another order, eh?' Jimmy said, with a sly grin across his face.

'It's Michael, actually. And less of the lip or you'll not be getting another order. Mind, I'm doing you a favour by taking this off your hands,' Michael replied, a stern look in his eye.

'Aye, aye, you'll want more of the stuff when you see how quickly it flies off yer shelves.'

'Don't push your luck, Jimmy. Trust me, I will cut you off. I can find another supplier at the click of a finger.'

I watched as Jimmy threw Michael a dirty look and got back in the van. Rab appeared back in line with the lens of the camera. He looked up at the camera which was above the back entrance to the club and I drew back. Of course, he couldn't see me, but my past had taught me to stay back as much as possible when Jimmy or Rab were concerned.

'Ye got yersel' some CCTV there?' Rab asked, suspiciously.

'And what about it?' Michael replied.

'Just askin' is all.'

Rab got into the van and I watched it speed out of view.

It didn't matter that I had managed to get out of going to the carnival with Michael and the kids. It looked like the carnival had come to me.

Michael appeared in the office moments later. I swallowed back the bile, pretending I hadn't heard or seen anything.

'So, where do you fancy going for lunch?' he asked.

'You know, I suddenly don't feel too well.' The lie came out quickly.

'You don't look too colourful if I'm honest. What's up?'

I was screaming inside. How the hell was I supposed to deal with this? I knew he'd turn up, I just knew it. But for him to be trading business at Michael's club was something no one could have guessed.

'I feel sick. Must've been something I ate last night. I'll pass on lunch, go home, and have a lie down. That might help.'

Michael held his hand against my forehead, the way I did with Lucia when I thought she was poorly.

'Good idea. I'll drive you home.'

I remained calm on the outside, so Michael wouldn't suspect anything. On the inside, I felt as though every organ, every nerve was quivering in fear.

Chapter Twenty-Eight

'I have something to tell you,' I said, holding my breath in fear of what I had to say.

'What is it?' Helen asked. 'You don't look so good, Katelyn.'

'I don't feel so good. Something's happened. Something bad.' I was beginning to shake.

I noted the change in Helen's expression. She couldn't know exactly what I was about to tell her, but by the look on her face, her guess was pretty close to the bone. It was almost as though the room had grown colder in anticipation of the information about to be passed.

'It's Jimmy, he—' Before I could finish, Helen blew up.

'Oh my God, he's found us! Holy shit, what the hell do we do now?' Already the tears were streaming down her face, a reaction I was not expecting at all. Helen was supposed to be the strong one out of us, and I felt I was the one trying to keep us calm.

'No, no, it's ok. He hasn't found us. Well, not yet, anyway. He turned up at Michael's club.'

Helen placed her hand on her chest and exhaled loudly. 'What the hell was he doing there? Did he see you?'

'Do you think I would be standing here telling you this if he had?' I couldn't bear to imagine what he would have done to me if he had known I was there. 'No, he turned up with a delivery of knocked-off booze. Honestly, Helen, I have never been so terrified in my life. I was already planning my funeral as soon as I saw him.'

Helen sat down on the arm of the couch, staring at me in disbelief. Her face had become pale and her neck had broken out in hives from the stress. 'So, what happened?'

I shook my head. 'I watched them on the live CCTV feed in the office. Rab was lifting boxes from the van, and Jimmy was being a cheeky bugger as usual.'

'Rab was there?' Helen asked, still in disbelief.

I nodded. 'Yeah, he looked up at the CCTV. I suppose he was trying to intimidate Michael. But it didn't work. It only sent shivers up my spine. I knew he couldn't see me but for a split second, I thought I was a goner.'

I couldn't believe I was saying these words and remaining calm about it all. I had almost just been discovered and I was acting as if everything was fine. Of course, things were not fine. Not only was Michael's club no longer a safe place for me to be; Michael was no longer a safe person to be with. If I knew Jimmy, he wouldn't take kindly to Michael's backchat. He might be selling dodgy alcohol, but Jimmy was no petty criminal. He was a thug and a monster and if Michael wasn't careful, he could get seriously hurt.

I thought about what Michael was doing and my stomach shifted. Did I want to get involved with someone who bought dodgy booze, regardless of the fact that he was buying it from Jimmy? Is it so bad? I'd been in worse situations. What Michael did with his business had no real bearing on how he treated me, so I push the thought to the back of my mind.

'What are we going to do, Katelyn?' Helen rubbed her chest. 'And what are you going to tell Michael?'

I picked at the skin around my thumb nail, causing it to bleed. 'I don't know what to say. How would I even start that conversation?'

I imagined how it would go: *Michael, you know the guy who delivers the alcohol to your club? Well, he's my husband, and I ran away from him a while ago because he used to batter me senseless on a daily basis.* I shuddered at the thought.

I looked down at my thumb nail. My cuticle was lined with dried blood. I got up and rinsed it under the cold water tap. The icy water was sharp as it hit my skin and brought me back to reality. I had to tell Michael what was going on, but I wasn't one hundred percent sure I could trust him with the information. I dried my hand on the towel next to the sink and pulled my phone out of my pocket. Helen eyed me suspiciously.

'What are you going to do?' Helen asked.

'I suppose I will have to tell him everything. But not right now. I can't. I need to prepare. I'll talk to Seb first.'

I wondered if getting involved in a relationship so soon after Jimmy had been such a good idea. My past had come right to his front door. It was only a matter of time before Jimmy and Rab found out about me. On one hand, I wanted to stay away from the club and from Michael for a while, and on the other, I hadn't had the freedom to live the way I wanted to until now, and I wanted to live my life. It was just that having Michael in it was a risk to us both.

–

Having calmed down and had time to think about what had happened and how Jimmy was closer than I ever cared to think about, I stared down at the contents of the box I had brought home from Elsa's house. It was the second box I now owned containing the life story of my dad up until the day he died. I was beginning to picture a storyboard of his life. I liked the idea that I could piece it together with the letters to Elsa and the rest of the photographs from the second box. There was a difference between a storyboard and a shrine though. I didn't want to create a shrine to my dad. That would have been too weird. And I was past the point of grieving and had accepted their deaths. However, it was always nice to remember and learn about them. Lifting out the photograph on top, I noted two children in the picture. I turned the faded gloss paper and read the note on the back.

David and John, day out at Ayr beach, May 1966.

I wondered who John was. Possibly a family friend? Or a cousin? I observed that my dad was wearing trousers rolled up to his knees, I assumed to prevent them from getting wet. Both children in the photograph were smiling from ear to ear, and in the background the waves were crashing against the shoreline. I began jotting things down to remind myself to ask Elsa about them the next time I was in her company. I placed the photograph to the side and took the next item out of the box. It was a wedding photograph. I didn't recognise anyone in the picture, so I turned it over and read the note on the back.

Aunt Mildred and Uncle Leonard's wedding, Killearn Parish Church, 27th July, 1967. Left to right, Oscar, Elsa (flower girl),

David (pageboy), Mildred, Leonard, Marianne (bridesmaid) and Peter (best man).

I wondered who Mildred, Leonard, Marianne, and Peter were in relation to the family. Were they still alive, maybe even in the country? It would be nice to meet extended family and build a family tree for Lucia. I faced the sad fact that I wouldn't be around for ever, and even if Lucia did have a family of her own in the future, it would be nice for her to have a bloodline. At the minute, my only true relative was Elsa, and she was an older lady now. I noted down the names to remind me to ask Elsa who these people were later.

I put the photograph to one side and reached inside the box for the next item. I pulled out another photograph. A young child and a man were stood in a garden pathway. The man had his hands on the child's shoulders and both were subtly smiling. Overleaf, the note read,

David's first day of school, August 1966.

It was obviously Oscar in the photograph. His smile was subtle. However, his stance betrayed his pride in his son. My dad looked nervous; the first day at school would do that to you. I looked into his eyes and saw a little bit of myself reflected in them. Not in the way of resemblance, but in his expression. The glimmer of nervousness in his eyes reminded me of myself. Whenever I looked at myself in the mirror, I always had that pale, sick look about me, as if I was nervous or worried.

He looked smart in his school uniform; his blazer with the logo sewn on matched his shorts. His backpack hung off his shoulders and was almost as big as he was. I felt proud of him, which is silly, I know, because he's my dad and the photograph was taken long before I was ever thought of. But I never knew about this part of his life, so already I felt like I had learned a little more about him. He had never talked about Oscar, or Aunt Elsa for that matter. I can perhaps understand why he would have never mentioned Oscar to me, because if he hadn't been happy about the relationship, then he wouldn't have been happy about a baby being thrown into the mix too. Maybe the idea of mentioning Aunt Elsa worried him into thinking that I would want to get to know the family and, in doing so, I would be rejected by Oscar the way he had rejected my mam.

I stared at this photograph for a while. I'm not sure why. I found it hard not to cry. I still missed them so much after all this time, but in particular, I missed my dad. I felt closer to him by searching through the box. I pulled out some more photographs, all of which contained my dad. Some of him playing in the garden, some of him posing with other children whom I assumed were school friends. As I dug deeper, my dad grew older. His face was changing in the pictures and he was becoming a young man, more like the man I knew and remembered. I smiled at the memory.

I set the box aside and got up to check on Lucia. She was fast asleep in her cot as usual. She never caused me any bother. I was lucky to have her. As I watched her sleep, I saw a slight resemblance in her to my dad. I smiled. This was something I would share with Seb. Something that would make me cry but for all the right reasons. Happy tears were something I could bear. It just frustrated me that, no matter what I was doing in life, Jimmy was never far from my mind. I hated him in every way possible.

I hated that I hated him, that I was wasting energy and emotion on him. I hated that he was getting in the way of everything. Even though things were going well with Michael, I hadn't been fully honest with him about my past. And now that Jimmy had turned up at the club, how were things going to move forward? It was possible that the next time Jimmy showed up to do business with Michael, I would be there. And if I was, what the hell would happen? I didn't know if I could trust that Michael would understand.

Chapter Twenty-Nine

Seb sat patiently in his chair. The glare from the bulb above us shone onto the lens of his glasses as he allowed me time to cry. The tears had become relentless since I had been visiting him. I was sick of crying, sick of hurting, sick of the fear. I hated crying. It was a sign of weakness and I had had my fair share of being weak. I didn't want to be this pathetic little girl anymore. I wanted to be strong, not only for me, but for Lucia too. I had to be strong for her in order to give her a decent upbringing. Being a nervous wreck wouldn't get us anywhere. I wanted to give her a home, a decent home where she would feel safe and loved. But what was home? I had never truly known the meaning of it. Not in relation to a place or a building. The only time I had ever felt close to 'home' was when I was with my parents, because they were the only thing in my life that had ever made me feel safe.

'It's ok to feel that way, Katelyn.' Seb repositioned himself in the chair across from me. 'You said you never felt like you belonged. Can you explain that?'

I lifted a tissue from the box on the table beside me and wiped away the tear which slowly rolled down my cheek as I searched for the words. 'Do you ever feel so lost that you worry you'll never find yourself, no matter how hard and long you look?' I asked. Seb didn't answer me; he just continued to look at me. 'I feel that way, all the time. Every day, I just want to find myself.'

Seb opened his mouth to speak but paused, like he was uncertain about what he was going to say next.

'What is it?' I asked.

'Do you think that, on some level, you're not searching for yourself, but for your parents?'

I regarded this for a moment. I hadn't looked at it that way before. I had never really known who I was, never known what I liked or disliked, never had a true opinion on anything. That part of my personality had been suppressed. Jimmy had never let me be myself; he made sure that everything I did, said, or wore was all his choice. I never had a say in anything. The only time in my life when I was encouraged to be myself was when my parents were still alive. More by my dad than my mam. She was happy as a traveller. And, to an extent, so was my dad. Deep down, I think he wanted more from life, but he knew that living at the site was the only way to be with my mam. My dad used to say things to me about finding my calling in life.

You can be anything you want to be, Kat. Just work hard and you'll be successful.

Was it any wonder he hated the fact I had fallen for a Denton? He knew if I ended up too deep with Jimmy, I wouldn't follow my dreams. And at that age, my dreams had become all about Jimmy. Teenage love was a strong obstacle to overcome and unfortunately I had fallen at the first hurdle and never got back up again. The worse thing about it all was that, at some point, my dad would have saved me had he still been here. So, maybe Seb was right.

In some way, was I actually in the never-ending search for my parents, in particular, my dad?

I parted my lips to speak but the words didn't flow, only tears. I bowed my head, hating that I was crying yet again. It was then that it hit me. I had not yet accepted the death of my parents, as I had previously led myself to believe. I was still very much grieving their loss.

'Why do you think this has only just hit you now?' Seb asked.

I looked up, wiping the tears from my cheeks. 'I don't think I was ever allowed to grieve for them, not properly.'

'Jimmy?' Seb queried, although he already understood that was what I meant. I nodded in agreement.

'Not long after I was forced to move in with them, Jimmy changed towards me. At first, he was actually supportive. He would comfort me whenever I cried. But after a few weeks, he would give me a look, like he was telling me to get over it. He turned colder towards me, which led me to search for comfort from him. He knew what he was doing. He was breaking me down when I was already broken, he was creating a new version of me that would soon rely on him and his attention. Jimmy was slowly beginning to make me push my parents to the back of my mind and bring him to the front. All he ever wanted was to have me all to himself, to share me with no one, not even my dead parents.'

Seb pursed his lips. Looking at him for words of wisdom, opinion, or purely for him to just listen, I noticed little things about him. How he was always cleaning the lens of his glasses, or how he would clasp his hands once he opened up the session to me. I left Seb's office feeling better each time I visited him. However, when I returned, I always had so much more to say.

'I think you're a lot stronger than you believe.'

'I'm not.'

'Why not?'

I sighed. 'If I was strong, I would have left him a long time ago. I wouldn't have put myself through the years of abuse.'

Seb smiled but shook his head. 'Katelyn, you didn't put yourself through anything. If anything, you pulled yourself out of it.'

I looked at him, doubtful that his words were true.

'You chose to leave, you chose to run with your unborn baby. You chose to get away from the abuse, the taunting, and the oppression of being in an abusive relationship. You did something that probably filled you with more fear than staying ever would have. You sought help to start again. You're building a life for you and your little girl and most of all, you admitted that you couldn't do it alone. You come here every second week and spill your guts to a complete stranger.'

I wriggled in my seat. I wasn't used to someone speaking of me in a positive manner.

'Sometimes, I think I am stronger. Other times, well, most times actually, I don't.'

I knew Seb was a professional therapist, trained in listening and providing an impartial ear. But I felt I had a connection with him. He knew me, understood my struggles.

'Jimmy got to you at the most vulnerable time in your life. It's normal to doubt your strength after everything he has put you through. Even now, when you're no longer in his grip, your behaviour shows me he still has an element of control over your life. You're still learning how to set yourself free from him. Something like that takes time.'

I folded my arms over my chest. 'I feel like I'll be doing that for the rest of my life.'

The memory of Jimmy and Rab came to me. Now that I knew they'd been in a part of the city centre that was so close to where I was living, I had become more cautious about where I took Lucia when I had errands to run. It was more likely now than ever before that I would bump into them, and I didn't want to have Lucia with me if that happened. It was just far too risky.

'Something happened the other day,' I said. Today, all I wanted was for my session to go smoothly and to talk about my parents. Yet here I was, concerning myself with Jimmy all over again. Seb was right; even though I had changed my life, Jimmy still had control over me.

Seb took off his glasses and cleaned them with a tissue pulled from a box next to his seat. I didn't wait for a cue to keep talking; I didn't have to do that with Seb. 'Jimmy turned up at Michael's work.'

Seb placed his glasses on the bridge of his nose before pushing them on properly. 'I'm sorry, did I just hear you right?'

I nodded, not quite able to believe the words coming out of my mouth were true either.

'How did this happen?' Seb seemed genuinely shocked.

I explained everything; how I had heard Jimmy converse with Michael, how I had backed away from the screen when Rab had stood just under the camera, glaring up at it. Jimmy hadn't found me, but he wasn't far from it. I was falling for Michael, much to my surprise, but I wasn't sure I could trust him to understand my situation.

'Do you believe that your life is in danger right now, Katelyn?' Seb sat forward, genuine concern etched on his face. Tears stung my eyes. My new identity, my new life, escaping the site and his clutches, keeping Lucia a secret… If he found me, it would all be for nothing.

'At this precise minute, no. But…' I stifled a sob, '… if he comes back and finds me, I'm done.'

'Does Michael know any of this?'

'Not yet. I need to come clean, though. I need to be honest with him. I've dragged him into my mess and if anything happens to Michael, it will be my fault. What if Jimmy has already seen me and is keeping a low profile?'

Seb handed me the box of tissues. I had shed so many tears I didn't think there would be enough tissues in the world to see me through. 'Seb, I'm so sick of this. He has robbed me of a normal life. Even two years after leaving him, I'm still ruled by him.'

I looked past Seb and out to the street. The sun was still shining, peeping out periodically from thick grey cloud. Just like my life; just when a little bit of sunshine appeared in my sky, thick clouds threatened to rain havoc down on my world. I shook my head, feeling defeated.

'You can get through this, Katelyn. You're stronger than you think. Look at how far you've come in two years.'

'I haven't come far at all, Seb. All I've done is run. And I'm still running. I can't do this anymore.'

Seb pursed his lips. 'Ok, so what do you want to do?'

'I want this to stop, I want Jimmy to go away.'

'Then, maybe tell the police. If you tell them every-thing you've been through, they might be able to help.'

I knew that wasn't true. How could I prove years of abuse? Contacting the police wasn't an option.

'The only way I will ever be free is if Jimmy were dead.'

Seb raised his eyebrows. 'You want to kill him?'

'No, but I wouldn't mind if someone took him out. You know, maybe someone could run him over with a bus or something.' I forced a smile.

Seb didn't return the smile, his eyes telling only a story of concern. I could tell that he believed I wanted to kill Jimmy. And why wouldn't he? Why wouldn't anyone?

Chapter Thirty

After my session with Seb, I decided that if I didn't tell Michael about Jimmy now, I never would. I walked to his club, which gave me time to process what I was going to say. There really were no two ways about it. There was no way to dress the situation up or down. I just had to tell the truth and hope that Michael didn't think I was a nutcase.

As I approached the club, a strange feeling hung over me. I couldn't put my finger on what it was. Uncertainty flooded through my veins as I noticed the club door was ajar as I entered the building. I felt my chest tighten, the air around me thickening with every step I took. I wanted to call out to Michael but something deep inside my gut stopped me. I imagined Jimmy hiding behind the bar, waiting to jump out and drag me back to the site. I tried to tell myself I was being irrational, but I knew Jimmy was capable of anything. I swallowed hard and took a deep breath. I stepped forward and stared in the direction of Michael's office. The door was slightly ajar and light from the window filtered through the gap. Relief lifted a weight off my shoulders as I approached the office. And then I stopped, a thought entering my mind. Michael never left the office door open even if he knew I was coming to see him. I remembered him telling me that he kept it closed because of the amount of money kept in the safe. That and the personal paperwork he kept on the staff.

I stopped just outside the door. Fear gripped my soul as I imagined what could be inside. I thought back to when I found out that Jimmy and Rab were delivering dodgy stock and wondered if in some way they'd known I was there as I watched them through the camera. Rab had looked up at the lens and I knew he couldn't see me, but something in his eyes said he was aware someone or something was watching them. I still found it strange that Rab made me shiver more than the thought of Jimmy. In some ways, he was more dangerous to me. Rab worshipped the ground Jimmy walked on, and would do anything to me if he thought it would score him points in Jimmy's book. All those years ago, there were things that Rab had done to me, or said to me, that when I look back at it now, Jimmy had undoubtedly put him up to. Things that were most likely to make Jimmy look like the hero when I told him about them afterwards. 'Don't worry, I'll have a word with him,' was the kind of thing Jimmy would say to me after I had had a run-in with his sidekick. His arm would hang around my neck and he would kiss my cheek to soften me up. I was so blind to his ways back then that I was clueless as to what was actually going on.

Rab did as he was told; his job was to assert Jimmy's authority. However, as the years went by, I started to wonder how much of what Rab did was on Jimmy's command, and how much was because he enjoyed the power.

I knew what to expect with Jimmy, knew what pushed his buttons and the trigger signs. With Rab, not so much.

He was often more threatening, the suggestive behaviours sending my stomach into turmoil. He'd be rough, the way Jimmy was. But then, he'd stroke my face, run his fingers through my hair. He'd make out that although Jimmy was his best mate, Rab could make things better for me if I just cooperated. The meaning behind his words were never spelled out, but I knew what he meant and I always declined. Rab never crossed the line, but I always lived in fear that he would. He got a kick out of seeing that fear in me.

It was something I never told Jimmy about. I couldn't trust either of them.

'Michael?' I called out softly. I waited for a moment but there was no response. I stepped forward and pushed the door open. Peering down at the floor, I noted a scattering of papers across the shiny tiles. My heart skipped a beat as I pushed the door a little further and saw legs sprawled out from behind the desk. A groan came from the floor space. I rushed over to find Michael covered in blood.

'Oh my God, what happened?' I knelt down by his side, not sure what to do. 'Michael?' I placed a hand on his arm. My hand felt wet as I touched him. As I lifted it, his blood dripped from my fingertips. The stench of iron that filled the air stuck in my throat. I swallowed back the bile which rose from my stomach.

His eyes flickered open, but took a few seconds to focus on me. There was so much bruising, so much blood. If he hadn't made a sound, I would have thought he was dead. His shirt was torn at the buttons, revealing bruising to his ribs.

Another groan barely escaped his lips before I realised I hadn't phoned an ambulance. I pulled my phone out of my bag and dialled 999. Before I could lift it to my ear, Michael knocked it from my hand. 'No,' he gasped. 'You can't.'

'Why not? You could die!' I wailed.

'I have to protect you,' he coughed.

It was only then that I realised. I was the one who had to protect him. I had been trying to stay off Jimmy and Rab's radar for so long, to keep them away from me and my daughter. But now, I had brought a stranger into my mess and here he was, lying on his office floor bloodied and battered, and it was all my fault.

'Why didn't you tell me?' He tried to sit up but the pain must have been too much to bear.

'Tell you what?' The game was up. It was obvious to me who had left Michael in this state. There were no coincidences in my world. I shuddered.

'Why didn't you tell me who you really are?' My phone was still in my hand, the numbers still waiting to be called. But time stood still at that moment. I thought back to when I was Kat, known as Kat, thought like Kat, worried every minute of the day like Kat. I couldn't go back to being that. I *wouldn't* go back to being that. My past was something I had fought harder than I had ever fought before to get away from. Now, it had found me, and it was going to ruin everything I had built up here in my new life. I looked down at Michael, bloodied and bruised. He deserved an explanation. Even though Michael knew the truth, I still couldn't bring myself to say it out loud.

'And who do you think I am?'

Michael coughed again. He looked up at me through swollen eyes, silently pleading with me to tell him the truth.

'Who did this to you?' The words left my mouth in a whisper. I squeezed his hand.

'Your husband and his stupid big mate.'

My heart lurched, the words making the situation all the more real. 'Jimmy and Rab?' Their names were forced through gritted teeth. I hadn't wanted to say them, just like I hadn't wanted them to find me. But I did and they had.

–

I sat on the chair in the waiting area of the hospital. Having decided to keep things from Helen until I figured out what I was going to do, I had told her Michael was taking me out and asked if she wouldn't mind watching Lucia. It terrified me to think that I was leaving my child at a time where her dad could turn up at any moment and pull me back to hell. But I knew she was safe with Helen, and the less she knew, the better. The main thing, I reminded myself, was that he had absolutely no clue that Lucia existed.

Michael and I hadn't spoken since the ambulance arrived. He knew who I was; from what I could gather, Jimmy had told him everything. And from what I had seen, he was not at all happy about it.

The assault had been a statement, made by the bold and fearless Jimmy Denton. He was not about to let me get away with what I had done to him, and if that meant hurting the closest people around me, then he would. All the more reason to keep Helen and Lucia out of sight.

A nurse approached me, a smile lifting the corners of her mouth. She was young, likely the same age as me, although she didn't appear half as troubled as me, and she was stitching people up for a living. 'He's asking for you.'

I followed her to Michael's cubicle. My heart hammered in my chest as I considered how to explain myself. I had lied to Michael about who I was. Would he ever forgive me? The nurse pulled the curtain back to reveal him lying in bed.

'He's in a bit of a state. The police will be back to speak to him later. But I've managed to fend them off for now.' Her voice was soft. I returned her smile before turning to face Michael.

'I'm ok.' His voice was hoarse.

'Why do I not believe you?' I smiled weakly before taking his hand.

He winced. 'Broken wrist.'

Silence surrounded us, aside from the beeping of machines in the cubicles around us. I didn't know how to start my story. 'I'm so sorry.'

'Me too. I'm sorry you felt like you couldn't tell me things.' Michael's expression was neutral.

'I didn't know how to. You weren't supposed to be part of this. I had planned to start again and just be me. Then I met you and things became complicated.'

'So, why don't you just tell me what happened. From the beginning.'

I shook my head. I needed to find out what Michael knew first. 'What happened to you back in the club, Michael?'

He didn't say anything for a few minutes. I wondered if he had forgotten, due to having been beaten so badly. He offered out his hand to mine. Relief flooded me. I held his hand gently. I decided to let him sleep, he could barely get his words out, his speech muffled due to the pain relief, I imagined.

–

I opened my eyes and Michael was staring at me. I sat up in the chair and took his hand in mine. Glancing up at the clock on the wall, I realised I'd been asleep for around three hours.

'Are you okay?' I ask, my voice cracking.

'I've been better,' he replied. I gave his hand a squeeze. 'You stayed here the whole time?'

'Of course I did. I wasn't going to leave you. Do you remember what happened?'

He nodded. 'I was working in the office. A delivery was due any minute.' His speech was slow but clearer than earlier. 'The office door was closed when I heard crashing coming from the bar area. I opened the door to find that stupid big guy trashing the bar. I shouted at him to stop, asked him what he thought he was doing. He just started laughing at me. I mean laughing uncontrollably, like he was crazy. Then the other one, Jimmy, came out from the toilets. He wasn't laughing.'

I swallowed hard. This sounded about right, Rab being the front man for Jimmy's game.

'Jimmy asked me about you. Said he'd seen you leave the club with me and wanted to know where you lived.'

'He didn't follow us?' I panic, realising that my change in appearance clearly hadn't worked the way I'd wanted it to.

'Apparently not.'

'What did you tell him?' I asked, panicking that he had told Jimmy who I was. If that were true, I had to get back to the flat right now and take Lucia to the refuge as quickly as I could.

'Nothing. That's why I'm in this state. The two of them were delusional if they thought I was going to tell them anything about you after they'd just trashed the place. Anyway, I told Jimmy to fuck off. He pulled a bat on me, the fucking bastard. I tried to close the office door but that Rab one is a solid. Jimmy gave the bat to Rab and held me down.'

'You didn't tell him about me?' I asked again, tears filling my eyes.

Michael shook his head. 'No, he just said he would be back. And if I was smart, not to tell the police.'

'You have to tell them. He can't get away with this.'

'And what have you let him away with?' Michael replied. 'Katelyn, he didn't call you by your name. He called you Kat Denton. It wasn't until he showed me a photograph of you that I realised who he meant. You were in the photograph with him. He told me he was your husband and that he had come back for you.'

I shivered. 'Shit.' Michael's eyes pleaded with me.

'What am I caught up in, Katelyn? Or should I be calling you Kat?'

'I never want to be known by that name ever again. Before this happened, I had decided to tell you everything. That time I was in the office and they delivered the alcohol, I saw them on the CCTV. I've been on the run from them for two years. I freaked out and decided that you deserved the truth. When I found you, I was coming to tell you everything.'

'So, tell me.'

266

My head was a jumbled mess. But now was the time. 'Before you met me, I was married. Actually, I still am married. And it wasn't a good marriage. In fact, it was a marriage made in hell. He wasn't a very nice person. I was what you might call a battered wife.' I paused, gauging Michael's reaction. His eyes widened a little but he didn't say anything. I told him everything.

When I finally finished, he was silent for a few moments, staring past me, as if taking a glimpse into the life I used to lead.

'Is that why you freaked out about those carnival tickets?'

'Sorry, I just couldn't risk you finding out. Obviously, I wanted to be honest with you, but in my own time. Now, I've had to tell you everything because he's turned up. He'll never give up looking for me. I want to tell the police what he's done to you. But I know Jimmy. He's a snake and has got away with so much in his life, has always been able to wriggle his way out of dodgy situations. He'll have destroyed your CCTV, there will be no proof. And if anyone saw them in your club, or hanging around, Rab will have dealt with them too.'

There was silence for a few moments while I allowed Michael to process the information I had just provided him with. By the look on his face, I wasn't sure how he was feeling about it. I didn't know if he was thinking that our relationship had changed and we wouldn't be able to carry on. Maybe he was thinking I was lumbered with too much baggage and, with his little boy to think about, we weren't going to work. I wouldn't blame him. I had just told him I was on the run from a thug who I just happened to be married to. Anyone with half a brain would leave me. The silence was beginning to worry me. I placed my hand on his shoulder, which seemed to jolt him back from his thoughts.

'What are you thinking?' I fought back tears.

'I think you've done amazingly, getting to where you are now. I know we've not been together for very long, but I know I want to be with you, Katelyn. So, we need to figure this out together, if that's what you want?'

'Are you serious?' I was stunned. 'You want to stick around after all this?'

'When my wife died after the wee man was born, I learned life's too short to run away from opportunities that have a million obstacles in front of the prize. But when I met you in the park that day, I just wanted to know you, whether that meant us becoming friends or more. Then when we bumped into each other outside the cinema, it was the first time I had ever considered fate. It was like we were meant to run into each other. Then when you turned up at the restaurant, I knew that I had to ask you out. Look at us now, a few months down the line and I can't imagine not being with you.'

Before I realised it, the tears were streaming down my face and I was smiling widely. I had almost forgotten about Jimmy. Nobody had ever made me feel wanted like that before. 'You want to stand by me and work at this?'

'There's no doubt about it. I'm not about to walk out on you after you've just poured out your heart and soul to me. We're going to work through this together.'

'You accept everything, just like that?'

'Katelyn, I love you. Isn't that enough? I just took a serious beating; I should be walking away from you. But I can't. I won't.'

Just when I was getting my life together, just when things were going my way because of the choices I was making, Jimmy had to come along and rip it from my hands. I held onto Michael and sobbed. I had never expected to get away from Jimmy. To have got away and made a new start was one thing; to have unexpectedly found someone who accepted me for who I was and wanted to help me, that was something else entirely.

'He won't give up until he finds me, you know,' I said after I had stopped crying.

'You mentioned an aunt. Could you and Lucia stay with her?'

I hadn't thought of that. Elsa was the one person that Jimmy had no idea existed. Finding out about that part of my life had been my escape from everything else that was going on. 'Yes, I suppose that is an option. But what about you and your wee one? Jimmy will do anything he can to hurt me, and that means getting to you again.'

'Well, I'll probably be in here for a few days for observation. I have family who I can go to. Or, we could come and stay with you until we figure this out?'

As much as I wanted to be with Michael, I knew I had to sort this on my own. I explained that I thought it would be best if Michael stayed with family until I contacted him. The further away from me he stayed, the better it would be for him. 'I'm so sorry I dragged you into all this.'

'I've never met anyone with so much baggage.' He smiled.

'I'd call it rubbish more than baggage. I have to deal with this in my own way. I hope you understand. I'm not just doing this for me. I'm doing it for my daughter and now you.'

I stayed with Michael for a little longer. We didn't say much but just being with him made me feel better even though I feared for the life of my child.

'What are you going to say to the police?'

'Nothing. I remember nothing. We need to protect you and Lucia. I think informing them will make things worse for all of us.'

He was right. Regardless of whether the police were involved or not, Jimmy would walk away from this.

–

'So, now what?' Helen asked, her shaking hands cradling a mug of now cold coffee. I looked down at my daughter, who was playing with stacking cups and oblivious to the world she had come from.

'We go to my aunt Elsa's out in Killearn. She will look after us until we figure everything out.' I didn't want to think about what we would do if Elsa turned us away. But I remained positive until I had the chance to speak to her. After dinner, I ran Helen a bath, put Lucia to bed and held on to my mobile phone, staring down at Elsa's phone number for longer than I needed to. I pressed 'Call' and waited for her response. My stomach churned as I told her about the events which had unfolded. She was horrified.

'You come here right away and bring that bonnie lass of yours,' Elsa said. 'You mustn't feel like you're a burden now, we're family. Too much time has passed already for us to be wasting any more. You get the next available bus out here. There's plenty of room.'

I explained the situation concerning Helen, expecting Elsa to tell me that Helen wouldn't be welcome. 'You bring the people who mean the most to you.'

So that was that. I packed up our things and Helen, Lucia, and I were on the next bus out to Killearn. Lucia would have the freedom she deserved, instead of being cooped up in the flat because I was too terrified of Jimmy seeing us to take her out. Jimmy knew nothing of my connection to Killearn, so I knew we would be safe there.

Chapter Thirty-One

I lay curled up on what had once been Oscar's chair. Of course, I had asked Elsa if it was ok before I sat down. It had been a long first day at Aunt Elsa's house, and now that Lucia was settled and Helen had retired to bed for the evening, Elsa and I had some time to talk. I hugged my knees close to my chest and rested my chin on them. I had always wondered why, if my aunt Elsa had been in contact with my dad via letters for all those years, she hadn't come to find me after he and my mam died in that fire? I didn't know how to drop it into the conversation without offending or upsetting her.

'How are you feeling, dear?' Elsa asked.

'I'm exhausted, mentally and physically. I feel like I've done nothing but move around since my parents died. After getting semi-settled in the flat with Helen and Lucia, then finding Michael at death's door because of Jimmy and Rab, I just feel like I'll always be on the run. And now I have dragged someone else into my problems. I really thought that once I had left him, I would be able to move on and concentrate on family.'

Elsa sighed. 'Oh sweetheart, you have been through so much. If your parents were here…'

I interrupted. 'If my parents were here, I wouldn't be in this mess. Or maybe I would. Maybe if they were still here, I would have become the stubborn teenager who did what I wanted to do. I mean, I fought my parents' wishes that I stay away from the Dentons. I would sneak out to see him as much as I could. So maybe this is all my own doing.'

'You could never have foreseen what a monster he would become, Katelyn. Your dad was a good man and he knew what was best for you. But you were exactly like he was, stubborn. Your dad knew what he wanted from life and he went out and got it, at the expense of his relationship with his dad. We can't predict the future. If we could, we would all be in a much better place.'

Elsa looked at me with sad eyes as she spoke of my dad. She clearly missed him.

'How long did it take for you to find out they'd died?'

'I only found out because it was on the local news. If it hadn't been for that, I may never have known.' Elsa looked frail.

'But I thought you wrote to each other all the time?' I asked, bewildered. 'Surely you would have known something was wrong if you hadn't heard from him in a while?'

'As you know, my father, Oscar, felt the need to control all aspects of the family. He wasn't able to control your dad, so when he found out I had been in touch with David for all that time, he became very angry. He was even angrier at the fact that you were on the way. As he saw it, if Michelle was pregnant, your dad was trapped and would never return from the travelling community. So, he insisted that I stop all contact.'

'That's awful, how could he do that to his family?'

'It was just his way, dear. Oscar was a strong-willed man, knew his own mind and believed he knew what was best for his family. In the end, it tore us apart.'

'So, did you stop contacting him?' I felt a sadness for my dad. It was as if Oscar was against everything that made him happy.

Elsa nodded. 'I regretted it, though. Unfortunately, I had never been to see my brother and he had never come to see me. So, I knew you existed, but of course, you didn't know about me. You see, I never replied to your father's letters. It was too hard to tell him that Oscar never mentioned him, didn't seem to care. I thought that David would eventually stop writing to me when I didn't respond. But of course, he didn't. I regret my ignorance.'

I wanted to blame Oscar for everything that had gone wrong in my life. Had he just accepted my mam into the family, I could have been brought up in Killearn, with a family around me. But because he had been so stubborn and closed off to my mam's different lifestyle, I had been lumbered with a truly pathetic existence. But then, I reminded myself, my dad *chose* to live that life. Just like I chose to stay with Jimmy.

'Have you read all the letters?' Elsa asked.

I shook my head. 'I'm making my way through them, I don't want to get to the end.'

'When you do get to the end and you have read every last word, I think you'll finally be able to let go, dear. I truly believe that those letters will set your soul free from all the misery life has thrown at you over the years. I'm just sorry I didn't fight for you.'

I wiped away the tear that had managed to trickle down my face without me realising it. 'What do you mean, you didn't fight for me?'

'I came for you once, just after the funeral. I asked around to see if anyone knew where you were. I wasn't allowed into the site. Nobody would entertain me, I was told to go away, in some rather colourful language.'

In the very pit of my stomach, I felt rage like I had never felt before. The anger turned to nausea and I swallowed hard, desperate to stop myself from vomiting right there in the sitting room.

'You were coming to take me away from the site?' I wiped away more tears.

'Yes,' Elsa nodded. 'You were just a young girl, and in one of the last letters, David said you'd become mixed up with the wrong crowd. When he died, I decided that enough was enough and you had to come home to your roots. Sadly, that didn't happen.'

I wondered what else that letter had said. I stood up and stretched my legs. The sun had disappeared from the clear sky. 'Elsa, as much as I would have loved for you to have taken me home with you, if I think back, I wouldn't have gone with you. I was so consumed with grief and already so messed up because of Jimmy, I wouldn't have left the only place I knew to be my parents' home.'

I bent down and kissed Elsa on the cheek before going to my bedroom. I had no intention of going to sleep even though I was exhausted. I wanted to find the very last letter my dad had ever written to Elsa. My gut told me something wasn't right and I had to find out what it was. My eyes screamed for sleep but my mind called on the information I felt I needed to find out. If Elsa had come to the site after my parents' funerals, who was it that hadn't let her in? Why would anyone do that? My gut was telling me the answer. I knew exactly who wouldn't have let her in, and there would have been more than one. But they would have all gone by the surname of Denton, I was in no doubt about that.

Chapter Thirty-Two

After my conversation with Elsa, I locked myself in my bedroom and began rummaging through the first box of letters Elsa had given me on my first visit. I wanted to find the most recent letter from my dad to Elsa. Something in my gut said something wasn't right with their last days, and with Elsa saying she had been refused entry to the site to find me after the funeral, I wanted to know if there was any truth to my gut feeling.

I pulled every envelope from the box, looking at the dates on the stamps to find the one closest to their deaths. When I finally found it, I held it in my hand for several minutes before I built up the courage to open it.

> Dear Elsa,
>
> I haven't heard back from you in so long. Has something happened with Dad? Or you? I wanted to speak to you in person, face to face. I have something I want to ask you. But because I can't get a hold of you, I've decided to put my question in this letter. I wouldn't ask if I wasn't desperate.
>
> Something has happened at the site, a disagreement between the Dentons and ourselves. Kat has started seeing Jimmy

Denton, Stan's son. You'll be aware of him from my previous letters. He is one little thug, taking right after his dad, and when Stan eventually hands the site down to Jimmy, my poor Kat is going to be the next Denton wife. I do not want that for her. I have told Kat that I forbid her from seeing him, but she just won't listen. You know what teenage girls are like, and you'll remember what I was like with Dad when I met Michelle. But this is very different. I have even had a word myself with Jimmy, asked him to end things with my daughter, but he just laughed in my face, told me that Stan would 'make things difficult' for us living on the site. You know me, Elsa, I am not a forceful man, but at that moment in time, I lost it with Jimmy. I told him to send Stan to me if he had a problem with it. Before I knew it, Stan and the rest of his cronies appeared at my front door. I was warned straight down the line, if I didn't shut my mouth I would be taught a lesson that would affect my daughter for the rest of her life.

I had no idea what they meant, but I have a feeling my life is in danger. It wouldn't surprise me if they dragged Michelle into this too. I don't often doubt my confidence in a situation where I am at loggerheads with these people, but I am very doubtful of my family's safety in this instance.

My favour is this. If anything happens to me or Michelle, I want Kat to come and live with you and Dad. I know Dad still doesn't approve of my marriage to a traveller, but at this moment in time I really couldn't care less. My daughter is the single most important thing in my life, other than Michelle, and I will not allow anything to happen to her, even if I am no longer on this planet to protect her myself.

I really would like to see you or speak to you as soon as possible. I have never feared for my life before, Elsa, but today, I do.

All my love, David.

I stared at the letter, the last ever letter that my dad had written to Elsa. And he was begging for her help. My eyes stung with tears. I was transported back to the day they died. I felt the same emotions now that I had back then. This was why I could never move on. My parents didn't die under tragic circumstances. They were murdered. The question was, who killed them? It could have been any one of the Dentons or the Brannigans. For the first time in my life, I no longer feared losing my life to Jimmy. No, I wanted to take *his* life, and there was nothing or nobody who was going to stop me.

–

I left a note on the dining table before I left the cottage that morning. I got up earlier than normal and decided that if I was going to put an end to my suffering, then I had to do it now or it would never stop. And I had to do this on my own. I wasn't going to allow Helen or Lucia to be dragged into it.

After reading my dad's letter, pleading with Elsa to come and take care of me, and knowing that someone had murdered my parents, I didn't know where my head was at. I was angry at Elsa for not being straight with me from the start. I was furious with myself for not realising sooner that the circumstances of my parents' deaths were suspicious. I mean, of course the fire was suspicious; how had I not seen that before now? Jimmy had never been flavour of the month with my dad, and when you went against the Dentons, you paid the price, regardless of who you were. I was thrown in a belly box for expressing my opinion, battered senseless because another man looked at me, and raped for attempting to leave Jimmy. If my dad had gone up against Stan and his family, there was absolutely no doubt in my mind that the Dentons or the Brannigans had something to do with his death, and my mam's too. I didn't have much of a plan, but I knew I had to go back to that site and find out what happened the night of that fire.

I'd wanted to believe on some level that the fire had been an accident, that my dad asking Elsa to look after me just before the fire happening was just a coincidence. But how could it be?

I cast my mind back to when I was in the hospital, lying in the bed with Jimmy by my side, while Stan was in the corridor talking to the nurse. There was a high possibility that they both knew exactly what had happened to my parents. In fact, there was a high chance that most people on the site knew exactly what had happened and everyone was too scared to speak up. My life had been ripped apart, but I was so blinded by love that I hadn't been able to see what was staring me in the face.

I looked back at the dining table where I had left the note for Elsa and Helen to find. I crept into Lucia's room and kissed her gently on the head. I knew I was leaving her in safe hands with Helen. I would speak to Elsa when I returned, but right now, grilling her on why she didn't fight for me was down on my list of priorities. My head told me to stop what I was doing, climb back into bed, and move on with my life. But my heart told me that this was the only way I would ever be able to get closure on the whole situation. I wasn't looking forward to seeing Jimmy, or Stan for that matter. But I couldn't just sit back and do nothing after what I had read in that letter.

I left the cottage, tiptoeing as quietly as I could past the bedrooms of the people who cared about me the most in the world. It broke my heart to leave without telling them, and somewhere in my mind, I knew there was a high chance I wouldn't ever see them again. There was a time when I would never have put myself at risk like this, but I knew that I was doing this for Lucia. If I could find out what had happened, and somehow deal with it, maybe Lucia and I wouldn't have to run or look over our shoulders for the rest of our lives. I closed the door very quietly behind me and made my way to the terminus, having timed the first bus of the day. I would think about what I was going to do during the journey. What was I going to say, how was I going to feel, when I saw him for the first time since I left?

Jimmy would certainly be surprised to see me, and hopefully it would catch him off-guard. I considered phoning Michael to tell him what I was planning. But

I knew instantly that he would try to talk me out of it. And when Elsa and Helen found my note, I imagined Elsa would tell Helen everything and Helen would know where I had gone. By then, hopefully it would already be dealt with, in whatever way it needed to be.

I stood at the terminus, wrapping my coat around me. It was a crisp, spring morning. Killearn village was silent, aside from a few birds chirping overhead. I imagined what it would be like to soar above the tree tops, looking down on the mess that is our world, to be able to fly off to the next spot, wherever took your fancy, escaping the clutches of your responsibilities and problems. I looked around the village. Every so often, a car passed, its tyres crunching the stones and gravel lying on the road. The sun shone just above the outline of the Campsie Hills and highlighted the undersides of the lonely clouds floating in the sky. Everything was so peaceful here. The exact place where I wanted Lucia to grow up, the exact place where I should have grown up. I sighed, a stream of air leaving my mouth and swirling in the air before dispersing. I enjoyed the moment before I heard the bus approaching. It pulled into the terminus, the doors already open. It was the same driver who normally took the route, and I had become friendly with him.

'Good morning, Miss. Early rise for you, you off some-where nice?' he asked, climbing out of his cab for a cigarette break.

'Not particularly.' I smiled. I sat down, waiting on his return so I could pay my fair.

As the bus pulled out of the terminus, my stomach began to lurch. This was it, the beginning of the journey where I would face Jimmy for the last time. I wasn't sure if, when it came to it, I could go through with killing him. There had been plenty of times where he had almost killed me, so in theory it should be relatively easy. But I knew myself and when it came to it, only the survival instinct would push me to do it. I wasn't going to think about it until I was approaching the site. All I knew was, I wanted to surprise him, so I would enter the site the way I had left. In secret.

I admired the sights of the country through the window of the bus. I sincerely hoped I would be back here to admire them again.

–

Pulling into Buchanan Street Station, I watched as swarms of bodies poured off buses and out of taxis. The bus station was rammed with people in suits carrying bags and brief-cases, and they all looked like they were in a rush to be somewhere important. I was in no rush to get to where I was going, and on several occasions on the bus, I had almost rung the bell to alert the driver to stop and let me off. The city centre was a far cry from the peace and tranquillity of Killearn. The sound of the bustling traffic travelled along the street, joining more traffic at the next junction. I exited the bus station and faced the Royal Concert Hall, heading right towards the cinema where I had bumped into Michael for the second time. I took a sharp right again and noted the bus stop I needed to be at to head for the site. The number seventeen bus was due along in the next five minutes, so I sat down on the narrow bench to await its arrival.

The final destination was Duntocher, a place I had truly believed I would never set foot in again. It was a mile or so from the site, heading down the A82. I was coming closer to my personal hell on earth, but I knew I couldn't turn back. I looked down the street and in the distance I could see the bus approaching. The number seventeen bus was the same one Helen and I had used to escape the site after creeping our way through the back streets of Duntocher.

I remembered sitting there, while the bus came to a stop, and hearing Jimmy and Rab's voices, thinking it would be the last time I'd hear them. We had only been separated by metal and glass, and he had only been a metre or so away from me, but he had no idea I was there. I shuddered at the memory. I stood up and held my hand out, signalling to the driver that I wanted him to stop. Climbing on, I paid for a return fare, determined that I would return, for my daughter, if no one else. I leaned my head against the glass and peered out at the city as it receded from my view. The bus took me further from the busy roads and crowded streets. I watched as passengers came and went, going about their daily business. Not one of them looked much different to me, except for a less pained expression, perhaps.

The sun had risen, casting an orange glow across the tops of the buildings that whizzed past the window. Before I knew it, the bus pulled into the terminus in Duntocher and I was the last passenger. The driver switched off the engine and got out of his cab.

'This is the last stop, hen,' he said.

'Thanks,' I replied. I didn't want to get into a discussion as to why I hadn't got up yet. I stood and stretched my legs. I left the bus and stood by the shelter. Duntocher village was busy with bursts of people and traffic moving along the main road. I froze, not wishing to head towards the site just yet. I walked along the main road in the opposite direction, not entirely sure of where I was going but glad that I had my back to my fears. I passed the florist on the left and I could smell the scents of the flowers as they floated on the spring breeze. The café up ahead was open, so I went inside to gather my thoughts. I ordered a coffee to keep my wits about me for when I approached the site. I sat in the far corner, facing the entrance. I was never keen to sit with my back to a door. Doing so made me feel vulnerable. I paid for my coffee and ordered a sandwich.

'Excuse me?' I said to the waitress. 'Would you mind if I stayed here for a while?' I needed time to compose myself, to charge my bravery. I also needed the darkness of night to shelter my approach. I contemplated that today could quite possibly be my last day. I was surprisingly calm about that.

The waitress, whose jaw clicked each time she chewed on her bright pink bubble gum, responded with a shrug. I supposed she didn't care who came or went. So long as she got her wages at the end of each week, she wasn't fussed who sat in the café. I noticed my hand shaking slightly as I lifted the mug from the table. I quickly placed the mug back down and wrung my hands together. I didn't want to attract any attention at all, even with something as small as a shaky hand.

–

'Excuse me, are you ok?' My daydream was interrupted by a concerned voice. It was the waitress. I looked up at her face, noting that she looked more confused than concerned.

'Oh, sorry, I was miles away,' I replied.

'Missus, you've been here for about four hours. I don't mean to sound rude, but don't you have somewhere else to go?'

'Yeah, I do have somewhere else I need to go there now,' I said. 'Unfortunately for me.' I got up from my seat. 'No time like the present,' I muttered. I headed for the door, aware that I had been only one of around six customers for the four hours the waitress had stated. It was then that I wondered why she would want anyone to leave at all.

'I didn't mean to be rude, it's just, we haven't allowed anyone to sit in for too long since the travellers came up a few weeks back. They were causing all sorts of problems, so they were.'

'The ones from the site down at Dalnottar?' I asked, knowing full well that was exactly who she was talking about.

'Aye, the younger ones have been up here, hanging around. Smoking, even drinking in here. And when the boss spoke to them and told them to shift, the dads and the uncles came up and started giving us all grief. I know I was ok with you staying earlier, but I don't want any come back from the boss.'

I smiled, said thank you and left. As I made my way along the main street and onto the boulevard heading towards the site, I worried that I was walking into something worse than I had left. I wasn't sure I was ready for it just yet. So, when I reached the cemetery, I decided to stay there until it was beginning to get dark. As morbid as a cemetery sounds, I felt like it would be the most peaceful place I could be until I was ready to face the site.

Chapter Thirty-Three

I stood at the top of the hills which surrounded the cemetery above the site. I would have never imagined myself back here, especially now I was settled and Lucia was coming along so well. And not only that, I was also building my confidence when it came to the opposite sex, with Michael. He had helped me to realise that not all men were like Jimmy, as hard as it was to believe considering the amount of shit that man had put me through. Looking down at the site, I felt the familiar sensation of nausea rising into my throat. How was I going to face this evil without reverting back to my old ways and simply accepting his behaviour because I was too scared to stand up to him? I remember how I used to try to plan exactly what I would say, how I would behave and how I would react to his explosion of anger. Sometimes all I would have to do was breathe the wrong way and he would kick off.

I took a deep breath and closed my eyes as I exhaled, envisioning the anxiety leaving my body along with my breath. How would he react once he saw me? Surely, he would be shocked? He wouldn't be expecting me after all this time. I wondered what he would have to say about my new look. He wouldn't like it.

I felt stronger than I had ever felt, but at the same time, I had never felt more terrified. I had to be on my guard.

He could kick off as soon as he saw me; he was bound to be angry that I had the gall to leave him in the first place. Then there was the added problem of having to explain his sister's involvement in my disappearance. If Helen knew I was here, she would kill me – so long as Jimmy didn't kill me first.

I could smell the smoke from the barbeques down below the hill. I looked around the grounds and saw a few children running around and instantly felt relieved that Lucia wasn't living in that hell. I couldn't begin to imagine her living there, in among the other kids and families, getting into all sorts of trouble. But the thing I could least imagine was her being witness to her mother taking a beating off her father. Her innocent little mind would be tainted with visions of me with black eyes, a broken nose, torn clothing, and a trailer wrecked by his antics. Even thinking about it made my skin crawl.

I began my descent, taking slow, deep breaths as I steadied myself on the steep hill. Luckily, the night sky had faded to purple as the sun had begun to set, so nobody would be able to see me coming down to the site even though I felt so exposed. The last time I had been on that hill, I had been going in the opposite direction, running for my life. I must be crazy to be heading back this way. But there was no way on earth I could let this go. That bastard had got away with murder for long enough; there was nothing that would stop me from facing this. Nothing.

I found myself at the bottom of the hill, staring at the familiar wagons and trailers. I felt rooted to the spot. I couldn't move, couldn't think. Jimmy could walk around the corner at any second and I would be standing there, face to face with the devil himself. I closed my eyes and took a deep breath, allowing myself to release the fear, otherwise I would not be able to go any further. I wasn't going to waste my time standing here when I could be taking everything back from him that he had taken away from me: my pride, dignity, confidence, self-esteem, among other things. I stepped forward. I turned back towards the hill and as I looked up, I could see the old me, the shell of what I once was, staring down at me, screaming at me to climb back up and run as fast and as far as I could.

I smiled and shook my head. I wasn't going to sink back into my former self; I was not going to allow him to fill me with fear any more. I turned my back on the hill and my last chance to escape. I had become the devil on my own shoulder, pushing me to face Jimmy, even though I knew it could end so badly. I pictured Lucia. If anything, she was one of the main reasons I was here. I had to end this and I had to end it now. As I began to move, the sounds around me faded. I fixed my eyes on Jimmy's trailer and refused to look in the direction of where my parents' one once stood. A light was on inside and I could see the back of someone's head, but it wasn't Jimmy's. Time seemed to stop as I approached the door. I lifted my hand and before I could change my mind, I banged my fist on the door. This was it, no going back. My heart was beating so hard I was beginning to think that when Jimmy opened the door, he would find me lying on the ground, having a heart attack.

I saw a silhouette appear behind the glass door, and the hand rise to meet the handle. I watched as the door opened, and when I lifted my head so that my eyes would meet his, I drew back, astonished at the sight before me.

Chapter Thirty-Four

'What the fuck are you doing back?' Mandy asked, with little emotion in her voice.

I couldn't take my eyes off her beaten face. She looked so worn and tired. The way *I* used to look.

'Mandy, what the hell has happened to you?' The words came out in a whisper.

She shrugged and stepped back from the door. 'Are you coming in or what?'

I hesitated. Seeing Mandy had caught me off-guard. When I was sure I had gone unseen, I made my way inside.

The familiar stench of beer and cigarette smoke flooded my mind with unwelcome memories. I looked down at the floor where I had been raped. I remembered Jimmy spitting on me once he had finished, and thinking that he had robbed me of dignity, or at least what was left of it.

'Mandy, do you live here?' I turned to face her, pushing the memories from my head.

She nodded. 'After you both fucked off, Jimmy was a mess. Dad said I should move in to keep an eye on him.'

I shook my head. 'And he did this to you?'

Mandy sniggered. 'Are you kidding? Who else do you think would do this?'

I don't know why I was surprised, after everything he had done to me, and Helen's revelation just before we left. Why hadn't we taken Mandy with us?

'Anyway, like you care what happens to me? If you or Ellie gave a shit about me, I wouldn't be in this mess. You would have made me go with you.'

'I'm sorry, Mandy,' I said. 'I had to leave straight away. It was too risky for your sister to convince you to go with us. Jimmy was a king in your eyes.'

'Ha, aye, maybe back then.'

Mandy sat down, hanging her head. 'What are you doing here, Kat?'

I winced at the sound of that name.

'I've a few things that need sorting.'

Mandy looked up at me. 'With Jimmy?'

I said nothing. I didn't want her knowing anything. That way, he wouldn't be able to get anything out of her.

'Where's Ellie?'

'I don't know.' I had to lie.

'Bullshit. You don't trust me not to tell him.'

I shook my head. 'I don't trust that he won't beat the shit out of you *until* you tell him.'

Mandy sighed. 'Take me with you when you leave.' Her eyes brimmed with tears.

'Let me deal with him first.'

Mandy stood up, as did I. I didn't expect her to hug me. But she did, and she cried like a baby.

–

The trailer was in darkness, the moonlight cascading down onto the grit lining the grounds of the site and in through the window. The gun was cold as I held it tightly in my hand. Jimmy had left it in the very place he had told me about, years ago. Foolishly, he hadn't changed the safe place after I'd gone. I listened as footsteps approached. My heartbeat was steady and my breathing calm. The door opened and I heard him enter the trailer.

'Mandy, get me a fucking beer,' he grunted. 'I've had a fucker of a day.'

When there was no response, he looked over at the sitting area, where I sat in the darkness in front of the window, my silhouette highlighted by the light of the moon.

'Why are you sitting in the dark, you idiot?' he said, flicking the lamp switch. When he looked up, he stared into my eyes. He didn't blink, he didn't move. He didn't speak.

'Get your own fucking beer,' I said, startled at the venom in my voice.

Jimmy straightened, tilted his head, as though a better angle would help the realisation that his estranged wife was sitting in front of him after all this time, and with attitude too. He opened his mouth to speak but nothing came out.

'Surprised to see me?'

'You're brave, I'll give you that.' He casually sat down on the end of the sofa. 'Mandy know you're here?'

I shook my head. 'Nope. No one does.'

Jimmy began laughing hysterically. I let him have his moment. He wouldn't be laughing by the time I had finished with him.

'So, to what do I owe this *fucking* pleasure?'

'What do you owe?' I said, without moving. I was firm in my place. I wasn't the twitchy, terrified little wife I had left as. 'You owe me a lifetime of explanations.'

Jimmy erupted, springing up and lunging at me. I had expected it, so I matched his movements and got up and out of the way in quick motion. He fell forward onto the couch. When he composed himself, he turned to face me, ready to pounce once more. I could see that he hadn't expected to be staring down the barrel of a gun. He stopped suddenly.

'Kat, what are you doing?'

Both hands holding firm and steady, I didn't lower the gun. Neither did I hesitate with my words. 'I'll tell you what I'm doing. I'm getting justice for something that happened a long time ago.'

He stared into my eyes. 'What are you talking about?'

'Arson, Jimmy. I'm talking about the night you killed my parents.'

Chapter Thirty-Five

His eyes were fixed on mine. Our bodies were still. I relished the fear across his face; it was usually the other way round. Feeling in control, I knew that with the barrel of the gun aimed at his forehead I was going to get answers. I hadn't actually decided if I would shoot him. On the one hand, I had too much to lose if I pulled the trigger. On the other, I would be forever free from looking over my shoulder, forever free from the fear that he could turn up anywhere and find out about Lucia.

Then, he spoke. 'Mandy will be back soon. She won't be too happy to see you pointing that in her big brother's face.'

I bit my tongue and shook my head. My upper arms were beginning to ache from holding the gun up for so long.

'You look, well, amazing.'

Was he serious? He thought I was going to fall for that? He'd lost his charm along with that fire. I wasn't stupid. 'I know.'

Jimmy laughed. 'Oh, you know, do you?'

I wanted to punch him. He was trying to force me into a conversation that I didn't want to have. He'd do anything to turn things back to me. I wasn't about to let that happen. How could he sit there and still try to belittle me, even with death staring him in the face? My stomach turned. The fear had gone from his face.

'Start talking, Jimmy.'

He adjusted himself to a sitting position, shoulders relaxed, left ankle casually resting over his right knee. This was the way he would sit on the couch, beer in hand, watching television after he had knocked lumps out of me. I refrained from shuddering at the thought. I could feel my arms willing themselves to lower with the weight of the gun. I resisted. This was my defence and I wasn't about to let myself become exposed.

'What exactly do you want to hear from me? I could agree with you and your stupid idea that I set that trailer on fire. But then, I'd be telling lies. So I'm not going to.'

The images of that night came flooding back to me. The smoke, the flames, the unbearable heat. I wasn't going to let this go.

'You can't hide from this anymore, Jimmy. I know.'

He smirked. 'You know what?'

'I know what you said to my dad a few weeks before the fire.'

Jimmy continued to smile, the evil shining out from his eyes. 'I said a lot to your dad before that fire. You'll have to be more specific than that, sweetheart.'

I suppressed my urge to vomit. After all this time, he was still trying to grind me down. I pulled the letter from my back pocket with one hand, while holding the gun in the other. The gun felt so much heavier in one hand. I threw the letter at him and he let it fall onto the seat beside him. Reluctantly, he picked it up and peeled back the seal. The sounds of the paper creasing gently under his fingers were elevated over our silence. My heart pounded and I could hear the blood rushing through my ears. I kept my eyes on him as he began to read. I waited until he had finished before I said anything.

'Well?'

Jimmy looked up at me with eyebrows raised. He shrugged. 'Of course he's going to say this. He hated me. Thought his little Kat was too good for me.'

'I *was* too good for you. I still am.'

That wasn't the point. He was still sitting there, denying it all.

'You were never too good for me, Kat. You needed a bit of shaking up. You were a daddy's girl who needed to see what a real man was like. I don't remember you complaining at the time.'

The bile began to rise again. This time it reached my throat. I forced it back down, willing myself to stay strong in front of him. If I let my guard down now, I could only imagine what he would do to me. I couldn't risk anything happening to me, for Lucia's sake.

'I was young and naive back then; you took advantage of that.' I gripped the gun harder. I wanted to pull that trigger so much.

'You were slim and sleek, too. I couldn't resist that little body of yours.'

I tried to block out his words. I failed to remember why at one stage, I was attracted to the scumbag. I couldn't remember the person I used to be when I actually became excited at the thought of his touch. He was a different person back then. I was a different person now.

'Well, you'd better hold on to that memory, because it's all you're going to have of me for the rest of your pathetic little existence.'

Jimmy was stunned by my new-found confidence. He tried to hide it, but I could see it written all over his face.

'You know, Kat, there was a time I'd have belted you for talking to me like that.'

'What, staring down the barrel of gun changes things, does it?' I replied.

He shifted his position but remained seated. 'No.'

'Then what is it? Don't tell me you're a changed man.'

He shook his head. 'I don't know, maybe just seeing you standing in front of me after all this time has made me realise what I had, what I lost.'

I laughed. He was stalling. I could read him like a book, he was hoping that the longer time went on, the less confident I would become and that I would lower my hands.

'Why is that so funny?' Jimmy asked, his brows furrowing as the words left his mouth.

'I have to say, Jimmy, I've known you for a very long time and this is the first time I have ever seen you genuinely shit-scared.' My arms were hurting now. I had to make this quick, whatever *this* was.

'I can't say I'm thrilled to have a gun pointed at my face, Kat. But I'd rather be talking to you like this than not at all.'

He still had the nerve to try to draw me back in to his bullshit.

'You told my dad that Stan would make things difficult for him. Then Stan said he would do something that would affect me for the rest of my life. You set out to murder them, didn't you?'

Jimmy shook his head. 'You've some imagination, Kat.'

'You set out to murder him and then pretended to save me from the fire so you could keep hold of me.'

Jimmy began to rise.

'Sit the fuck down!' I shouted, jutting the gun at his face.

Jimmy held his hands up and sat back down again.

'Tell me the fucking truth.'

I could feel myself shaking. Every nerve shuddered and every muscle twitched as I waited to hear the words come out of his mouth.

'Ok, you want to hear it? I'll tell you. First, let me get a beer. It'll help calm my nerves with you waving that fucking gun around.'

I considered this. I was still in control; I could end this at any moment. Was I brave enough to let him get up and take the few, short steps to the fridge to retrieve the beer he needed so badly?

'You so much as breathe in my direction, I swear to God I'll kill you right here,' I said.

Jimmy nodded, got up, went to the fridge, took out a bottle of beer, and returned to the couch. He twisted the lid off and tossed it to the side. After taking a large gulp, he rested the bottle on his knee. He glanced up at me.

'Start talking,' I said. 'Before I lose my patience and shoot you anyway.'

Jimmy took another gulp of beer. 'Sweetheart, you won't shoot me.'

'And what makes you think that?'

'Because if you shoot me now, and I die, how will you ever be sure what happened to your precious Mam and Dad?'

I stared straight into his eyes. He was right, I couldn't shoot him, not now. And the question was, could I shoot him at all? I had to let him see that he hadn't created doubt in my mind.

'I'll take that chance. Like I said, start talking.'

Chapter Thirty-Six

'We had been seeing each other a few months. You doted on me, hung on every word I said. You were the sexiest little thing I'd ever seen. I had to have you for as long as I could.'

My skin itched at the memory.

'Get to the fucking point, Jimmy.'

He rolled his eyes at me, clearly irritated at the way I was speaking to him, and even more so that I was getting away with it.

'So, one afternoon, I went to your trailer looking for you. Your dad said you weren't in but would be back later. But while I was there, he told me that he wasn't happy that you were spending time with me.'

I remembered that day. I remembered watching them as I hid from their view.

'What happened?' I asked.

Jimmy shook his head. A look of disgust fell over his face. 'I said I was good enough for you, that he had nothing to worry about. But he stood there and told me that no Denton would ever be good enough for his precious daughter.'

I looked out of the window behind Jimmy. It was so dark outside that it looked black.

'Well, he wasn't wrong,' I replied.

Jimmy shot me a glance. 'Watch your mouth.'

In previous years, such words would have silenced me. However, with a gun in my hand and Jimmy before me, I felt no fear, no anxiety. All I felt was hatred.

'Don't tempt me to shoot you before I've heard all I need to hear, Jimmy.'

Jimmy smiled, but it most definitely did not reach his eyes.

'You don't have the fucking guts,' he snarled.

In the time I had been away from Jimmy and built up my life with Lucia, I hadn't realised how strong I had actually become. I was once a timid, pathetic little female, with no mind of my own. All Jimmy had to do was look in my direction and I would crumble with fear. That was then. Things were different now.

'Are you willing to risk it? Trust me on this, *do not fucking push me.*' I pushed the end of the gun against his face. He tried to hide it but I saw him flinch.

He held his hands up in defeat. I loved watching him squirm. But was this really me? Could I really go through with this? I thought back to that day in the field when he shot down the crow. I had felt sick at the sight of the bird falling through the air, wings splayed out. I had wondered how anyone could hurt a living creature. Standing here now, I was the gun and Jimmy was the crow.

'Get to the point,' I said, pushing the doubts to the back of my mind.

Jimmy looked at me, the rage burning in his eyes. This was frustrating for him, not to say humiliating. He must have wanted to get off the seat and start smashing my face in, like he would have done in the past. I hadn't thought anything could stop Jimmy Denton from doing what he wanted with me. I supposed staring down the barrel of a gun somehow changed that. Now it was my turn to have things done my way. I needed Jimmy to tell me the truth and I wasn't leaving without it. How the tables had turned.

'I tried to tell him that I would be good for you, I would be able to look after you and treat you with respect. But your dad was having none of it,' Jimmy said, shaking his head.

'So you decided to set our home on fire and keep me for yourself?'

'No.'

'You're a liar. The whole thing screams Jimmy Denton. My dad tells you to stay away from me and then a few days later he ends up dead?'

'I always get what I want, Kat. I wasn't going to let your dad tell me I couldn't have you. I wanted you.'

The smirk across his face was enough to send me into a frenzy. I butted him in the face with the side of the gun as hard as I could. He fell back and put his hands up to his face. I stood over him, adrenaline cascading through me like a raging river. I was ready to hit him again, but as I lifted my hand, Jimmy shot out an arm and curled his hand around my wrist. His strength took me by surprise and I opened my hand, letting the gun fall from my grasp. Before I knew it, Jimmy had risen from the couch and pushed me down onto the floor. His weight as he held me down was paralyzing, but I managed to turn my head and I sank my teeth into his wrist. He screamed out as I struggled out from under him. We both made a dash for the gun. Fighting against each other, he won the battle for the revolver and this time, I was pinned to the couch. Jimmy held the gun to my head.

'Wrong fucking move,' he breathed, as he tugged at his belt with his free hand. 'One last moment of fun before I blow your fucking head off, eh?'

'I'd rather die than let that happen, you piece of scum,' I said, through gritted teeth.

He leaned down and put his lips to my right ear. 'Not an option, darling, I'm the one in control now.'

He pulled at my jeans and I continued to struggle. I glanced up at his face and he had a look of pure evil in his eyes.

'Jimmy, stop!' Mandy's voice came from above.

'Mandy, get the fuck out of here.' He grunted as he stood up. I felt his weight lift from me and I scrambled to my feet. I stood still as Jimmy turned his back to me. Everything seemed to be moving in slow motion. He still had the gun in his left hand.

'No.' Her voice weakened as he moved closer to her. Her eyes widened when she saw what was in his hand.

'This is between me and my wife. You don't need to be a part of this. Now, do as I say and fuck off out of here.' He grabbed at her wrist and started to push her back towards the door, holding the gun in front of him. Mandy gasped.

'Is this what you do to the women in your life? You get off on having power over them?' My heart was beating so hard, my voice trembled in my throat. He turned, still holding Mandy's wrist in his other hand. 'You're nothing but scum. Look at you, backed into a corner so you'll use power and violence to get out of it. She's your sister, for fuck's sake.'

His lips parted as if to reply, but instead he cried out in pain and fell to his knees, grasping at his crotch. The gun fell to the floor. Mandy stood by the door, panic written all over her face at what she had done.

'Fucking bitch,' he gasped, as he tried to get to his feet. I caught Mandy's attention and glanced at the door, gesturing for her to leave. She shook her head and remained by the door, reaching down and grabbing the gun in her hand.

'You don't want to do that, Mandy. Come on, give me the gun,' Jimmy croaked as he got to his feet, hunched over by the pain delivered by his sister's right knee.

'So you can kill me? No thanks.' She lifted the handgun and pointed it at his face. 'Or so you can shoot her and I go back to being the good little sister?'

'Don't you get it? This bitch broke my fucking heart. She left without a word and now she's come back and started accusing me of all sorts of shit. What am I supposed to do here?'

Mandy shook her head and then looked at me. 'Let's go.'

Jimmy held his hands up in surrender, still hunched over slightly. 'I'm not exactly in a position to argue, am I?'

But those words were just too easy. Jimmy wasn't going to let us walk out without a fight. Mandy walked a few steps towards him and told him to sit down on the couch. Jimmy obliged, which unsettled me.

'Now, you're going to let us walk out of here and you're not going to come after us because if you do, I swear to God I will shoot you square in the head and I don't give a shit who sees me do it. Do you understand?' Mandy's voice was quivering in time with her shaking hand. Jimmy shrugged, his hands still in the air. I moved to Mandy's side and took the gun from her. She turned to face the front door, but a sudden heaviness hung over me. As I faced Jimmy, the sound of the door opening behind me sent my stomach into a spin as I saw Jimmy's expression change. He was smiling widely now.

'What the hell is going on in here then?' Rab's voice made my skin prickle. His presence was strong, his footsteps heavy on the floor.

'Rab, my man. Come in and join the party.' Jimmy raised an eyebrow at his friend's unexpected presence. 'Look who it is.'

I turned around, knowing that there was only one barrel but two targets. I had no choice but to take my eyes off Jimmy. I trusted Rab less.

'Kitty Kat, how the devil are ye?' he said, his broad frame blocking the door. Mandy's head hung low. She looked as defeated as I felt.

'I've been better.'

'You're no happy to see an old pal?' Rab did not seem fazed by the gun pointing in his direction.

'She's not too happy at all, Rab. Seems as though Kat blames me for the fire that killed her folks.'

Rab smiled. 'Oh, we can't be having that now.' He looked down at the gun and then at me. 'Hand it over, don't make this harder than it has to be.' Before I could do anything, Jimmy was at my back. I felt a sharpness press into my spine. I knew the game was over.

'Good girl,' Rab said, taking the gun from my hand. I eyed Mandy again. She was still looking at the floor. 'Now what do we do?'

Jimmy's breath was heavy in my ear. 'Sit down.' He pushed the sharp object into my back with more pressure and I moved towards the couch. Mandy stayed by Rab and said nothing. My heart ached to watch her go into herself when they were both around. I would never forgive myself for leaving her behind. I sat down on the couch and Jimmy sat beside me. I watched as he placed a knife down on the seat beside him. Bile climbed from my gut. I swallowed hard. My knees trembled as I glanced up at Rab, who was holding the gun down by his side. 'So, why don't you tell us what you've been up to, Kat?'

Jimmy laughed like a hyena. 'Like we don't know.'

I thought about Michael, still lying in a hospital bed. They had found out about me and Michael had suffered because of my past.

'Looks like you landed on your feet with that one, Kat.' Jimmy patted my knee. 'Big shot who runs his own business, nice catch.'

'Not so much of a looker now though,' Rab sniggered. 'Did he survive, by the way?'

My blood boiled at the sound of their laughter. Everything was funny to them. Death and violence was nothing to them. 'Oh, he survived. He's under police protection right now. They know everything. So they should be coming for you both pretty soon.' I lied.

Jimmy grabbed at my throat. 'Oh, you think so? Funny how they've not been anywhere near. You don't have the fucking balls to grass on a Denton.'

I gasped for air as his grip tightened. Rab looked on, his eyes sparkling with pleasure at watching me suffer. He had as much control over me as Jimmy had during my time as a Denton. I was as good as married to both of them. I clutched at Jimmy's hands, trying to peel his fingers from around my neck. He was on his knees, applying more pressure. My vision began to blur, the sounds around me becoming duller. I clawed at his skin, trying to release the pressure. Rab was by me now, pointing the gun in my face. I closed my eyes, picturing Lucia. I wanted her face to be the last thing I saw before dying at the hands of her father. I heard Mandy's screams and a door hammering against a wall. Fingers released from my throat. Jimmy's voice roared in my ear. 'Fuck!' I heard a click.

'Shit, the thing's not fucking loaded,' Rab said. I opened my eyes. Jimmy was at the door of the trailer.

'Mandy's done a bunk. If we don't find her before she goes to the police, we're fucked.'

Jimmy was out of sight. I was on my feet and Rab was pulling me outside.

'Must be your lucky day, Kat.'

I gulped down the fresh air. The stench of bad memories filled my nostrils as I left the trailer. Rab pulled me towards a car and opened the passenger door, forcing me inside. I had no energy to fight. My head slumped against the headrest as Rab got into the driver's seat. The engine roared to life. The car sped through the site, towards the exit.

'Where are we going?' I muttered.

Rab either ignored me or hadn't heard me. I noted the headlights weren't on. We were hurtling into the darkness of the road beyond the site, venturing deeper into the black night. My stomach lurched and I vomited into the footwell.

'Urgh, Kat, for fuck's sake,' Rab shouted.

'Sorry,' I said, before I could stop myself. I wasn't sorry for throwing up. But I was used to saying sorry so many times for lesser crimes than being sick.

I was thrown forward suddenly, my head hitting off the dashboard before falling back in my seat. A crunching sound came from somewhere under me and I was mildly aware of an array of swear words coming from Rab. The car halted.

I lifted my hand to my forehead. It was wet. Blood dripped from my head onto my knees as I looked down. 'What the fuck was that?' I looked up.

The windscreen resembled a frozen spider's web. Cracks in the glass spread like threads of silk, obscuring the view ahead. My heart skipped. We had hit something. Or someone.

Rab gripped the steering wheel, his face drained of all colour. The stench of blood from my head and bile from the footwell made me gag again. I opened the door and fell out onto the gravel. Gripping the door, I climbed to my feet. I peered over the top of the passenger door. A figure lay on the ground a few feet ahead of the car.

Spinning from the head bump, I concentrated on walking. I heard a car door open behind me. I turned around. Rab had got out of the car. He was running towards the person lying on the road.

'Naw, it cannae be,' he said, as he passed me. I watched as he stood over the person. I shook my head, unable to make sense of what was happening. I approached them, peering around me for anyone else who may have seen what happened.

'No, no, no.' Rab's hands were on top of his head, clutching at his hair.

'Kat?' Mandy called from the other side of the road. She ran towards me and clung to me like a child.

I looked down at the person on the ground. Blood trailed across his face, eyes wide and looking up to the night sky. Rab dropped to his knees next to the body. Mandy collapsed to the ground. Sobs left her lungs as I continued to stare down at Jimmy's body.

'Mate? Jimmy, can you hear me?' Rab panicked over Jimmy's body.

Jimmy lifted his hand and clutched at Rab's collar, pulling him closer. I watched in disbelief as my husband lay dying at the hands of the one man he had truly trusted throughout his whole life. Rab was the one person Jimmy could always rely on, the one person Jimmy could make do anything.

'Where is she?' Jimmy's voice barely made it out of his throat. Rab glanced up at me, and I moved closer to them. All I had wanted since leaving Jimmy was to be free from him. But now that he was dying on the ground in front of me, the teenager in me who had fallen for him was screaming for him to hold on. Not only was I fighting the demons in my head from years of abuse from the man I was supposed to be able to trust, I was fighting the stupid little girl I once was.

Jimmy was at my feet, blood on his face and death in his eyes. I kneeled down beside him and he grabbed my hand, squeezing it tight as he looked into my eyes. I didn't know what to say. What *could* I say? As much as he had put me through hell, I couldn't just walk away and leave him to die on his own.

'Jimmy,' I managed.

'Kat, it wasn't me who killed them.' His voice weakened. His eyes darted to Rab, who was still being gripped by the collar.

Rab's expression changed from anguish to confusion. 'But, you said...'

'Aye, I did say it was between us,' Jimmy winced in pain. 'But I'm no' going to die with her thinking it was me, when really it was you.'

I shook my head. 'You two are pathetic. You're both as culpable as each other.'

Jimmy cried out in pain again, letting go of my hand and placing his own on his stomach. I eyed Rab. He was staring from me to Jimmy. 'Rab, did it never occur to you that Jimmy was not your friend but your boss? You were the easiest one of us all to control. He said jump and you asked how high.'

I should have known all along that Rab was the one who had set fire to my trailer. I should have known Jimmy would never get his hands dirty like that. If one wasn't there to keep an eye on me, the other one would make sure I didn't step out of line.

'Jimmy?' I said. Lucia was on the tip of my tongue. I wanted to tell him in his dying moments that he had a daughter he would never see. But that was one part of my life I knew he would still be able to control even from the grave. If he knew about Lucia, if Rab knew about her, then Stan would find out and I'd never be free from the Dentons. Lucia would never be safe.

His breathing slowed, eyes rolling. I stood up and turned my back on him. Rab called after me. The pain in his voice almost reached my conscience, but I had to keep walking. I didn't want to be with Jimmy when he died, as much as the teenager inside my head did. There were two versions of Jimmy in my life. The one I fell for, and the one I hated. The one lying on the ground was the one I hated, and he deserved to die at the side of the person who killed him.

'Kat!' Rab called again, his voice cracking with emotion.

I sat down by Mandy and allowed her to cry into my shoulder. My head still ached. I dabbed at the wound with my hand, feeling the blood trickling down my face. In a way, it was as if the blood leaving my skull was taking all the bad memories with it.

I lifted my phone out of my pocket and called for the police and an ambulance.

Mandy's tears fell in silence. I wasn't sure what she was thinking. The sirens blared in the distance. I tried not to look in the direction of Rab and Jimmy. As always, Rab never left Jimmy's side. He was with him to the bitter end, apologising over and over. Jimmy gave no reply to his words.

As the sirens came closer, the flashing blue lights illuminated the trees down the road. Crowds had begun to gather at the site gates a few yards beyond the car. People would soon find out what had happened and Rab would suffer for it. And soon, they would find out why I had left and what had been happening to Mandy. I planned to tell the police everything. About Michael's attack, about my parents' death. The legacy of the Denton family would come crashing down.

The ambulance appeared from the bottom of the road, the police following closely. The blue lights lit up the road and the faces from the gathering crowd. I glanced over at

Rab, who was now cradling Jimmy like a baby. He let out a blood-curdling scream. It was then that the weight of seventeen years was lifted off my chest. Jimmy Denton was finally dead.

Epilogue

Two years later

I signed my name on the last page of statements and placed the pen to the side of the paper. I sat back in my seat. For some reason, I felt as though I would cry if I looked at Seb. I had done enough of that in his office over the past few years.

'So, how does it feel to have completed your counselling?' Seb asked, with a big smile on his face.

'It feels...' I searched for the words, '... about time. I didn't think this would ever have had the impact it has, Seb, but you have been a godsend to me. I finally feel like I have a place in the world now, like I can make a decision without overthinking it. I don't feel scared to walk out of here, wondering who I will come across. I can walk into a crowd of people now and hold my head high.'

'That's all down to you,' Seb replied. 'I've just been lucky enough to be witness to the change in you. I feel honoured to have worked with you, Katelyn. I wish you all the best with your future. I really do.'

I couldn't hold back the tears now, but I wasn't ashamed of them anymore. I wanted to hug Seb. I felt like I owed my life to him. We stood up together and Seb held the door open for me. 'You're free to go and enjoy your life now. Make the most of it.'

I smiled at him and took a deep breath before crossing the threshold of the clinic and out to the open world. I turned back towards Seb, who smiled and waved. I walked on, leaving Kat behind me. The sky outside was blue, the temperature slowly creeping up and I could feel the warmth of the sun on my face. I wrapped my scarf around me and zipped my coat up as far as it could go. Crossing the busy road, I decided not to look back at the clinic. As much as I would be forever grateful to Seb and his work, I never wanted to see that place again. Today was about moving forward.

The door to the café on the other side of the road was held open for me by an older man. I smiled, thanking him as I passed him on the way in. I sat down at a table and glanced over the small menu. I heard the bell ring as the door opened and when I looked up, Lucia came rushing towards me with the biggest smile on her face. 'Mummy, you beat us!'

'Looks like it. Where's your dad?' I asked, giving her a squeeze.

'Can I have cake?' She beamed with happiness at the thought of cake.

My eyes moved to the door once more and I watched as Michael struggled through with Lucia's new bike. His son, Scott, was hunched over like a grumpy teenager, staring into the matrix of his mobile phone screen. 'Ah, you're here,' I said.

I stood up and kissed him on the cheek. I ruffled Scott's hair. He pulled away and continued tapping his mobile device. Helen appeared from behind the counter, wearing a white apron and a pair of blue vinyl gloves. 'First week has gone well. The customers are raving about the cakes,' she said.

I looked down at Lucia, who was jumping up and down, trying to see which cakes caught her eye. 'They're not the only ones.'

Bringing Mandy home two years ago hadn't been easy. She'd gone off the rails after what had happened. She blamed herself for Jimmy's death, even though it was a freak accident. It hadn't been her fault Jimmy had run out in front of Rab's car.

Helen and I had managed to help her. We put her in touch with Louise at the refuge, who in turn had put her in touch with a therapist who did a lot of work with her. She never really spoke about the therapy. I knew she would be fighting demons of her own, and we decided to give her space.

Elsa died not long after I found Mandy again. She had left the cottage to Lucia and me, in a new will she had written after we met. She had included a letter which said she couldn't apologise enough for letting me and my dad down all those years ago.

Mandy had decided to live by herself after the therapy and was rehomed in Aberdeen. We don't see much of her any more. She found it too difficult to be around us. Helen and I would never forgive ourselves for leaving Mandy. In hindsight, it was obvious that Mandy would have been Jimmy's next target. I had just been so terrified for my own life and that of my unborn child that I wasn't thinking of anyone else.

I should have felt guilt for Jimmy's death. But I didn't. He had deserved to die. Rab, however, had been so consumed by guilt about killing his best friend that he blurted out everything to the police. He was arrested for dangerous driving resulting in the death of a man. With his guilty plea, there was no need for us to appear in court. I haven't seen Rab since then.

I had wanted to kill Jimmy, but the best possible outcome had become reality. His best friend and puppet had been the one to finally cut his life short. What a humiliation. Jimmy had been so angry in his final moments that he had thrown Rab under the bus and revealed that Rab had been the one to start the fire. I knew he wouldn't have been the only one involved, but I had had enough of searching for all the details. Things had moved on. Things were finally getting better.

'So, how was the last session?' Michael asked.

I nodded. 'It was fine. I cried, as per usual.'

Michael smiled. 'Only happy tears from now on?'

I nodded again. 'Maybe not even those. I don't think I can cry anymore.'

I watched as Lucia pestered Scott to let her have a turn on his mobile. Helen wrote on the board above the till about a lunchtime special deal and Michael sat down to a mug of coffee and a newspaper. Five years ago, if someone had told me I would be living this mundane yet blissful life, I would have never believed them.

I went outside, just to have a moment to pinch myself to realise it was all real. This was all I had ever wanted. I finally had the life *I* had chosen. I turned to my left, where the children's play park was situated. I could hear the birds singing in the trees just a short distance along the road.

Finally, I was at peace.

The flower boxes which lined the windows of the café were in full bloom; I had planted them all with white flowers, as I'd read somewhere that they absorb negative energy.

As I admired them, a little robin landed on the edge of the furthest flower box. I stood perfectly still so as not to scare him away.

I thought of my dad. I believed the bird was his way of showing me they were ok and that we could all move on now. My heart swelled in my chest as the robin took flight and disappeared from sight.

I looked along the road as the parking spaces began to fill up. The lunchtime rush was taking its course. A few work vans and various cars passed by, some stopping to pick up lunch.

There was a time when I would have watched each one intently, looking for Jimmy or Rab. I supposed that feeling would never leave me, even though Jimmy was dead and Rab was in prison. But I wasn't going to allow it to consume me. Not today and not tomorrow.

Not ever again.

Alex Kane – Writer...

Firstly, I would like to thank you for choosing to read my debut novel, *No Looking Back*. It really means so much to me that people are taking the time to read the book I have spent so much time writing and creating.

If you enjoyed it, I'd be thrilled to hear your thoughts via a review. I love to see the reader reviews, they are inspiring and help me to know how the story was received, and it's also a wonderful way to push me on in writing my next book.

I began writing this book in 2013 and I found it took on a mind of its own. I never imagined it would ever be published, but I'm glad that it has. I found writing Katelyn's story stressful at times, but also invigorating. Thankfully, I have never had to face what Katelyn did in this story, however I thought it was important to depict what can be possible with the right support, that women or men can leave an abusive relationship and start to rebuild their lives.

Some research went into several elements of this book, and I found learning about the travelling community very interesting and the lady who helped me is a traveller herself, which gave me the confidence I needed to ensure that certain language and descriptions were as authentic as possible. With that being said, the story is completely my own invention, the characters are entirely fictional and I had a lot of fun (and stress) creating them.

I hope you were able to go along with Katelyn throughout this story and championed her ability to find herself after a lifetime of terror and abuse. It was a rough time for her but I hope that you enjoyed the story.

Again, thank you for your support on this journey and I hope you'll continue to follow me as I work on new releases.

You can get in touch on my Facebook or, Twitter or through my Instagram, if you'd like to talk about this book, or anything else!

Best wishes and happy reading.

Alex Kane

www.facebook.com/alexkanewriter

www.twitter.com/AlexKaneWriter

www.instagram.com/alexkanewriter

Acknowledgements

First of all, I'd like to thank Keshini Naidoo and Lindsey Mooney at Hera Books, for taking a chance on me and my work, for all the advice and support on my first novel with Hera. I have been writing for almost a decade now and am still in disbelief that this has happened. I am so immensely grateful for this opportunity. Thank you to you both.

A big thank you to Jennie, for all the work you put in to helping me make *No Looking Back* the best it could be. It was a really great experience to work with you and you helped me to see things clearer than I thought I could.

Thank you to Emma Mitchell, my proofreader.

Thanks to Danielle, who helped me with important details about the travelling community.

To all the book bloggers and readers who have supported me from the beginning, especially Noelle Holten and Sharon Bairden.

Casey Kelleher, for encouraging me to submit to Hera Books. I owe you a gin.

To my friends and family for their support over the years, for listening to me talk endlessly about my dream of becoming a writer and encouraging me to keep going.

Thank you to my husband, Chris, who pushes me to keep writing, every day.